RIPPLE EFFECT

J. BENGTSSON

Save the Date
July 23, 2022

To my future daughter-in-law, Samantha Meyer (soon to be Bengtsson—yay!). It's no secret I adore you. The minute I heard your big, hearty laugh I knew you were the one for me... I mean, for my son. I love that you will be a part of our lives forever and am beyond giddy for all the beautiful things to come. I promise to always treat you with the love, devotion, and respect that you deserve. You're an amazing woman. Thank you for saying yes.

WIKIMUSIC

AnyDayNow is an American boy band formed in Los Angeles. Under the direction of famed manager Tucker Beckett, the group is composed of **Bodhi Beckett, RJ Contreras, Shawn Barber, Dane Makati,** and **Hunter Roy.**

Propelled to global success after the release of their first album, the five members of *AnyDayNow* are considered teen idols and, as such, are often the objects of fan hysteria. Their followers refer to themselves as *Dayers.*

AnyDayNow broke up following the near-death experience of band member Bodhi Beckett in a California firestorm. His story can be found in Like the Wind (J. Bengtsson, 2019)

PROLOGUE
RJ: BORN READY

THE LIMO PULLED UP TO THE CURB. CROWDS GATHERED ON ALL sides of the vehicle, held back by flimsy, plastic barriers and burly security guards well versed in young female hysteria.

"Marry me, RJ," screamed one woman with brightly colored locks.

Another held up a cardboard sign reading *Follow me* with her handle in big block letters.

Crushed up against the barricade, a crying girl called out, "I love you, RJ."

The funny thing about fame was you got used to it. Things that might have seemed foreign to you before, like women professing their love with their very last breath or a marriage proposal screamed through tinted windows, became so commonplace you barely registered the words. It didn't seem that long ago that I was a nothing—a throw-away skateboard kid from Idaho with a tiny social media following and a non-existent bank account. What happened next was what teen male dreams were made of—hand-plucked from obscurity to become one of the five members of this century's biggest boy band, *AnyDayNow*.

Brought together by the spin doctor himself, manager Tucker Beckett, we were manufactured in every sense of the word. From the songs we sang to the clothes we wore to the food that passed through our digestive systems, everything we did had to be cleared through handlers. Scheduling our shits, although not required, was highly encouraged. As much as I hated the oppression, I couldn't deny the results. Tucker had made us into exactly what he'd promised—internationally revered superstars.

Five years we performed together. Traveled together. Got stinkin' fuckin' rich together. And the fame? My god. It was beyond any of our wildest dreams. Me, Bodhi, Dane, Hunter, and Shawn. Goddamn, I loved those guys. None of us shared the DNA that defined a bloodline, but we were family all the same. It was that bond, one I'd never felt with my own brothers, that I missed the most after our breakup. But I didn't miss the rest— the estrogen-fueled mobs, the micromanaging middlemen, the saccharine lyrics I was forced to sing.

AnyDayNow had inevitably run its course, and the way I saw it, we'd gotten out just in time. Here's the problem with boy bands—they're never meant to last. In fact, there's a simple mathematical formula, puberty + eight, that accurately predicts how long a boy band can thrive in the wild. Our little girl fans didn't want us to grow old. They wanted our youthful faces and smooth skin to stay frozen in time. But there's no aging in reverse. Inevitably, we had to grow up, get hairy, and move on.

I shook off the memories threatening to derail my big day. Today wasn't about the band or the guys or Tucker Fuckin' Beckett. It was about me and my new sound. I'd been working non-stop since *AnyDayNow*'s demise six months ago to polish my solo album, and now, finally, the day was here.

"Look at that," Roland beamed. "They love you, RJ."

Unimpressed, I didn't bother looking his way. Roland Akers

was my new manager—a yes-man through and through. He did whatever I said, when I said it. With Roland, there was no micro-managing. No rules. Roland said yes. Roland listened. Roland made things happen. For example, the three-song mini concert I was about to perform on the pier. Okay, look, I'll admit to having my doubts when Roland had first proposed it to me. Sure, I knew my shit was good, but was it smart to unleash it on my teeny-bopper fans who weren't used to this type of music? These tunes were harder, deeper, and heavier than the pop songs they knew and loved. But I also understood what Roland was saying. I needed these girls. They were the buzz required to launch my solo career.

Tucker Beckett would've said no. He would've told me that celebrating the release of my album with a concert on the pier in front of a hand-picked selection of *AnyDayNow* superfans was too splashy, too ego-fueled. He would've tried to stifle my creativity. Well, fuck him. Where was Tucker Beckett now? Oh, yeah—he was dying a slow post-*AnyDayNow* death, while I was on the cusp of superstardom all over again... with the cowering Roland Akers by my side.

No one could say I lacked confidence. Even as a child, I'd wanted to be seen. To be heard. To be loved. And that meant I needed to excel at everything I did. There was no better way to stand out in a crowd then to be better than everyone else—or at least better than my older brothers. And so I embraced my skills, whether that meant sports or skateboarding or singing, and showed them off, earning myself more than a few enemies along the way. But what did I care? There were always more 'friends' waiting in the wings to skim a little off my shine.

I'd concede to being a cocky bastard—*bastard* being the key word here. As a matter of fact, I was the result of a 'break' in my parents' marriage, or at least that was how my mother described it. My father might not fully agree. According to *his* recollections of my illegitimate beginnings, they had been happily married with two kids, a dog, and a cat, and floating cherubs singing love songs in the rain. Obviously, the truth lay somewhere in between.

All I knew for sure was that Mom got pregnant with me by some traveling musician who'd played a few gigs at the bar she used to frequent with friends. His name was Greg or Gary, or possibly Jack. She couldn't remember exactly—damn those Mojitos—but she did remember having sex with him once or twice or possibly three times in the back of his van. And then, after he was long gone, Mom found herself pregnant with a busker's baby and desperately trying to cover it up.

How did I know the gritty details of my mother's infidelity, you ask? Because it came up every time my parents fought... like every fucking time.

How many times do I have to tell you to put the toilet seat down, Renato?

I don't know, Heather. How many times did you fuck that musician in the back of his van?

Yeah. So, that was how I knew.

Mom hid the truth for as long as she could, the two of them preparing for my arrival just as they had for my brothers before me. But when the doctor handed me to my father in the delivery room, Dad took one look at my light skin and bright blue eyes and handed me back, insisting he'd been given the wrong baby. But no, I'd come straight out of his wife's birth canal and into his waiting arms. There was no mistake, buddy.

He just takes after my side of the family, Mom insisted, offering up her Irish freckles as proof. But no one in the birthing room believed her. Hell, I was minutes old, and *I* didn't believe her. There wasn't a drop of Renato's side of the family in me. That much was easily confirmed in our first party of five photo. Ah yes, it was a classic. My father with the look of death on his face.

My mom nervously looking his way. And me, translucent, in the middle of my two older brothers. I was the human equivalent of the childhood game, 'Which of these things just doesn't belong?'

But Mom wasn't willing to part with her lie so easily, even naming me after him—Renato Junior—n her continued effort to deceive. How was that for a consolation prize? *Sorry I slept around but here, I'll name him RJ after you—just so you'll never ever forget what I've done.* As you can imagine, nothing about my existence sat well with the man. He'd gone from a proud, expectant father of three boys to a bitter man with another mouth to feed. This was no Hallmark movie. Renato never 'came around.' He never accepted me as his. And we never lived happily ever after. At least, *I* never did.

Uhhh...not now. I couldn't think about shit like that, not on the biggest day of my life. Three songs. That was all I needed to sing to have my adoring fans bowing down once more. That would show my family and all the other haters out there who took one look at me and immediately thought *loser*.

"RJ, have my baby."

I glanced out the window at the woman offering me up fatherhood like it was such a simple endeavor. What she didn't know was that there would never be little RJs running around in this world, not if I could help it. I hated kids; or at least I hated the ones who came to *AnyDayNow* concerts. The little screamers who burst my eardrums with their high-pitched squeals, the tiny tyrants who stomped their angry feet and demanded their mommies and daddies keep buying them more of our over-priced merchandise—the cash boxes that kept me in the goddamn lap of luxury. Also the ones I was now counting on to blast my solo career into the stratosphere.

The car door swung open and Roland stood there, his megawatt smile nearly blinding me with its splendor. "You ready for this?"

Ready? This wasn't amateur hour. I knew how to work a crowd. Really, this was just like any other night's work. I'd have these girls eating out of my hand before the night was through. I could barely wait to read the industry reviews the following day.

Stepping out of the limo, I plastered a smile on my face and waved to the crowd. Fans surged, forcing security to form a barrier between me and the overexcited females.

I turned to Roland. "I was born ready."

1

RJ: DEATH OF A HEARTTHROB

Five Months Later

My eyes are open, but I can't see. A chill prickles my skin as I inch forward, one small step at a time, using my hands as guides even though I have no idea what I'm reaching for. It feels expansive— dangerous—like at any moment I might plunge over the edge of a cliff. Intermittent pulses of light flash like the pops of a camera shutter. Darkness and then light. A low murmur can be heard from some- where in the shadows. I tilt my head in the direction of the sound, trying to make out the words. A chant? The lights suddenly flick on, flooding my eyes and giving me the first view of my surroundings. I'm on a stage, microphone in hand, but I'm silent. Paralyzed. The audi- ence studies me from their place of safety. The sound grows louder until I recognize it for what it is—booing.

Beep. Beep. Beep.

Jolting upright, I panted wildly as my brain worked overtime, shifting me in and out of that nightmare world and dumping me here...into a not-much-better waking one. Reaching for my phone, I silenced the alarm before dropping back onto my bed and cursing the audience that mocked me whenever I closed my eyes. I wanted to scream, or throw things at the wall. But instead I just lay there, silently seething.

"Fuck you," I grumbled to the haters in my dreams. "Fuck you all!"

Dragging my ass out of bed, I wandered into the bathroom to take a piss, and inadvertently I caught a glimpse of myself in the mirror. *Whoa! Shit!* I twisted my head around to make sure there wasn't an axe murderer with my likeness sneaking up behind me. Nope. Just me. Damn—at least I looked the part of a pathetic, washed-up has-been. No one could say I wasn't living up to my potential.

God, what happened to me?

No, seriously. What happened?

I looked like I'd crawled out of a manhole. What was up with my hair? It was like there was a party going on front, back, *and* center. And to think there was a time when these bitchin' tresses had inspired Instagram accounts and caused little girls to faint dead away. Yeah, those were the days.

I sighed. This, right here, was why I avoided mirrors. They were a reminder of how far I'd fallen. Back when I was a bona fide heartthrob, industry people lined the block, eager to help me look the part. The hair, the clothes, the...okay, we weren't going to talk about the man makeup. I'd bought into the hype, reveling in the thrill of being included with the heavy hitters, like with *People* magazine's sexiest men alive. But now, examining my blank canvas up close, I saw that much of my looks had been manufactured through the Hollywood spin machine. I wasn't all that. Hell, I wasn't all *this*.

Maybe if I shaved off the nastiness covering three quarters of my face, I'd feel better about myself. I mean, I wasn't a bad-looking guy on a good day. But that beard—dude. I didn't even know where to begin describing it, other than to say it ate other beards for breakfast. Migrating north and south, the unrestrained growth was climbing not only up my face but down my throat. It was only a matter of time before my wily whiskers joined forces with the lonely, south-of-the-equator happy trail, and then I might as well throw in the towel. This was not good. Even if I wanted to get back in the beauty-obsessed music business, the doors would be deadbolted shut for the new and unimproved me.

Not bothering to flush, I slammed the lid down and sidestepped to the sink, never taking my eyes off the asshole in the mirror.

"What the hell did you do to me?" I accused my reflection.

It answered back with a flip of its middle finger.

"Very mature," I mumbled, as I made my way back into the bedroom/living room/kitchen combo area of the space I now called home.

I almost laughed at that one. *Home.* Let me be clear. I had a home—three, to be exact. One lavishly appointed mansion for myself in Los Angeles, one gigantic eyesore in Idaho for my blood relatives to squat in, and one ritzy penthouse suite in New York. Yet I preferred to lick my wounds here, in this bare-bones apartment. With its white walls and dull brown fixings, the 450-square-foot holding cell was no one's idea of a relaxing spot to prop up tired feet after a long day of moping. If it weren't for my guitar, my keyboard, and a pile of scribbled songs scattered over the Yeti cooler I was using as my coffee table, there would be nothing in this suckass studio apartment that felt like home. I'd conceded defeat, and this was my place of worship.

I think both me and the shithead in the mirror would agree. We'd hit rock bottom. Problem was, I didn't know how to pull myself out of the crevasse I was now wedged in. I needed outside help; someone who could objectively analyze the situation...and maybe offer up some worthwhile suggestions.

Sighing, I realized I was going to have to use a lifeline.

"Alexa, make me not want to stick my head in the garbage disposal today."

"Playing grunge music," her automated voice replied, as screaming melodies instantly blasted from her speaker.

I stood there a moment, stunned at the lack of communication we shared before realizing maybe Alexa was on to something. Maybe I needed more shrieking in my life.

"Ah, yes." I nodded. "Perfect choice."

But by the end of the three minutes, I wanted to drive my car into a lake and *not* try to get out. No, this was the opposite of help. I needed something less 'blow your brains out' and more 'keep that chin up, bud.' So I asked Alexa for something upbeat, and she delivered by serving up a big healthy serving of bubblegum pop...and not just any bubblegum pop, but *my* bubblegum pop.

Of course, Alexa would choose this song—the one *AnyDayNow* tune that gave me crippling anxiety and depression every time it came on the radio. "Desperate for You," our biggest hit, was the last song we'd performed that night. Our final bow. And once we walked off the stage after performing it, *AnyDayNow* was no more.

I dropped into a chair, instantly morose as I tossed an old band shirt over my head and listened to the lyrics of the song that had ended it all. I took a deep breath in and remembered— my brothers and me standing at the edge of the stage, arms linked, as the screams from the stadium grew louder and more persistent. Emotions were running high. We couldn't even look each other in the eye for fear of breaking down.

God, how I missed them... and the nights we'd spent rolling down those lonely highways, sprawled out on the leather sofas, exhausted from consecutive nights of performing. It was in those quiet moments when our bond was tightest. The laughter. Our dreams. Even sharing some of our deepest fears. Okay, maybe not Shawn... that dude was a dumbass... but even he had been a necessary part of our dynamic. I'd never had bonds with other guys before. My brothers had always been competition. They'd never had my back, and would just as soon have pushed me off a cliff if they thought their names might be in my will.

Looking back, it was hard to believe we'd once been strangers; teens brought together for the ride of our lives. We'd strapped in and gone wild—some of us more than others. Look, I'd be the first to admit, I let it go to my head. After a lifetime of being a second-class citizen in my own family, I'd emerged into a whole new world where I was important and girls worshiped the ground I walked on. I'd become a cocky shit, thinking I was invincible and that anything I touched would turn to gold. Time —and an ill-fated solo career—had proven me wrong. And now I'd come to the inevitable conclusion that I was only great as one tip on a five-pointed star. I missed touring and performing. I missed the guys. I missed my whole life.

We should've stayed together.

I know what you're thinking—that I was the cause of the breakup. That was, after all, the headline splashed across tabloids the world over. "Jealous RJ Quits *AnyDayNow* Over Bodhi's Rising Fame." That never happened. Sure, I'll admit to having one foot out the door well before the band actually imploded, but it was Mother Nature who'd dropped the final shovel of dirt on *AnyDayNow*'s grave.

If you somehow missed the story of our destruction, a quick Google search would pull up the cautionary tale of my band-mate Bodhi and the swift-moving firestorm that nearly ended his life. But it was the chaotic aftermath, with the news falsely reporting Bodhi's death, that made the four of us remaining band members unanimously call it quits. At the time, it seemed impossible for the band to weather his loss. Of course, that same Google search would tell you Bodhi showed up alive the next day, having survived the fire by the hair of his chinny-chin-chin. But by then, the damage had already been done.

My phone buzzed. I swiped it off the counter, saw it was Bodhi, and set the phone back down. This was a pattern that had repeated itself daily ever since I'd walled myself up in this suck-ass fortress.

"Sorry, dude, not today," I said, hitting the ignore button. Keeping Bodhi and the boys at arm's length was essential if I wanted to continue wallowing in my own misery. They had a way of lifting me up, and I had no interest in such positivity.

Speaking of which...

"Alexa, play 'Apologies.'"

Yeah, I was pushing it now. "Apologies" was the first single off my debut album, and the one I'd been sure would catapult me into a successful solo career. I'd put everything into its creation, nurturing it to perfection. And once it was ready to share with the world, I'd sent it off like a baby bird learning to fly. God, I'd been so proud. Never in my wildest dreams could I have imagined my songbird would slam into a closed window and plunge to the earth with a sickening thud. But that was exactly what had happened following that disastrous concert on the pier—with the added horror of watching "Apologies" barely slide into the Billboard Top 100 charts before dropping away soon after.

Yeah. Too bad I couldn't swipe left on *that* memory.

I listened to the lyrics, trying to decipher just what it was about the song that people hated, but as hard as I tried to find fault, I couldn't. Despite what everyone else thought, I still loved my baby.

"Alexa, do you like this song?" I asked.

"Hmm...if you like this song," she replied, "maybe try Nickelback."

"Fuck you!"

I shot up from my chair and threw the shirt across the room. Everyone was a goddamn critic. Silencing the shrew, I headed for the kitchen and tossed all the ingredients into my blender for the perfect smoothie. Even as everything was collapsing around me, I held onto my fitness routine, eating clean and continuing my workouts, because as my life spiraled out control, my body was the only thing I had left to count on.

My cell rang again. Bodhi. *Answer the damn phone,* I told myself. *You can count on him. You know you can.* But try as I might, I couldn't get myself to answer. Grimacing, I let Bodhi's call go to voicemail. I loved the dude. He was my best friend. We'd done everything together, including being the dueling heartthrobs in *AnyDayNow.* Ours were the names screamed from the stands. RJ and Bodhi. Bodhi and RJ.

But then he'd gone on to bigger and better things, leaving me stuck spinning my wheels in the mud. I should have been where Bodhi was, slowly building a solo career with a kickass woman by my side. But instead, I'd been overconfident, rushing things in order to be the first *Day*er to release a solo album. And now here I was, paying the price for my arrogance. Fuck me. Fuck all those armchair critics who reveled in my despair. And fuck Bodhi Beckett.

Whoa! Easy, son. This wasn't Bodhi's fault. Not even close. He was only calling me because he was worried. They all were. How could I blame them? I'd basically dropped off the face of the earth, ghosting the guys I'd claimed would always be my brothers. But here was the deal: they wanted me to be fine. And I wasn't fine.

So I hid, holing myself up in this shitty apartment and living under the alias Chad Woodcock—one of the many fake names the guys and I had dreamed up on our multiple tours together. Back then, it was funny as shit. Now it just seemed sad. Maybe, deep down, I wanted them to find me, and that was why I'd picked Chad Woodcock. It was a clue—a piece of low-lying fruit ripe for the picking. If my buddies were really motivated, if they put their collective brains together, then maybe, just maybe, they'd find me.

I wasn't holding my breath.

"Shit," I whispered, disappointed in myself. I was such a bad friend. A bad singer. A bad human. I should just go back to bed, pull the sheets up over my head, and drift away. But there was nowhere safe for me. Not asleep. Not awake. Not work. Not home.

I flicked the blender switch to 'on.'

Here's to the start of another wasted day.

2

DANI: REPEAT AFTER ME

WHY DID HE HAVE TO BE SO PERFECT?

I dropped my forehead to the table and did a little no-hands head bang. It seemed appropriate, given the circumstances. Last night, I'd been on my first date in months; but somehow, I'd managed to ruin a perfectly good evening by slut-shaming the dude's mother over a slice of cheesecake.

"Uhhh," I groaned, smacking my head against the table one last time. What was wrong with me? Most girls would feel so lucky to get a date with a man like Jeremy. Set up through mutual friends, he and I seemed perfectly matched—so much in common. Some might even say too much. Both driven, articulate, and, dare I say, attractive, we really should have had instant chemistry.

Jeremy was a catch in every sense of the word. He was gainfully employed *and* loved his mother—like, a lot. Maybe even more than most. But you know, there was nothing wrong with a strong parent-child bond, even if the son was in his late twenties. Right? I mean the fact that I found it even remotely creepy spoke more to my less-than-stellar relationship with my own mother than it did Jeremy's with his.

And don't even get me started on my father. Let's just say he wasn't in the picture—nor on my birth certificate. My father was nothing more than a vial of sperm, yet he'd still managed to wreak havoc on my personal life. In fact, if my dad hadn't been such a Lothario in his early years, I wouldn't be in this predicament with Jeremy. And, yes, I understood that made me sound like I was shifting the blame for my own bad behavior onto my father, but his bountiful right-handed tug-and-pulls in the sterile back room of a fertility clinic really was the bane of my existence.

Last night was a perfect example of what I'm talking about. Within minutes of the start of the date with Jeremy, I began noticing little things about him... eerily similar things. The way he used 'so' as a filler between pauses. The way he traced his finger along the table top. The color of his eyes. The brightness of his hair. The dimple in his cheek. It was then I realized—Jeremy and I could be siblings. And once the thought permeated my brain, there was no shutting it off. Suddenly all I could do was picture us finishing each other's sentences, and not in the cutesy, unrelated sort of way. Or us celebrating the birth of our future daughter, who would arrive in this world sporting an extra nose protruding from her belly button. Dating in the city was hard enough without having to worry that every man I met might actually be my brother.

The sound of the blender next door pulled me out of my thoughts.

"Chad," I mumbled under my breath, steam venting through my ears.

Every morning, like clockwork, Chad's NutriBullet roared to life, and given that the wall separating my neighbor and me was as thin as a seaweed wrap, I got to be right there for the action. Living next to Chad was like interactive live theater. If he was watching sports, I heard the cheers. If he was taking a shit, I heard the plops. And if the muscle man next door was making a protein shake, I heard the high-powered crushing. What the hell was he grinding in that thing anyway—a sliding glass door?

When I first moved in, I'd tried to give Chad the benefit of the doubt, even slipping a reverse-psychology 'good neighbor' contract under his door, promising to keep *my* noise levels down for his comfort—when in reality *he* was, and always had been, the problem. Not that the strategy worked. If anything, the contract only made him louder and more difficult. The guy had an ornery side to him that I found nearly as off-putting as the shaggy brown carpet covering nearly the entire landscape of his face. But why stop there? Since I was currently on the subject of Chad, I'd be remiss not to mention some of the weird shit he did, like avoiding all face-to-face contact. Look, I'm all for maintaining some distance, but this guy's aversion to eye contact bordered on obsessive, especially when he covered his face with his hand as I walked by.

Um...okay, weirdo. You do you.

I'd originally just shrugged off Chad as one of those antisocial video gamers who'd been weaned off the teat not with a pacifier but with a controller in hand. I imagined the poor guy had only recently discovered the outside world. It was a plausible theory, for sure, but it didn't account for the muscles I spied every time he came home from the gym. Nor did it explain that heavenly voice of his when he sang along to his guitar. Or the tattoo sleeve that traveled up his arm and over his broad shoulder. Or those striking aqua blue eyes that occasionally peaked out from under a feather duster of lashes.

Wait. Why was I thinking about my hairy, jacked-up neighbor? Chad was nothing like clean-cut Jeremy—my possible genetic twin. Oh man, I had to stop thinking of him in those terms.

Repeat after me: Jeremy is not your brother.

I mean, come on. Get a grip, girl. There were four million people living in Los Angeles. What were the odds I was related to a good percentage of them? Deflating at the thought, I realized for the average girl, the odds were very slim; but for me the probabilities were surprisingly high.

See, I was the offspring of a woman who was too picky to settle down with 'just any man,' so instead, she'd hand-picked the perfect one—Sperm Donor 649. Don't get me wrong—'d never had a problem with my artificially inseminated beginnings. On the contrary, I was proud to share my story, even playing the papa game with the other kids in school until the principal called my mother into the office and put a stop to it. *My dad's a doctor. My dad's a fireman. Yeah? Well, my dad's a test tube.*

Yep, it was all fun and games until I got an email from a lawyer two years ago warning me that just as my mother had found Sperm Donor 649's profile irresistible, so had lots of other women—in total birthing one hundred and eleven artificially inseminated offspring. To date, I had forty-four confirmed half-siblings. Plus, thanks to the rise of the DNA testing sites and our accompanying Facebook page, The Lucky Swimmers Club, the numbers were continuing to rise. And because more than half of us had yet to be identified, that made Jeremy guilty until proven innocent.

Certainly, my life on the dating front would have been so much easier if my dear ol' test tube dad hadn't financed his college education one ejaculation at a time. I don't want to brag or anything, but the man was a bit of a rock star in the semen-seeking world. Who knew in the mid-90's that blue-eyed med students with above average intelligence and six-foot-one frames would be all the rage? My prolific pop's 'contributions' were so sought after, in fact, that an unscrupulous doctor kept his seed in rotation long after it should have been retired, making Sperm Donor 649 the unwitting commander of a small army.

Sometimes I imagined my father and wondered if he knew he'd had a part in bringing so many humans into the world; but more specifically, I wondered what he'd think of me. My whole life, I'd tried to live up to his ideals, excelling at school and getting a degree. Would he be proud? God knows, my mother never was. It really didn't matter what I did in life, it was never good enough for her. Hell, I could bring home Neanderthal Chad to meet the fam and that still wouldn't come close to the disappointment she'd felt when I'd failed to get accepted to medical school.

But then I went and totally ripped her heart out by refocusing on another profession—teaching. I swear my mother would probably have preferred I slide up and down a pole rather than have to tell her friends I taught first-graders Common Core curriculum and modeled for them how *not* to hold their crotches when they had to go pee pee. If I was going to disappoint, Mom wanted it to be something grand, something she could then blame on my father's side of the family. *Obviously, Danielle got her severe acne from her father's side of the family.* Or, *Of course Danielle is a stripper. What did you expect when her great-great grandmother, on her father's side, liked the feel of metal between her legs?*

Don't get me wrong—my mother could be sweet and loving. If the sun and moon aligned just right. But it was her disappointment in all things 'me' that had led to our mini estrangement and my accepting a job in Los Angeles, where the inflated rents forced me to seek out cost-effective housing and live next door to a dunderhead like Chad.

The blender continued to whirl. Jesus, how long did it take to grind up kale and broken dreams? I got up from my chair, made a fist, and pounded on the wall. In true meathead fashion, my neighbor defiantly switched the blender setting to high and let that baby churn. Such a colossal jerk. Why couldn't he just fall in line, like all twenty-six of my sperm brothers?

My phone buzzed on the kitchen table. I picked it up and raised a brow. *Well, I'll be damned.* Speaking of sperm brothers, a text had just come through from possible number twenty-seven: Jeremy.

Had a great time last night, he wrote.

Really? How? If my excessive incestuous sweating hadn't turned him off, I was sure the Ancestry.com survey request of his mother's sex life just before his conception would have done him in. Wow, Jeremy was a hardy fella—like a drought-resistant weed.

Yes, it was fun

Can't wait to see you again. How about tonight? Does a movie sound good?

Tonight? Huh, let me think. I did have plans to practice knuckle-knocking Morse code on the wall I shared with Chad, but I supposed I could put it off for one more day.

Um, okay that sounds fun, I typed. *What theater? I'll meet you*

How about I come pick you up instead? Around six

Pick me up? Given the considerable amount of time Jeremy had spent detailing his high-end apartment, I found it a rather bold move on his part to now freely volunteer to venture over to the dark side of Los Angeles living. But bolder, still, was that he assumed I'd give out my address to just any old serial killer.

You live in the Freeport Building, right?

My eyes rounded. What the...? I was going to die. Right here. Tonight. And it wasn't like I could count on Chad to save me, what with Wednesday being *American Ninja Warrior* night.

But as if reading my mind—don't siblings have a weird form of telepathy? or is that twins—he followed his text with. *Not a stalker. Ainsley is my cousin, remember?*

Oh, right. Ainsley. Lives in the apartment complex across the street. Ainsley. My coworker. His cousin. The matchmaker. See? He wasn't Ted Bundy. Silly me.

I know, I wrote back adding a crazy-face emoji to throw him off the trail of my craziness.

We spent the next few texts discussing what movie we'd like to see before he ended our digital chat with:

I dig you, Dani. Haven't stopped thinking about you since last night

Oh. I hadn't stopped thinking about him either. Did he have banjo toes like me? Did he grind his teeth in his sleep?

Stop, I chided myself. This was going to be great. Jeremy was great. There was absolutely nothing to worry about.

Again, repeat after me: Jeremy is not your brother.

RJ: POST-IT NOTES

Damn that Dani. She thought she owned the wall. And the balcony. And the world. The woman had an opinion about everything and never passed up a teaching opportunity. Needless to say, we were not Mr. Roger's sugar-swapping neighbors. Before either of us had moved into the apartment complex, some corporate genius had decided that it would be more cost effective to erect a wall the down length of a single 1150-square-foot apartment and call it two. Dani's side got most of the square footage, along with the bedroom, the original kitchen, and the bathroom. I got the stripped-down Spirit Airlines version on the other side.

Still, the cramped quarters and paper-thin wall separating us weren't the reason for our feud. That honor went to our shared balcony. Before Dani, I'd never once seen the person living next door. Whoever it was had kept their blinds drawn at all times, so that meant the balcony had essentially been mine alone, and my stuff was strewn everywhere—until the day she moved in and turned my bachelor oasis into an Urban Outfitters outdoor living space complete with a Boho wall tapestry, string lights, and an organic vegetable garden.

Don't get me wrong, I wasn't opposed to a little luxury, but Dani wasn't inclined to share. In the middle of our balcony, like she'd actually measured the length with a yardstick, she'd erected a barrier in the form of a brightly colored masking tape strip dividing our two sections. She'd even taken the initiative to stack my shit into neat piles on my side of the line with a Post-it Note attached reading, Please respect my space.

I responded with my own Post-it Note: I'd rather be drilled in the ass by a woodpecker than respect your space.

To which she responded, I don't care what sort of kinky shit you're into, just don't touch my basil.

And so began our passive-aggressive Post-it Note war. At any given time of the day, I could expect to find notes on my door or out on the balcony, alerting me to her disappointment in my existence. She didn't like my music or my smelly gym shirt hanging over my chair on the terrace or my trash bag that had been strategically placed outside my front door to remind myself to take it to the garbage chute in the morning.

I winced at the memory of the garbage chute misstep. That incident had led to an entire novel of one-word Post-It Notes pasted all over my front door that read, Your. stinky. trash. belongs. in. the. dumpster. Chad. Do better!

I wasn't sure what the woman did for a living, but I was fairly certain it had something to do with torturing small animals. Or maybe she worked at the DMV. All I knew was I needed to avoid her this morning at all costs, because after Alexa's heartless Nickelback diss, I didn't have the patience to deal with finicky women today.

Pressing my eyeball to the peephole before exiting my apartment, I searched for the little five-foot-two spitfire on three-inch heels. On workdays, Dani always wore her hair pulled back into a high ponytail and was clad in smart casual clothing. She was pretty, in a pretentious, know-it-all sort of way. She had killer hazel eyes and long, caramel-colored hair that flipped up at the ends and reached all the way to the small of her back when she let it down at the end of the day. I'll admit to accidentally spying on her on occasion when she was out on the balcony soaking up the sun. That was when I liked her best—when her mouth wasn't moving.

After taking the necessary precautions, I determined the coast to be clear and pushed open the door, breathing a sigh of relief. The day was looking up. But then, like a bomb blasting it off its fucking hinges, the door beside mine burst open and out tottered Dani. Goddamn, this woman couldn't do anything subtly. I held back my whimper.

"Oh," she said, startled. "I didn't see you."

Clearly, she'd been doing her own keyhole surveillance.

"Did you get my note?" I asked, without looking up.

Feigning ignorance, she replied, "What note?"

"The one I pushed all the way through the crack in your door last night until it disappeared inside your apartment."

"Oh, *that* note."

"Yeah, that one. Did you read it?"

She skipped answering my question in favor of her own inquiry. "Did you run out of sticky pads, Chad?"

"Actually, I did—I'm surprised you haven't run out yourself, given how liberally you abuse them."

"I bought in bulk after meeting you."

"I'm sure you did," I sighed. "Just answer the question, Dani. Did you read my note or not?"

"Yes, I read your note. But then I was forced to burn it because I don't want there to be any evidence pointing toward me when management finds your dead body."

This was the attitude I dealt with on a daily basis. It was like living next door to a disgruntled postal worker, only more hostile.

"And? Did you?" I asked, careful to keep my face covered in my pullover hoodie.

"Did I *what*?" She spun around to face me, and my pulse quickened. God, how I loved riling her up. Dani was one of those law-and-order girls who thought the universe revolved around her, when in reality, she was just getting in its way. How she'd ended up here, on the edge of extinction, I couldn't guess, but I'd watched her thrive with fascinated ambivalence. This was not a woman who hid out and felt sorry for herself. She was a go-getter, even if, based solely on her living conditions, she wasn't really getting anywhere.

"Are you asking me if I stole your package, Chad?"

"No. I'm simply following the evidence. According to the delivery information sent to my email yesterday, the package was left on my doorstep at 9:15 a.m. Saturday morning. But by the time I got home at 11:35 a.m., it was gone."

"Wow," she said in sarcastic amazement. "Your detective skills are spot on. Where did you learn your trade? From Riverdale?"

"I don't need high quality investigative training to tell me you're the most obvious suspect," I countered.

"Oh, yeah? And why is that? Please provide details."

"That's confidential."

"Oh, no. If you're accusing me of kleptomania, I have a right to know your evidence."

"Look, Dani, I don't care if you're into whips and chains. Your private life is none of my business," I replied, scratching my temple. I knew damn well what she was talking about, but I also knew I'd be lighting her fuse.

"No, Chad, kleptomania—a compulsion to steal. Seriously, dude, your teachers need to line up and apologize to you."

We have a flame.

"Or, at the very least, pummel you with a bat, dumbass."

Click. Click. Boom, baby!

She was just that easy. In some ways, making Dani crazy took the edge off. By stripping her of her sanity, I was restoring bits and pieces of my own. My eyes narrowed in on her. Obviously, she hadn't comprehended the joke. Typical. Fancying herself a scholar, Dani regularly chose intelligence-shaming as her weapon of choice, but seeing that she'd graduated from one of those Varsity Blue campuses where the rich mommies and daddies routinely bought their children's way into the school, I wouldn't have put it past Dani to have a fake athletic profile floating around out there somewhere with her face photo-shopped onto a rower's body.

"You want evidence?" I said. "Fine. There are two reasons why I've concluded you're the culprit. One: we're at the end of the hallway, and no one comes back here. And two: you're the only person who wishes me dead."

"Oh, Chad, don't sell yourself short. I'm sure there are plenty of people who want to throw you over the balcony."

I laughed at her snappy comeback, one of the few chuckles to pass my lips in months. Dani rolled her eyes then returned to the near-impossible task of fitting her key into the lock while agitated.

After witnessing several failed attempts, I stepped forward to offer my assistance.

"Back off!" she hissed, angling her hip to block me from advancing.

Holding my hands up, I took a step back. "Whoa, I can see that stuffing holes isn't your thing. I was just trying to help."

She glanced up at me, blowing a strand of hair from her

eyes. "Clever word-play there, Chad. I can see you've been practicing. Bravo. Oh, and if that hair on your face is any indication, I can't imagine little Chad is doing much stuffing himself. He probably can't see over the shrubs."

"Don't you worry about little Chad. He's a grower."

"Well, that's good, because he certainly isn't a show-er," Dani said, shifting her eyes downward and over my gym shorts before turning and walking away. "Have a shitty day, Chad."

"Thanks. You too. Oh, and Dani? I'll expect my package to be waiting for me when I get home."

She spun back around to face me. "Yeah? Well, you'll be waiting a long time because—say it with me, Dickweed—Dani. Did. Not. Steal. My. Package."

"Dani did *for sure* steal my package," I repeated after her...sort of.

"Uhhh..." she roared. "I can't even. Think whatever you want, but just know that I have no interest in a box stuffed with lube and tube socks."

Oh, damn. Shots fired.

"Actually," I volleyed, "it was a box of loneliness and desperation. I ordered it as a gift for you."

My neighbor's eyes widened. She was reaching her limit; and yet still I kept poking. Dani was the only thing in my life that made my pulse race the way it had when I was on stage. I needed her anger like I needed my life back.

"Ooh, you're hilarious," she replied, employing jazz hands just to showcase how unamused she really was. "Can you do me a huge favor, Chad? Can you never speak to me again?"

"Sure, I'll give it a shot," I said brushing by her in the hallway. "Oh, and can you keep the noise down this evening when you gobble up that Ben & Jerry's ice cream? I can hear your spoon hitting porcelain every fucking night, and it gives me headaches."

"Sure. I'll try to be more considerate." She smiled through clenched teeth.

"Awesome. Thanks."

"Oh, and Chad? You be sure to hydrate properly after aggressively masturbating tonight."

"I would," I called over my shoulder, "but you stole my lube."

4

RJ: THE AMBUSH

CHUCKLING ALL THE WAY TO MY CAR, IT WASN'T UNTIL I WAS strapped in that I caught the devious expression on my face in the rearview mirror. I didn't like what I saw—that self-righteous smirk. A little too familiar a sight for my taste. My smile faded. What was it about Dani that made me want to pick her apart piece by piece? The girl hadn't done anything to deserve my wrath. I was bored and unhappy with my life, and Dani's misery had become my serotonin.

Damn. What had happened to me? What had happened to that hyperactive kid who self-calmed through music? Fame—and a man-made ego the size of football field—that was what had happened to me. With women throwing themselves at my feet, it was easy to adopt the idea that I walked on holy water. But these past few months had proved I was nothing if not mortal.

And Dani... oh, Dani. This morning, she'd stumbled onto a land mine in not the most sensible footwear. There was no way the poor girl wouldn't take a step in the wrong direction and explode. I often wondered if Dani would hate me as much if she knew who I was. Probably not. People tended to give celebrities the benefit of the doubt even when we didn't deserve it. Still, it did surprise me that, after all this time, she hadn't pieced it together. Could it be that I'd come face-to-face with one of those rare women under the age of thirty who was not a card-carrying *Dayer*? I'd always heard such females existed, but I'd never met one in person.

Although... maybe she actually was a fan of *AnyDayNow* but had been thrown off my scent by the pelt on my face, as well as the habitat in which I was currently living. This was, after all, the very last place on earth anyone would expect to find a multimillionaire pop star. And that was precisely why it made this apartment complex the perfect place to hunker down for the rest of my natural born life.

What frustrated me about Dani, and maybe why I picked on her relentlessly, was because she viewed me through unbiased 'Chad Woodcock' eyes and had clearly found me wanting. Goddamn story of my life. Strip me of all the ladders I'd climbed and all the awards I'd won and you were left with that little boy who ate his dinner on a TV tray away from everyone else because there was no room at the four-person table. I was twenty pounds, soaking wet. They could have scooted the fuck over.

My fingers curled around the steering wheel, and I gripped it like two steel clamps. This was precisely why I avoided trips down memory lane. They never led anywhere good. But now that I was locked and loaded, I couldn't get *them* out of my head. My neglectful mother. My resentful father. My two manipulative brothers, who'd thrilled in watching me punished for the things that they would do themselves. Something as small as a misplaced candy wrapper could provoke my parents' wrath. It didn't matter how much I protested or tried to defend myself against the allegations—no one was listening.

And so I grew into an unruly kid who sought attention at every curve. I wanted to be heard, and if that meant bouncing off the walls with enough energy to light a city block, that was just what I'd do. A brat, I was called. Hyperactive, I was labeled. If I didn't receive the loving attention I deserved, then I'd damn well get it anyway I possibly could—even if it came at a cost, like bent over Renato's knee with his hand slapping me on the ass.

And yet, I preferred the corporal punishment over the mental abuse he and my uncaring mother doled out on a daily basis. She was more subtle in her distaste, slipping in small insults here and there—things that wouldn't seem inflammatory on the surface but would burrow into my skin and slowly fester. But Renato, oh yeah, he never passed up a chance to laser me with his hateful eyes as he cursed my existence under his breath. If only those two had understood their spiteful seething hurt me more than if they'd just gotten it over with and lashed me with a belt.

I could have folded my hand and let them win, but that had never been my style. I had to prove my worth, make something so big out of myself that not even they could deny me. And so, I carved out my niche in the world—something that was uniquely my own in this family of underachieving duds. Music. I'd shown a propensity toward it from as early as my toddler years—able to carry a tune into the next county and back. Given that my brothers would be hard-pressed to sing the Meow Mix song, it was safe to assume my talent came from Gary or Greg or whatever the hell his name was.

But even as I made my talent known throughout the town and then the county, I still could not best my brothers.

Yes, RJ, you won the county-wide talent competition, but Luis here, he just farted the National Anthem. Can you get through 'the rockets' red glare' without shitting your pants? I don't think so."

My brothers contributed nothing of value to the family unit, yet still they were the apples of my father's eye. Me? Nothing I did impressed Renato. In his eyes, I was different. Musical. Artistic. Wild. Another man's son.

And my mother? How dare she. I belonged to her and only her. She should have protected me. Loved me. But the day I was born, she picked a side. It was them or me...and she chose them.

———

Driving into the back alley, I parked my car in the small lot behind the gym. Technically this was employee parking, but I was given certain privileges because of my celebrity—a status that was quickly fading. I wondered how much longer these perks would last before I'd be forced to park out front with the rest of the washed-up boy banders who'd come before me.

I pulled on the handle and was about to step out of my car when the door swung forcefully open, shocking me.

"Outta the car!"

Two men with black ski masks covering their faces gripped my shirt and dragged me from the cab. My heart battered against my chest as self-preservation took over.

They just want the car, I told myself. *Don't fight them. You have eight more where this one came from.*

"What do you want?" I managed to coax the words from my bone-dry throat.

"Don't play dumb, Contreras, you know what we want."

My name. He'd used my name! This was no car-jacking. Could it be a kidnapping for ransom? If so, who was going to pay up? I'd bought the house in Idaho for my family and provided to them the required living wage for keeping their mouths shut about our rickety family history, but I certainly wasn't stupid enough to grant them access to my fortunes.

One of the men shoved me up against my car and twisted my

arm behind my back. I turned my head to get a look at my assailants, but the other one palmed my head and shoved me down onto the hood. It was then I snapped out of the shock that had rendered me temporarily stunned. These fuckers had picked the wrong guy. I was already at the end of my rope, but no way was I going to let someone else take the credit for hanging me.

Determination pumped through my veins, and with a forceful grunt, I flung my arms out to the sides, knocking both my assailants backward. They instantly released their grip, which allowed me to flip around and ready myself for battle. Neither one had expected my brute strength, that much was clear. During my boyband days, I'd been lean and sinewy—just what the girls had wanted. But months of regret all pounded into punching bags or lifted over my head with heavy weights had added a good thirty pounds of muscle to my frame.

Both accosters attempted to flee, but I grabbed the closer of the two and slammed my fist into his stomach.

"Mother dick, that hurts," the man grunted on the way down to his knees. I cocked a brow, recognizing that voice. It couldn't be. But then my eyes narrowed in on the dad bod of the other attacker. Now I knew exactly who I was dealing with: the Tweedle-dee and Tweedle-dum of former bandmates. Dane and fucking Shawn. And they were about to meet their maker.

Planting the sole of my shoe against Dane's chest, I shoved him hard and watched as he tipped to his side and crumpled to the ground. Satisfied he was down for the count, I lunged for Shawn, but he'd been expecting my revenge and sprinted toward the door of the gym. Perhaps if he'd sprinted to the gym more often in his everyday life, I wouldn't have been able to so easily catch up to him. I took Shawn down like the third-string quarterback he was.

We spent a moment wrestling on the ground before I

trapped him beneath me and raised my fist in the air, ready to pummel him into the concrete.

"Uncle!" he scream-laughed, pulling the mask off his face. "Uncle! Uncle! Uncle!"

My fist shook. Just one punch. He deserved it. But instead, I lifted him up and then dropped him like a weight back to the ground.

Shawn held up his hands in surrender. "Jesus H. W. Bush, RJ! I called uncle!"

"And I heard your pathetic cries; hence the reason I'm not rearranging your face. But only because you're ugly enough as is."

"Tell that to my body count."

"And then credit that body count to your bank account."

Shawn responded with a smile before flipping me off.

"Seriously, dude. Can you be any dumber? Can you, really?"

He stared up at me defiantly. "You know I can!"

Oh yes, I knew he could. Having spent five years with him in the tour bus, I knew a thing or two about this dude's IQ, and let's just say he wasn't smarter than a fifth grader.

Dane had recovered enough from the stomach punch and foot shove to get up off the concrete and make his way over to us.

"You really need anger management classes, dude," he grumbled, rubbing his gut. "We were just having fun."

"Surely there's another way to have fun that doesn't require committing a felony kidnapping?"

"If there was..." Shawn shrugged. "We didn't think of it."

"I told them not to," Hunter said, stepping out from behind the dumpster. What the hell? Was this an *AnyDayNow* reunion? All we needed was Bodhi to round out the fivesome.

"So did I," Bodhi said, following Hunter out.

And now we were complete.

"What are you guys doing here?" I asked. "How did you find me?"

"Chad Woodcock?" Bodhi raised his brows. "Please—give us a little credit. We're not complete idiots."

"Well, it did take you five months, so..."

"You're an asshole." Dane shook his head. "Why were you hiding from us in the first place? Did our blood handshake mean nothing to you?"

"It was ketchup... so no."

"It was the symbolism behind it, RJ!"

"Look, I'm sorry. I wanted to be alone."

"You can be alone but still answer the phone," Bodhi said. "If you'd just picked up, Dumb and Dumber here wouldn't have concocted a plan to abduct you."

"I was hiding out. By definition, that means I hide."

"For five months?"

"For as long as I feel like."

"Yeah, well, you might want to come up with a better hiding spot because if our stupid asses can find you, so can anyone else with half a brain."

"Maybe I will."

"Or maybe you pull up those big boy pants of yours and face the music."

"Or...," Shawn weaseled out from under me, and dusted off his expensive clothes. "Maybe you can be a groomsman at my wedding."

I whipped my head around. "Your wedding? I thought you were already married."

"Not to that one. This is a new one."

"Wait. Angel?"

"No, Angel is baby one's mama. Not marrying her."

"Yvette?"

"She's the baby two's mama. Not marrying her either."

"Reese?"

"Married her, but it was annulled, remember?"

"Then who?"

"Laura."

I shook my head. "I'm going to need more than that."

Shawn sighed. "You might remember me referring to her as Quiet Sex Girl."

"Quiet Sex Girl?" My eyes rounded. "Dude, I thought you said she creeped you out—that you were worried she might mutilate bashful Shawn in the act."

"With two whole inches of dick?" Bodhi smirked. "I hardly think that's possible."

"Exactly," Dane agreed, chuckling. "No one is that skilled with a cleaver."

Shawn shook his head. "Oh, right, I forgot this was dick-shaming day."

"Actually, there's no need for a national holiday," I said, patting his shoulder. "Every day with that little Mini Cooper in your pants is cause for embarrassment."

"And to think, I came all the way out here to kidnap you—and this is how you treat me?"

"I never asked to be abducted, and I never asked you to get married to Quiet Sex Girl. That was all on you."

"Watch it. Laura is the love of my life."

Bodhi and I exchanged knowing grins. There had been so, so many *loves of his life*.

"Uh-huh." I said. "And how far along is she?"

Shawn grumbled under his breath. "Four months."

"Dude," Hunter gaped. "Another baby?"

"What? I might need a kidney in thirty years. This just increases my odds of a match."

I smiled, almost forgetting how much I'd missed these guys. "Okay, so, let me get this straight. It took all four of you to come down here and ask me to be the best man at Shawn's wedding?"

"Whoa, hold up, dude. Who says you get to be best man?" Dane scoffed. "Do you really think you can hide from us for five months and then suddenly reappear only to slide into a starring role? I don't think so."

"Shawn," I turned to him. "Who's your best man *this time*? Because I seem to recall last time you picked Bodhi. And the time before that was Dane."

"Right, but I never got to serve because the paternity test came back just in the nick of time," Dane reminded.

"But you were asked," I snapped back. "So, by the process of elimination, I'm next in line."

"Um, hello, assholes. I'm right here." Hunter reacted with indignation. "Am I not even in the running?"

"You don't need to be the best man," Shawn said, gripping Hunter's shoulder. "You have a much more important role to play in my life. You know you're the only one I trust to delete my browser history if something bad happens to me."

"I..." Hunter shook his head. "I'm honored."

"Anyway, RJ," Bodhi said. "Shawn's wedding isn't the only reason we've been trying to get in touch with you."

"Then what?"

"We're getting back together," Dane jabbered.

My eyes rounded to epic proportions. What was he talking about? *AnyDayNow* had run its course. They all had to realize that by now.

"Dane, you can't just blurt shit like that out," Hunter admonished. "Gotta ease the skittish ones in."

I looked back and forth between my former band mates. "You guys are delusional, that's what you are. Do none of you remember the misery of the last year in *AnyDayNow*? How could you want to go back to that?"

"I told you he wouldn't go for it," Bodhi said to Dane.

"He has to," Dane said, shrugging. "It's all or none."

"What's going on?" I demanded.

"We're getting the band back together for a documentary series," Hunter explained. "About our time together. They already have all the footage from that time when the crew followed us around during the 'Listen Up' tour. All they really need from us is interviews, both together and separate."

"And why would we do that?" I asked.

"They are offering us bucketsful of cash, that's why," Shawn replied.

"I already have bucketsful of cash."

Hunter's face soured. "I don't. Dane doesn't. Shawn doesn't."

"Please—you get the same percentage of royalties Bodhi and I do."

"Right, but your royalties are supplemented by the outside endorsement deals the two of you receive. The rest of us didn't get that windfall. We've never had the same high profile you guys have. You do realize that Shawn, Dane, and me haven't even landed a record deal yet, right?"

I didn't know. And now I felt bad. Bodhi and I had always been the favorites, but I'd never realized it was to the detriment of the others.

"Look, I know you want to hide out," Hunter continued. "But we need you. It's been over a year, and things are drying up for us. I got a wife and kids, man. And Shawn, he's got a kid in every state. Dane…I have no idea what extracurriculars he's got going on. But here's the deal, RJ. If you really are our brother, then this is the time to show it."

My eyes jumped from one to the next as my resistance wavered. How could I turn my back on these guys when they'd always been there for me? Five years we been stuck to each other like glue. We'd gone our separate ways, yes, but that didn't change the way I felt about them. I loved these guys, and no matter how broken or lost I currently was, I was never too broken or lost for my ketchup-blood brothers.

5

DANI: EYES ON ME

THE CHATTER CREPT UP ON ME. ONE VOICE. THEN TWO. A THIRD from across the room. This would not do. Isolated chitchat in a classroom of twenty-five first graders could easily spiral out of control. Six- and seven-year-olds were like rolling thunder. If you gave them the chance to join forces, there'd be no stopping their explosive storm.

"One-two-three, eyes on me."

"One-two, eyes on you," my students responded to my chant —all except the culprits in the back, who'd been the reason for the intervention.

Stepping around my desk, I made my Cruella De Vil catwalk down the aisle, watching as the two offenders spotted me coming only to right themselves in their seats, fold their hands on their desks, and seal their mouths shut.

That was better. *Now* I was back in control—just where I liked to be. It was a place that Chad had callously denied me this morning, and a place I would never allow him to take from me again. *Ugh. Stop thinking about Chad!* I had a classroom of students to teach, and I refused to allow him to derail me from educating the youth of America. They deserved better.

"Thank you, girls." I winked.

Their nervous faces dissolved into smiles, and a spattering of giggles filled the room. That, in a nutshell, was my 'milk dud' teaching style—hard on the outside but soft and gooey in the center. I had a reputation as a teacher who cared, and after only three years as a credentialed educator, I'd landed into the enviable position of being the first-grade teacher all the PTA moms fought over.

Sure, tough love had its time and place, but I was proof positive that it was not the only way. My mother had thought otherwise, almost always dishing out the *tough* without the *love* when dealing with my perceived failings. The result was I'd become sneaky, hiding things from her to keep the peace. And now, as an adult, I could clearly see that *tough* only worked if it was paired with its forward-thinking partner.

"Okay, friends, I can see most of you are finishing up your assignment in the math workbook. Great job. But does that mean it's playtime?"

A high-pitch chorus of 'no-s' erupted.

"That's right. Playtime comes *after* the bell rings. Until then, we work. So, for those of you who are done with the subtraction classwork, you may get an early start on the writing assignment. Today we'll be writing a letter to our Star of the Week. Do we all remember who this week's star is?"

"Sophie!" My students yelled out the name of our Star Student. That was what I loved about kids. They were always genuinely happy for their classmate. Ah, if only grown-ups got such recognition. Yes, perhaps we needed an Adult Star of the Week.

I knew who wouldn't be its first recipient—Chad. If he were in my class, he would've lost points for all sorts of infractions after our hallway confrontation. Lying. Not being a good friend.

Unkind words. Not following directions. Heck, I might even have taken the drastic step of calling his mother.

"You're all so smart," I praised my students. "All right, then, let's get back to work."

Since I was already in the back of the classroom, I took my show on the road, moving from desk to desk to check the progress of my little charges. One such girl sat starting off into space.

"Nelle, is there a problem?" I asked.

"I don't know what to write about Sophie."

"Just write something that you like about her."

Nelle peered down at her blank sheet of paper, like her immature brain was struggling with the fairly straightforward concept.

Ever the patient nurturer, I nudged her in the right direction. "What's your favorite thing about Sophie?"

Nelle thought for the longest time before finally coming up with an answer. "Can I write that she has nice teeth?"

"Um... let's try not to focus of physical traits. Instead think of something interesting about Sophie. Is she a good friend? Is she an amazing singer?"

And as if a light bulb had flicked on in her head, Nelle perked up. "I know."

I smiled. It was moments like this that made my job so rewarding—to be able to mold young minds and watch as ideas blossomed into something beautiful.

"I'm going to write that Sophie had lice."

My brows shot to the ceiling as I struggled to hold back the laughter. "Oh, sweetie, I don't think Sophie would appreciate that."

Nor, I guessed, would her mother.

"But..." Nelle crinkled her nose. "She *did* have lice, remember?"

Oh yes, I remembered. The little critters had crawled out of her hair and were in the process of making their pilgrimage across the desk when Johnny, her seat partner, screamed so loud the school nearly went into lockdown mode as the office staff tried to assess if there were an imminent threat to the facility.

With the giggles already threatening to spill over, I patted Nelle on the shoulder. "Just write that she has nice teeth."

———

Reigning supreme over my rapt audience, I concluded the latest installment of the 'I hate Chad Woodcock' saga.

"So, I said something like, 'Have fun aggressively masturbating tonight.' Then he said 'I would, but you stole my lube.'"

It was only then that I looked up from my Cookie Butter latte and into the stunned silence of my siblings. A split second later, uncontrolled male laughter roared through the coffee shop. Of course, my sperm brothers would think that story was funny. Chad had become their unofficial mascot—the guy they loved to hate.

"Shut up," I said, fighting off my own desire to giggle. Chad was quick-witted; I'd give him that. "You're supposed to be on my side."

"I know Chad Woodcock is your arch enemy and all—but is it wrong that I wanna have a beer with him?" Ross replied. "Hell, I'll even buy."

"Dude, me too," his identical twin brother agreed.

"Am I the only one who's tired of hearing Chad Woodcock stories in the middle of our meetings?" my sister asked. "I mean, my god Dani, either bang him or move!"

"Ugh." I fake vomited. "I would rather watch Thomas the Tank Engine blow snot bubbles than bed that parasitic worm."

"Tell us how you really feel," Charlie chuckled.

"Fine," Simone huffed. "Whatever you say. But let's agree to hold all Woodcock chatter until after the meeting from now on."

"It *is* after the meeting," I replied. "You asked, 'Is there any other business?' and we all shook our heads. See? Over."

"Actually, the meeting is never over until the president adjourns it. I'm the president, and I didn't adjourn it. And just FYI, Dani, that whole sordid story you told is now a matter of public record."

I glanced around at my silent brothers. They were all looking away. Cowards. She wasn't even that scary.

"No, it's not," I challenged.

"Yes, it is. Your tiff with Chad is part of the minutes now, and as such, it is open for all members of the organization to read."

"Except"— held up a finger—"I'm the secretary, and I wasn't taking notes."

"Which, I might add, is a derelict of your duties," Simone shot back.

Not ready to concede defeat, I said, "Duties that were assigned to me out of no fault of my own."

Simone narrowed in on me, annoyed. She liked being in control even more than I did. Even more than Chad... or King Joffrey.

"My god, Simone," Conrad grumbled, finally having had enough of her dictorial ways. He reached over, grabbed her tiny wooden gavel, and thumped it against the table. "There, it's over. Problem solved."

Simone's eyes doubled in size. She ripped the gavel from Conrad's hand. "No one, and I mean no one, touches the gavel."

She proceeded to tap it on the table three times.

"Whew." Conrad stretched out in his chair. "Now anything we say can't be used against us in the court of Simone law."

"There are rules, Conrad. If you don't like them, you're free to go."

"Am I?"

"Actually, yes. I don't recall ever asking you to join, so bon voyage."

From the look on Conrad's face, he wasn't going anywhere. "I don't know if I say this enough, but you're the most annoying human I've ever met."

"And you make me want to sanitize up to my elbows."

I laughed, glancing around the table at the siblings I hadn't known existed only two short years ago. Now, as irritating as some of them might be, I wouldn't trade any of them for the world... okay, maybe Simone and Donny and Landry... but not the rest of them. Say what you would about my father's unorthodox choices, but he'd done something very right—he'd inadvertently brought these quirky siblings into my life.

And there were more. Enough, in fact, to form our own organization, the Lucky Swimmers Club, and have an actual governing board, which the five of us at this table were a part of. The LSC was an organization committed to the cause of uniting every last one of Donor 649's offspring. And, as Simone maintained, equally as important was to keep the riffraff wannabees out—as if there were a backlog of twenty-somethings clamoring to be a part of our sticky society.

But how could I argue with her methods? It was Simone who'd set up our Facebook page. And Simone who'd arranged the first annual 'swim' meet and greet. And Simone who'd created the ruling body of the organization, claiming the role of president for herself even though no one had asked for a leader. When it came time to pick her cabinet members, it really just depended on how close you were in proximity to her when the positions were being assigned. I just happened to be walking by, and bam! suddenly, I was Dani—the Lucky Swimmers' secretary.

Ross and Charlie had similar stories to mine. They'd

committed the grave error of being seated beside her when Simone began asking for volunteers. Ross became Vice President and Charlie, Treasurer. Not that I was complaining. It was certainly no hardship to spend time with my two identically dreamy sperm brothers. Whoever said that guys made in a petri dish couldn't be drop dead gorgeous had never met the Kosinski brothers. See, while most of us had inherited an acceptable mix of DNA, or at least enough that small children didn't scurry away in fear, the Kosinski twins proved that not all semen was created equal. I could only assume our father had been well-rested and feeling fine the day he'd strode into the clinic and jacked out my glorious brothers.

Sure, Charlie and Ross were attractive men, and yes, I was sometimes mesmerized by their charm, but my interest in the Kosinski boys was purely platonic—despite what some of my coy coworkers might have you think. Believe me, I understood well that the twins were off-limits. And not the type of off-limits one might find in a daring romance novel either. No, Charlie and Ross were the type of off-limits that produced children that looked like the monster in the Goonies.

And then there was Conrad— Sergeant of Arms—and the only member of the Lucky Swimmers' governing board to have freely volunteered for the position. Why? None of us knew. He didn't seem to enjoy coming to the meetings, and his 'duties' consisted mainly of taking the opposite opinion of whatever decision the rest of us made.

Unlike the handsome and agreeable Kosinski twins, Conrad had that gloomy, WTF factor going on. Where Ross and Charlie were easy on the eyes, Conrad was... well... *not*. Or, if he was, it couldn't be determined under the dark eye makeup, black slicked-back hair, and signature trench coat—an accessory that had the ability to clear of room of skittish onlookers. I'll admit to having checked for the nearest exit when I'd first met him too.

Certainly, Conrad wouldn't have been Simone's first choice for a board member—or its last, either—but when no one else stepped up, Count Dracula did. No doubt he'd only volunteered because he knew no one wanted him—a challenge, if you will. He wanted us to kick him out; to prove we weren't the inclusive group we claimed to be. But Simone refused to play his game. She wasn't like me, the dumb-dumb who wasted way too much time giving fuel to Chad's fire. She'd invited Conrad in. Made him one of us. Kept her enemies close.

And a funny thing happened on his way to humanity. Conrad softened. His scowl relaxed. His heart started beating. Maybe, like the rest of us, he just needed a place where he could belong.

I glanced down at my phone, checking the time. Oh, good. I still had two hours before the date tonight. Just enough time to do something bouncy with my hair. The idea was that my mood would magically match my hairdo. I know, it was probably wishful thinking, but I had to try something, because it had become clear after I'd accepted his movie date this morning that I really wasn't feeling Jeremy at all. He was just—how could I put this nicely? He was just... blah.

I wished I could cancel the whole thing, but that would have been rude. Besides, in the era of online dating, where everyone wanted a hookup, you took notice when good guys came along. I was convinced that was Jeremy. So why, then, was I feeling so conflicted? I should want a good guy, right? But Jeremy? There was just no spark. Nothing at all. Maybe tonight. Maybe he would step up his game and absolutely knock me on my ass. If not, I was prepared to walk away.

An image of Chad flashed through my brain. Now there was an ass-knocker if I'd ever seen one. *Oh, no. Don't you dare, Woodcock!* I soured at the thought of that man getting even one more second of bandwidth inside my head.

"So?" Charlie grinned in that teasing way I loved.

"So, what?"

"Did you take the package?"

"Of course not!" I punched him. "Now I'm offended."

"Hey, I'm not calling you a thief; I'm just saying I wouldn't put it past you."

"Well, I didn't." I laughed out loud. "But the next one that drops at his door is mine."

Conrad sat up a little straighter. "Has it ever occurred to you that maybe Chad Woodcock isn't who he says he is?"

"What do you mean?"

"He doesn't work. He hides his face. He's being shifty. And his name is Chad Woodcock. That's the kind of name you'd find on a frat boy's fake ID. All I'm saying is, it's a little too convenient. If you want me to come over there and rough him up, just say the word."

I scanned my brother's long, skinny frame. There was no way he was taking on the mountain of a man Chad was—unless he was bringing a knife to the fist fight. I cringed. Yeah, that was probably what he was meaning. "Oh, that's sweet of you, Conrad, but I can handle him. Chad is harmless, like a stink bug."

"You sure? Because I can squash that fucker. Just say the word."

Ross and Charlie exchanged alarmed expressions, one of them even kicking me under the table.

"No, no," I said cheerfully, pretending my sperm brother hadn't just proposed contract murder. "I've got this. But thank you for the generous offer."

"You know," Simone said, totally ignoring Conrad's threat, "stink bugs aren't actually harmless. They've caused significant yield losses in fruit and nut crops around the world."

"Right, but should they be exterminated from the face of the earth, like Conrad is proposing?" Charlie asked.

"I'm looking out for my little sister. Is that so wrong?"

"Not in theory, but I'm telling you right now, Conrad, I'm not going down as an accomplice to murder," Charlie said. "So, if the stink bug population is significantly reduced this harvest season, I'll know where to send the cops."

"Go for it," Conrad challenged. "But you might want to go into hiding afterward, narc."

I shook my head, only barely following along. "Boys. My goodness. The testosterone is especially potent today, isn't it? I'll make this very easy for all of you to understand. No one touches Chad Woodcock. You hear me? I'm the only one who gets to crush that man under my shoe."

6

DANI: NOT CHAD

TAPPING MY FINGERS ON THE STEERING WHEEL, I SPEWED impatient curses at the woman callously making me wait for her parking spot in the underground garage of my complex. It wasn't like I had unlimited time. My hair. My bouncy hair. I now only had just over an hour to make it happen. This motorist's decisions could mean the difference between Jeremy getting the boot or becoming my future husband.

"Move it, Pokey!" I barked at the driver.

I needed to chill. The confrontational mood I'd been in since my morning run-in with Chad had my panties all twisted in a knot. You'd think a day filled with sweet-faced first graders would be enough to unravel them from my ass, but no, Chad still held his grip. I could feel my blood pressure rising at just the thought of running into him in the hallway. How dare he accuse me of stealing! Or of being some old maid just because I enjoyed the occasional night in with a bowl of ice cream. I mean, please. Not everyone needed to live on the edge with 650% more protein than the recommended daily allowance.

Now I wished I actually had stolen his package, because then I could stomp it into submission. Submerge it in water.

Then allow it to dry out before setting it on fire. Finally, I'd deliver his precious package all bloodied, bruised, and smoldering to his doorstep. Chad didn't deserve nice things.

Movement drew my attention back to the woman in her car, taunting me with her lack of consideration. She knew I was waiting, but clearly she didn't care about other living, breathing human beings. Her tire would roll a half a rotation and stop. Half a rotation and stop. It was a good goddamn thing that I'd put my running shoes on after work today because I was going to have to take the stairs Rocky-style.

Now we were in a holding pattern, painfully idling. This woman was wearing on my last nerve. Maybe she was related to Chad. I normally considered myself a very patient person; I even owned a crock pot and everything. But this stop-and-go action was just uncalled for. I should already be upstairs reapplying my makeup and getting dolled up for my date with Jeremy, not down here in the parking garage slowly dying.

The woman backed almost halfway out of her spot before inexplicably stopping *again*. I blinked once. Twice. Then I exploded.

"Oh...my...god," I articulated each word in a low growly threat. "I've seen baseball games played faster!"

My hand hovered over the horn, just daring me to blow the whole operation.

Breathe, I lectured myself. *You can't afford to piss her off—not when you've come this far.*

But maybe if I could tap the horn lightly enough, it might actually make her aware that I'd been waiting on her long enough for the earth to orbit the sun. Just one tiny honk. Surely she wouldn't take offense to that—a friendly toot that said, *Hey, sorry for bothering you, LOL, but are you backing out anytime soon, you fucking bitch?*

Whoa... where had that come from? Now I really needed to

chill. I knew as well as every other person in this apartment complex that patience was key to a successful changing of the parking guard. Parking swaps were a delicate dance, and I couldn't for one second forget the fluidity of the situation. Turtlepoke over there held all the power. She was, for lack of a better term, the man in this particular cha-cha-cha. And if I did anything even remotely off-putting to her, she might deny me the spot I'd been waiting so impatiently for.

This right here, the parking lot hunt, was the worst part of my day, and that included run-ins with Chad. I'd honestly rather have conversations about his bushy twig and berries than try to find a parking spot after work. I equated the experience to that of the old carnival game the Cake Walk. You know, the one where everyone is circling as chairs are removed, and then when the music stops, anyone left standing scrambles for that one open spot? This right here...this was my daily Cake Walk.

The brake lights flickered, and as slowly as a snail creeping through peanut butter, her tires again began to roll. *Here we go. Almost home.* My eyes darted in every direction, checking for lurking adversaries. There was a car one row over, but it was too far away to be a real contender. No, it looked like I might be home free. My mouth began to water.

Squealing wheels snapped my head to attention. What the shit? Oh, no! The non-factor car over on the other aisle had suddenly come into play and was angling to ruin my day. My heart rate quickened as the vehicle sped around the bend.

"Oh, no... no, you don't," I warned, flicking my blinker on and inching closer to the woman's car. It was then I saw who was trying to steal my spot—and of course, it had to be booger-flicking, name-calling Chad Woodcock. The woman pulled free of the cars on either side of her, and it was then she made the fateful decision to turn her bumper in my direction—blocking me from the spot and essentially welcoming in the weasel with a heart of coal.

"Don't do it!" I hollered, heat hop-skipping up my spine. Our eyes locked, mine flashing him a warning and his not giving a crap. I swear I saw him grin as he swung a hard right and slid effortlessly into my spot.

Oh, he was so dead!

Pulling my car up until my front bumper nearly touched his back one, I flattened my palm against the horn and I held it down in one continuous *fuck you*. I could even see Chad inside his vehicle holding his hands to his ears, and I pictured him laughing. I'd had enough of his bullshit. This was war.

But before I could take matters into my own hands, I felt my car jolt like it had been hit by solid steel.

Had Chad backed into me? My god, the dude was just asking for dismemberment. I checked out my driver's side window, puzzled. Our bumpers were right where I'd left them...still a good inch apart.

Another jolt.

"What the...?"

I checked my mirrors, but there was nothing behind me. And then it started. Violent shaking so intense it scrambled my head with confusion. Another jolt, but this one unlike anything I'd ever felt in my lifetime. There was the sudden sensation of dropping, as if the undercarriage of my vehicle had completely given way. The swaying walls in the parking garage rumbled and quivered, chunks of concrete breaking free from their berths and crumbling onto the cars below.

"What's happening?" I cried out, even though I knew full well what this was—a Richter scale-busting earthquake. And I really couldn't think of a worse place to ride out this once-in-a-lifetime event than in an underground parking garage...with *Chad*. The standard recommendations of hunkering under a table or taking shelter in a door frame did not apply in this setting. The only thing I could do now was wait for relief... and hope and pray I would still be alive once the earth had had its way.

The sound of ripping steel caught my attention. I swung my head around just in time to see the upper floor near the garage exit come crashing to the ground a hundred feet behind me. I watched in shocked horror as smoke from the collapse billowed toward me like a rampaging beast. Covering my head with my hands, I closed my eyes as fast-moving projectiles slammed into my car with the force of a bomb.

Only after the wave had passed over me did I dare open my eyes. My back window was shattered, and I was blanketed in glass and dust. And still the earth continued shaking. I wasn't going to survive this. This underground hell would very likely become my grave. Then, in what I believed to be the final moments of my life, I thought of him—Chad—the man I was about to die with. Our feud seemed so childish now; so petty. I wished I could take it all back. Start anew. But we might not have that chance...ever again.

It was his face I focused on seconds before a concrete slab ripped free of its mooring and dropped from the floor above.

———

My body settled as the earth ceased its quaking. The car alarms, which had been going wild a few seconds before the collapse, seemed to have leveled off into a polite whimper—their final cries as they lay dying under the weight of thousands of pounds of concrete.

It was as if the earth were observing a moment of reverence for what it had destroyed. I sat stunned in my car, the strange unnerving moans giving the sensation of being underwater. I kept my eyes closed, too afraid to face what lay ahead.

Open your eyes, Dani. I had to know what I was dealing with. I had to find my strength.

Reaching up with shaky hands, I cleared the dust from my eyes before slowly opening them to the new world order. Nothing looked familiar. The landscape around me had totally shifted in a matter of seconds, and now I was in a desolate wasteland, covered in destruction. The ceiling, once a healthy distance above, was now bearing down menacingly, trapping me in an eerie gray igloo of exposed rebar and crumbled pillars. It felt like I was in a hole, as if the ground had caved in and the ceiling was chasing after it.

Oh, god. Dragging in a raggedy breath, I tried to keep it together, but I was slowly unraveling. How could this have happened? Buildings didn't just fall. A quake this size could have taken out the whole city. Tightness spread through my chest. *Breathe, Dani.* Now was not the time to panic. A clear head, that was what I needed. And instead of focusing on the truly horrible situation I was in, maybe I should be grateful that somehow, amongst all the destruction, I'd been spared. Was this my wake-up call? Had I been handed a second chance to become a better, calmer, more introspective person? I could fall back on the weaknesses that held me back before, or I could look forward with strength and perseverance.

Not that I really had any choice. If I didn't find my inner bravery, I would surely die here in my car...or what was left of it. During those few short seconds of shaking, my Subaru had split in two. Where there had once been a dashboard and an engine, there was now just open space. The beam that had decapitated the hood of my car had worked like a seesaw, and now the mangled wreckage was elevated off the ground. I was still strapped in my driver's side seat, my legs dangling over the edge like a rider on one of those inverted roller coasters.

There was no safety plan for this, no accompanying handbook. This was all survival stuff—instinctual. If I wanted to get out of this, I needed to think like a wild animal caught in a snare. First things first: did I still have access to all my body parts? Just because I was feeling no pain didn't mean I'd escaped unscathed. Shock was a funny thing, tricking the body into thinking things were all hunky-dory when bits and pieces were actually hanging off you.

I took stock of my limbs, systematically testing various body parts for malfunction, and was relieved to find them responding properly—or at least they were from the waist down. Waist up was another story. Shards of glass were embedded in my skin; I must have looked like a shiny porcupine. Gritting my teeth, I went to work gingerly extracting those I could, even gathering the bravery needed to dislodge the one in my cheekbone. But a particularly jagged blade of glass rooted deep in my left arm proved to be beyond my level of expertise. Plus, if it was working as a stopper to prevent an artery from bleeding out, my instinct was to let it stay.

Slipping my right arm out my lightweight sweater, I used that as a tourniquet, tying it tightly around my upper left arm with my teeth. That would have to do until help arrived. If it did. I wasn't naïve enough to think my apartment complex was the only scene of destruction in this city of millions, nor did I think first responders would head here first. If it was this bad here, I couldn't help but wonder what a quake this size had done to the rest of Los Angeles. To my students. To my school.

To...Chad.

I whipped my head around. Oh god, how could I have forgotten he was here with me in this wasteland? My eyes darted from side to side. Where was his car? Had he somehow gotten away? And then I saw it... or what was left of it, flattened under mounds of concrete. The plank that had cut my car in two had also crushed his, only it had come to rest vertically—on top of a second beam that had fallen horizontally across the cab of his vehicle. I swallowed back a sob as I realized that no one could have survived that. He was gone, entombed under the intersecting planks that had fallen in the form of a cross to lie on top of what was now Chad's grave.

Shock. Horror. Every emotion grabbed hold as I slowly realized what I'd lost. Chad wasn't just the man I loved to hate. He was also the man I actually sorta *didn't* hate. There—I admitted it. It had taken this disaster to make me realize that I'd spent countless hours of my life obsessing over Chad for the same reason little elementary school girls the world over called boys names on the playground—I had a crush. Chad was the real reason I couldn't connect with Jeremy. The brawny jerk had hijacked my mind. At work. At play. At sleep. Chad was everywhere. And, as much as I tried to resist the icky attraction, I couldn't.

And now he was gone, buried under a pile of rubble. Tears welled as I tried to comprehend the loss. Twenty seconds was all it had taken to end his life, and now I'd never bicker with him again. I'd never instigate a knocking war on our shared wall or communicate with him through Post-it Notes. I'd never spy on his half-naked body through the sliding glass door or fantasize about those powerful arms pushing me up against the shower wall. If only I'd known how little time we had left, I would've treated those last minutes with more respect.

I dropped my head to my hands and cried for Chad. For me. For the sex-fueled life we'd never lead. He didn't deserve this. No one did.

"Dani?"

My lips parted in surprise. It couldn't be. I'd seen his car. He couldn't possibly have survived. But when he repeated my name, there was no doubt. That raspy voice, beset with pain, belonged to Chad.

Still, my brain could not compute. "Chad?"

There was a pause before he answered with his typical bluster. "Who else would it be?"

Oh, my god. Even in this life-or-death situation, Chad was being... a dick? If that didn't prove, beyond any reasonable doubt, that my tough-as-nails neighbor-crush had somehow survived the unsurvivable, I didn't know what would.

"You're alive?" I asked, confirming the obvious.

"Would I be talking to you if I were dead?"

"I don't know," I replied, falling right back into our comfortable mockery. "Maybe you're a ghost."

"No offense, Dani, but if I was a ghost, I sure as hell wouldn't be spending eternity with you."

"And, yet, for the last five months, I've been doing just that."

I waited for Chad's snappy reply. But he remained silent, which was not like him at all. He never missed a chance to volley. Something was wrong. No way would my surly neighbor waste a return of serve.

"Chad?"

"I'm here," he replied, but the sound came out more like a groan.

"Are you hurt?" I questioned, knowing immediately I'd asked the obvious. Of course he was hurt. No one could survive what he'd survived without injury.

"Well, let's put it this way. I'm not dead yet, but by the looks of it, you'll get your wish in a few minutes."

My wish? The hundreds of times I'd threatened his life had all been in jest. Those were the words of a frustrated girl with no other recourse against his force of nature.

"I don't want you to die, Chad," I said, maybe the first bit of honesty I'd ever spoken to him. "You know that."

"Yeah, I know that," he replied, with possibly the first bit of honesty he'd ever spoken to me.

"Tell me what's happening to you," I urged.

"Look for yourself."

"I can't see into your car. I don't even know how you survived that."

"I survived because I wasn't in my car."

"You weren't? Where were you then?"

"I was coming for you, Dani."

I let those words percolate in my brain for a second. My neighbor, the one who'd accused me of stealing, who'd stolen my parking spot, and who'd commandeered my thoughts at all hours of the day—and night—had been coming for me. Chad's face hadn't been a thought in my mind when I believed I was about to die. He'd actually been there, racing toward me, trying to save my life.

"Don't look so surprised," he said. "I have my moments."

"Wait—you can see me?"

"I'm right here."

I scanned the barren landscape but didn't see him.

"Look down."

Down? I stuck my head out of the missing window and there, about three feet from my car, was Chad, covered in grime and buried up to his shoulder blades in rubble. I gasped.

"Yeah," he said, pain etching lines across his sullen face. "That was my first reaction too."

I wanted to say something, anything, to make the situation better for him, but there was no silver lining. Chad was in serious trouble.

"Chad..." I began, my voice steeped in sympathy.

"Don't," he stopped me. "I know it's bad. I don't need your pity."

He was right. That wasn't how we worked. We'd never shown each other mercy before, so why start now? Our dysfunction made us stronger, and Chad needed that strength now. If he wanted 'normal,' I'd give him normal—starting with an insult. "I've been pitying you since the day we met, dude. So why stop now?"

He attempted a chuckle, but the pain proved a worthy adversary. I watched him clench his jaw as he drew in a shaky breath.

Now there was nothing but sincerity in my reply. "I'm coming, Chad. Breathe slow and steady. I'm going to get you out of there. I promise."

And I meant it. Taking my own deep breath, I reached for my phone, only to realize it wasn't where I'd left it in the cup holder. In fact, the cup holder wasn't where I'd left it either. Both had, no doubt, blasted off like rockets when the beam cut my car in two. I searched the area around me for my cell with no luck. It was gone, and so was any hope of a coordinated rescue. It was up to me now.

God help us all.

"Not to dampen your optimism," he said, before proceeding to do just that, "but unless you have a bulldozer in your pocket, I'm not going anywhere."

"Hey, check the doom and gloom, bud. I manage to Velcro and tie twenty-five first graders' shoes every day and still get them out to recess on time. I think I can dig one asshole out of a dirt hole."

"You're. A. Teacher?" he asked, every word punctuated with disbelief.

"Don't sound so surprised. What did you think I did for a living?"

"Well, I'd narrowed it down to a few contenders, with the top one being agent of Satan."

I laughed, relieved he had the energy to insult. That meant I still had time—but how much, I wasn't sure. Unhooking the seatbelt holding me suspended in place, I tried to ready my feet for the impact, but gravity took hold before I could steady myself, and I tumbled to the ground. I let out a cry of pain as a red raised abrasion instantly sprang up on my knee.

"Ouch. Dammit," I pouted.

"Are you okay?"

"Yeah. I miscalculated," I replied, pushing myself back onto my feet with my one good arm. "I'll live."

"That makes one of us."

"Enough with the negativity, Chad. Don't make me come over there and slap you."

"Not trying to be negative, Dani," Chad said, puffing out the words. "I'm actually having trouble breathing. The pressure on my chest is insane."

There was no snark left in my neighbor. His life was hanging in the balance, and he knew it. I had to get to him.

"Just focus on my voice. I'm on my way. I can't get out the driver side door, so I need to climb over the mountain of concrete in front of my car. It'll just take me a minute, and then I'll start digging you out."

He didn't respond, his silence an ominous predictor of his decline.

"Chad, don't fall asleep."

"I'm sorry, Dani."

His voice sounded defeated—done. I had to keep him talking.

"For what—stealing my parking spot?"

"No, I stand by that. Parking's a bitch in this garage."

I smiled to myself. He needed to work on his apologies. "Are you sorry for accusing me of stealing your package?"

"Yes, I am actually sorry for that."

"Oh, well, that's a start."

"Apparently it was delivered to the wrong floor. The neighbor lady below us brought the package up this afternoon."

I stopped, a frown forming. "You're a piece of work, dude."

"Don't I know it. Look, I'm going to be honest with you—and please don't get used to it—but I've been going through a rough time the last few months, feeling sorry for myself. I took it out on you, and that was a crappy thing to do. I wanted to say I'm sorry now, just in case, you know, I don't make it."

"Stop it, Chad. I don't want your apology. Don't assume you're the only player in this dysfunctional relationship of ours. You realize I sometimes make stuff up just to start a fight with you, right?"

"I knew it," he chuckled, his voice cutting out toward the end. I could hear him weakening with every passing second.

I squeezed around the toppled beam and got my first close up look at what Chad was dealing with...what I was about to deal with. And it wasn't good. Chad wasn't just buried in crumbled concrete and dust, he had actual cinder blocks holding him down.

"I'm here," I said, crouching down to eye level.

"Can you please not make that face?" he said, wincing. "I'm already freaked out."

"Sorry," I replied, heaving the smallest solid chunks of concrete off of him as I fought back a sudden onset of tears. Not here. Not now. My sorrow was the last thing he needed, so I swallowed the emotion and adopted a grimace. "Got my game face on now."

"Much better."

"Let's start over," I said, forcing a smile. "Hi, I'm Dani, and I'll be your hero for the day."

Chad managed a half-cocked smile. "Not that I'm dissing your superpowers, but you wouldn't by chance have a phone handy to call 911, would you?"

I shook my head. "I wish. You?"

"No. My best guess is it's somewhere near the earth's core by now."

I followed his eyes downward. Yeah, there was no phone. This was going to be a one-woman operation... and there was no time to waste. I continued with the rescue proceedings by creating a small pocket of wiggle room behind him, an area for him to lean away from the weight of the concrete boulders that were too heavy for me to move with one arm. With some of the pressure relieved, Chad dragged in deep, life-saving breaths, his first ones since the walls came crashing down.

Before we could celebrate that small step forward, an angry fault line conspired to take us two steps back. The ground rumbled.

Aftershock.

Chad and I locked eyes, and I knew before he spoke what he was going to say.

"Go!" he insisted. "Get out of here!"

He was right. I should go. This was my life we were talking about. But what about Chad? I couldn't just leave him to face his fate alone. With the earth quivering ruthlessly below us, I flung myself over him and together we rode out the lingering remnants of the half-hearted quake.

When it was over, I lifted my head and cautiously looked around. Everything had pretty much remained where it had fallen in the previous quake, even the assembly of concrete stacked pick-up-stick-style in front of him.

"Okay, well...*that* earthquake was a bit of a pussy, wouldn't you say?"

He shook his head, not appreciating my workplace humor. "You never listen, do you?"

"Seems like we established that fact long ago. Besides, I could say the same thing about you."

"I'm serious, Dani," he said. "If you don't go now, you're going to die in here...right beside me."

Like I didn't understand the risks. I knew what I was doing, and no one got to decide my fate but me...and maybe that bitch Mother Nature. "Sure, Chad. I'm going to die. You're going to die. But neither one of us is going to die today."

That silenced my quake date.

"Let me hear you say it, Chad. 'Dani is my hero.'"

Never had he repeated back one of my lines correctly, and I didn't expect it of him today either.

"Dani is my hero," he said without an ounce of mockery.

Well, I'll be damned. Miracles did happen. I smiled, liking the sound of his submission. Victory at last.

Chad clenched his eyes shut as he let out a slow breath.

"Hey, you okay?" I asked.

"Uh... it hurts to breathe. A lot of pain in my chest."

Not what I wanted to hear, but it did motivate me to dig faster, and not long after amplifying my efforts, I touched skin, making us both jump. "Is that what I think it is?"

"No," he answered, straight-faced. "Just my arm."

"Oh," I laughed. "Making funnies now, I see."

He smiled, his face registering the first real signs of hope. I doubled down then, wanting to see more of that faith in his eyes. Unfortunately, the excavation wasn't nearly as agreeable to the shard of glass still wedged inside my arm. With every movement, excruciating pain shot all the way to my fingertips. But the discomfort was all worth it when Chad's arm finally emerged from the earth... and he used it to hug me.

Both stunned and flattered, I slung my good arm around one

of his broad shoulders and hung on tight. I half expected him to squirm away like a skittish cat, but Chad seemed to be in no hurry to let go. Although, to be fair, he *was* trapped in a hole in the earth. It wasn't like he could get away from my public display of affection. He turned his head, his soft breath whispering into my ear, "You're my hero, Dani."

Okay, I was in love. No, seriously. If we both survived, I'd be stalking the shit out of his ass.

When we finally broke apart, things were different between us. We were no longer warring neighbors. Now we were full-fledged colleagues. And, working as a team, things moved faster, with his added arm strength helping to topple the concrete holding him in place. Within minutes, we not only had his other arm free but we'd also dug Chad out to his waist. And then to his thighs and to his knees. We were so close now. Just a little bit more and he would be free.

"Hey," he said, his voice cutting through the silence. I looked up to find his long-lashed blue eyes ringed in red. His words splintered as he spoke. "Just so you know, I'm not going to forget this. What you did for me..."

"You would have done the same for me."

"I would've tried," he said, holding my gaze. "But I'm no *you*."

"No, that's true." I grinned, loving this newfound side of Chad Woodcock.

"When we get out of here, I'm going to make it up to you in a big way."

"Yeah? And how do you plan to do that?" I asked, blowing the hair from my eyes as I continued my digging.

"By buying you whatever you want."

It was a weird thing for him to say. He lived next door to me, so clearly, Chad wasn't bathing in cash. Conrad was right. I knew nothing about this guy. I wasn't even sure if he worked. Did he have family? Friends? No one came to visit him...ever. I studied him now, getting perhaps my first full and unobstructed view of his shaggy face, and to my surprise, he looked oddly familiar. Not the neighbor-next-door familiar either. There was something about him...

"Oh, okay," I chuckled, pointing to my mangled car. "How 'bout we start with that?"

"Done."

My eyes widened. "Done? Just like that? You're going to buy me a car?"

"That's right."

"With what money? Do you have a trust fund that doesn't mature until you're thirty or something?"

"No, I'm a self-made millionaire."

I scoffed. More like self-made working-class poor, if you asked me. But what struck me about Chad was how effortlessly he could lie. All right, fine, I'd take the bait. "Wow, Chad, I had no idea I was living next door to such a big shot."

"That's right." He grinned.

Our eyes met. Even entombed, Chad was so full of shit. "Okay, Moneybags. Since you're waving your make-believe cash around, I'll take one of those new Broncos in steel-blue please."

"Two or four doors?" he asked, acting as if this little fantasy of ours was reality.

"Hmm..." I smiled. "What the heck, let's make it a four."

"Sounds good. Four-door it is."

I glanced up, smiling at our little game, but surprised to find him not returning the gesture. I stopped digging, confused by our conversation, but before I could question him further, Chad grabbed my wrist, and I could see the color drain from his face.

"What is it?" I asked.

"It's stuck."

"What do you mean, its stuck?"

"My ankle."

Crouched down into the hole we'd dug, Chad swept away a layer of dust to reveal a concrete slab pressing down on his ankle and completely enveloping his foot. Chad frantically tried pulling his leg free, but it didn't budge. These weren't the manageably-sized cinder blocks we'd been steadily removing either, this was a giant chunk of concrete and mangled rebar.

I dug deeper, trying to see how far it stretched and if I could dig him out from behind. But it was no use, his foot was locked in a clamp.

"What about your right leg?"

"I can move that one," Chad said. "I think maybe it's just buried and not entombed."

Redirecting our efforts, we dug around his right ankle until Chad managed to pull it free of the rubble.

Seeing our efforts paying off renewed my faith. "Okay, I can do this. Just one more foot and we're home free."

With him assisting from above, I pulled and pushed and heaved with all my might but it was no use. Chad was hopelessly shackled to the earth.

"Dani, stop."

"No," I cried. "I can do this."

He grabbed my hands, the tips rubbed raw from the coarse concrete. "You've done all you can."

"But," I gulped, a stream of tears cutting dusty ravines along my cheeks. "We can... maybe if..."

"No." Chad shook his head. "It's time for you to go and get help."

He was right. I knew he was, but I hated even the thought of leaving him alone, vulnerable, and in pain. We weren't just neighbors anymore. As weird as it sounded, we were bonded now, his fate forever tied to mine. Decades might pass without seeing each other, but neither of us would ever forget.

"Go, Dani. Find a phone. Call for help. I'll be okay."

I stood up, hesitant but resigned. It really was the only way.

"Okay," I said. "But I'll be back."

"No, you won't."

"Yes, Chad. I'll call 911, tell them where we are, and then I'll come back."

"Dani," he sighed. "You have to get as far away from this building as you can."

"I won't do that," I answered stubbornly.

"It'll be worse for me if I have to worry about you coming back here."

"And it will be worse for me if I have to worry about *not* coming back here."

Chad eyed me, contemplating his next move. "Look, I'll make you a deal. If you promise me you won't come back, I'll promise you that I'll come out of this alive."

He couldn't promise me that any more than I could promise him compliance. I understood that he didn't want to be responsible for my death any more than I wanted to be responsible for his, so if it made Chad happier to think I wasn't coming back, then I'd play along.

With my fingers crossed behind my back, I replied. "I promise."

"Thank god." He let a breath out. "She does listen."

I caught his eye. "Occasionally. Just don't get used to it."

"Never. See you topside."

I nodded, turning to leave.

"Oh, and Dani?" Chad called out to me. "Tell them RJ Contreras is trapped in the parking garage."

I spun back around, puzzled. "Wait, RJ Contreras—from *AnyDayNow*? Why would I tell them that?"

Chad raised a brow as he waited for me to catch up.

My mouth dropped open.

Oh, my god—that wasn't Chad Woodcock.

7

RJ: WORLD'S WORST LOIS LANE

"You're RJ Contreras?" she asked, not yet ready to believe her eyes.

"Yes," I confirmed.

"You?" she queried again.

"Yes," I reconfirmed. "I think we've established that already."

"No!" she snapped back. "We haven't established shit."

My eyes widened, surprised by her anger. What had I expected, that she would drop to her knees in worship after hearing my confession? Yes, actually that was exactly what I'd expected—what always happened when women realized who I was. But that wasn't how long-term deception worked in the real world. I couldn't expect Dani to forget the past four months she'd spent despising my every breath.

"Just because you say you're RJ doesn't make it true," she challenged, drawing her fingers over her smooth jawline, miming my beard as if the whiskers somehow disproved everything.

"Okay, then," I challenged. "How can I prove it to you?"

"Quick! Name an *AnyDayNow* song!"

"'Desperate for You'," I fired back.

She rolled her eyes.

"What?"

"Everyone knows that one."

To be fair, everyone knew a lot of our songs. We'd spent a lot of time at the top of the charts. Still, I tried again, rattling off one cheesy name after another like a semi-automatic weapon. "'She's my Truth.' 'Back it Up.' 'Dream Girl.' 'I'd Drop Dead for You.'"

Dani doubled down on the eye rolls. If I didn't know better, I'd think she was refusing to accept my word only because she didn't want to concede defeat. "All that proves is you have very bad taste in music, Chad."

"Watch it. I helped write some of those songs."

Her eyes widened, telling me—without saying a word—how she really felt about my songwriting abilities.

"Screw you," I fought back. "At least I don't have your exceptionally horrible observational skills. I mean, take a good look, Dani. You don't have to be a hardcore *Dayer* to see it's me under all the hair."

Emitting an offended squeak, she stomped back over to me, bending down and grabbing my face as she tilted it from side to side. Despite the pain roaring through my insides, I patiently waited for her to confirm my identity, and when the truth finally sank in, she let go of my jaw and backed away. Our eyes met and began a full-on stare down. She was pissed. She was shocked. And judging by the grimace Dani had adopted on that pouty face of hers, my neighbor was not the least bit impressed.

"Well, isn't this a treat. RJ Contreras in the house."

The way she said it through clenched teeth indicated she didn't find it a treat at all. I grinned at her faked enthusiasm.

"RJ Contreras in the parking garage," I corrected. "But yes, I agree, it is a treat."

Dani found no humor in my response, and I watched as she

folded her arms over her chest in indignation. Despite my life hanging in the balance, I couldn't help but take one last dig.

"You know, Dani, you really are the worst Lois Lane ever. I mean, I thought the fictional Loises were bad, not being able to tell that Clark Kent was actually Superman because he wore glasses, but you...Jesus... all I can think is you don't get out much."

"Uh-huh," she grimaced. "You have no idea how much I want to kick dirt in your face right now."

I laughed, but my amusement was short-lived as pain swept through me. My sudden change snapped Dani from her frustration and her forehead wrinkled in worry.

"Okay, here's what's going to happen, Chad."

"RJ," I corrected.

Dani's lips flattened. "Here's what's going to happen, RJ. I'm going to go now so that I can save your life. Then, once you're all healed up, I'm going to punch you in the gut for lying to me. Are we clear?"

I nodded to my savior. "We're clear."

As she turned to leave, her ponytail swung from side to side. Even her hair was full of life. Dani was a breath of fresh air in a world that had gone stale.

Overwhelmed with affection for this woman who was risking everything for me, I called out to her. "Dani?"

When she whirled back around, the confident woman was gone. Tears had replaced the anger in her eyes. Dani cared, more than she was letting on, and what surprised me the most was that her desire to help me had nothing to do with my fame. Dani didn't care about RJ Contreras, the superstar. She cared about some no-name asshole called Chad Woodcock. Somehow, somewhere, the two of us had connected, and now neither one of us wanted to let the other go.

We stared at each other, soaking in the moment. The tears

slipping from her eyes were only steps ahead of the ones pooling in mine.

"Thank you," I said, my voice cracking with the emotion the moment required. "For being there for me."

There was no playfulness. No mocking. Only genuine gratitude. This girl had become my lifeline. Her bravery might not save me, but I'd die knowing someone had cared enough to try.

She nodded, barely able to meet my eye.

"Remember your promise," she said. "You better be alive when the rescuers come."

"I'll try."

"No," she insisted, this time holding my gaze. "You will be."

I paused, drawing hope from her strength. If anyone could save me, it was this fiery and determined girl. "I will be."

8

DANI: THE SCOUT

I DIDN'T REMEMBER THE PARKING GARAGE BEING SO COMPACT... OR dark. Typically, I drove in, did my obligatory Cake Walk loop-de-loop with the mentality of a survivalist, and then went about my day, with no cave-ins and no life-or-death decisions to speak of. But this... Why had I always taken for granted that things would remain in the spots they'd always been? Everything was wrong now. Up was down. And down was—buried under a pile of rubble.

Remembering the concrete under my car dropping away, I realized then that we were underground and, to get out, I had to go up. Except there was no up; no opening. We were entombed. But I couldn't give up. RJ was counting on me. So, I continued on with purpose, every step I took away from him more urgent than the next. RJ was hurt. More than he was letting on, that much I was sure of. If I didn't bring help back to him, there was a chance he'd die. No. I couldn't think that way. RJ was going to be fine. He'd live another day. That blender of his would shred a thousand more sliding glass doors if I had anything to say about it.

After climbing over a wall of downed pipes and concrete pillars, I spotted the exit sign only to discover the exit was no more. Cars from the second floor of the garage were suspended precariously in the air, held only by the steel railing they'd crashed into on their way down. And on top of that were what appeared to be the upper floors of the apartment complex caving into the lower ones.

And then there was RJ and me, under all of that.

A squeak escaped me as my eyes tried to process the shock of what they were seeing. I'd promised RJ that I'd get help, but what if there was no help to be had? What if I couldn't find a way out? I would be as doomed as the man buried calf deep in concrete. The man who had a legion of fans to mourn him. Because he was RJ Contreras. RJ frickin' Contreras! Chad. RJ. Chad was RJ!

Okay, Dani. We got it. No need to repeat it a thousand times.

But the more I milled it over in my head, the more shocking the revelation became. The asinine man I'd been absently daydreaming about pushing in front of a stampede of bulls was actually one of music's biggest stars. RJ didn't just know the names of those songs he'd rattled off in record time, he'd sung them—nearly every night on stage with his generation-defining boyband.

Not that I'd ever been a worshipful *Dayer*, but you'd have to be living in a hole to not know the band *AnyDayNow* or to not be able to sing along to their songs when they came on the radio. For five years of my life, those *Dayer* boys had been pretty much unavoidable, appearing in magazines, on television, and on billboards, their music playing over the radio waves way more often than seemed necessary. And I'd just now discovered that I'd been living next door to one of them all this time? How dumb *was* I? No, really. On a scale from one to ten, I was like a forty-two. My god, I'd even been to one of his concerts, standing just below the stage, so close in fact that I'd sworn to my girlfriends that he'd sweated on me. That was the same RJ I was now trying to save. The same RJ Contreras from *AnyDayNow*! RJ was Chad. Chad was RJ.

Okay, so we're doing this again.

I spotted what I thought might be the turtle woman's car. It was pancaked into the ground. I didn't want to look because I was pretty sure I knew what I'd find—the woman dead in her car. There seemed no way she could've survived. But miracles did happen. I was still alive, and so was RJ. Although, he was only alive because he'd gotten out of his car just in the nick of time—to save me.

The thought gave me pause. For all the bickering we'd done, his first thought in the middle of an earthquake had been to save me. That said something about his character, something that hadn't been spoken in the past. I wanted to know this man; not Chad the dickhead neighbor, but RJ, the man courageous enough to risk his life for me.

And now I had to be courageous for him, for me... and for the turtle woman in her car. If there was even the slightest possibility she could be saved, I'd have to try. But one horrifying glance inside gave me the answer. Tears welled in my eyes. Had she backed out of her parking spot a minute sooner, she would have been free and clear of the garage before it collapsed.

"I'm sorry," I whispered, placing my hand on the twisted metal that had become her grave. "I'm so sorry."

I wanted to collapse to the ground and rage over the unfairness of it all, but I didn't have the luxury of mourning for this woman I'd never known, not when a man I did know was still breathing. In that moment of reflection, the tiniest ray of light caught my eye. A hole in the destruction. No, not really a hole, more like a precarious gap in a life-size Jenga game. Remove one piece and the entire thing comes crumbling down. But if I didn't take my turn, I would surely lose.

Ascending the precarious mound of debris on my hands and

knees, I used my fingers to dig out an opening wide enough to allow myself to squeeze through. *Head, shoulders, knees, and toes.* I repeated the childhood mantra over and over in my head as each part of me emerged into the outside world. It was only when I was finally free of the earth and standing on new colt-like legs that I saw the true scope of what I'd survived. My apartment was *gone*... as was a good chunk of the building where I'd once lived. I said *once* because it was clear I'd never live here again. A section of the west side of the complex had collapsed sideways, pancaking on top of the parking garage where RJ and I had been trapped—where he was still entombed. The rest of that wing tilted precariously to one side.

Looking out over the ruins of my former life, I now understood what people meant when they said 'Life changes in an instant.' Mine just had—the repercussions of this day, I was sure, would stay with me for a lifetime. And for one selfish moment, I mourned the inanimate pieces of my life that were gone. My vintage table thrifted at a flea market. My childhood stuffed animal. The bohemian chic balcony where I tortured RJ with my rules—the ones he'd never once abided by. All the things I'd thought so important once upon a time were now buried under rubble, and yet I was the lucky one. What of those who had lost loved ones? Their pets? Their lives?

My chest tightened just thinking of RJ's plight in the parking garage. If he knew what I knew now, would he have even a shred of hope? Somehow in all this destruction, we'd been spared. But how? The only explanation that made any sense was that the twisted metal had created a pocket, a lifesaving shell that had kept our fragile bodies alive. But with smoke and fire from exploding gas lines creating a hazard above ground, how much longer could RJ survive inside that bubble before the harrowing conditions outside came seeping through?

There was no time to waste. RJ needed saving right now. I

scanned the chaos. Firetrucks and police cars were already here, lining the street. Their ladders were extended, moving from balcony to balcony—or at least those that were left—as the rescue efforts got underway. I raced for the nearest unit and descended upon on a young man in yellow fireman pants.

"Please," I grabbed onto his jacket. "My neighbor needs help. He's trapped in the parking garage."

The fireman—so youthful looking I had to wonder if he'd been recruited to the force out of middle school—scanned me, my dust-choked hair, and glass-pocked skin enough to convince him that I was speaking the truth.

"In there?" He pointed to my apartment complex.

"Yes. The whole thing came down on top of us."

"How is he trapped?"

"His ankle. It's under a concrete block. And that block is being held down by another block."

The fireman winced. He actually winced. It was clear he knew more than I did about rescuing people in RJ's situation, but I didn't want to give him time to ponder the complexities.

"There's a small opening around the back side. I crawled out of it. Come on." I tugged on him. "I can show you."

The Doogie Howser of firemen stood his ground.

"Okay, hold on a second. I need to call my captain," he said, putting a hand up to stop my desperate rambling as he pulled a phone from his pocket. I waited as he made contact with someone on the other line.

"Cap," he said. "I've got a survivor from the garage. She says there's someone trapped inside."

There was a pause. I waited, my foot tapping impatiently. Every second of chitchat was another second RJ didn't have.

The fireman's expression shifted. Something was wrong. He turned away from me and lowered his voice like he didn't want me to hear.

"Is it?" he said. "Do we know how long?"

The conversation ended, and I could tell just by his body language that whatever he had to say I wasn't going to like.

So, I didn't let him say it.

"Let's go," I urged, starting to remind myself of Lassie trying to get the stupid humans to come help me pull Timmy out of the well. "I'll show you where he is."

"Miss... I'm sorry, but we have to wait."

My eyes bugged right on out their sockets. "What do you mean, we have to wait? I thought you people were all about rushing in and saving the day."

"Normally we are, but these are extenuating circumstances we have here."

"Uh... yeah. My friend is trapped in the parking garage. All the more reason to get him out now."

"There's nothing I want more than to go in there and save your friend—and all the others who are trapped inside too—but the building is too unstable. One of our guys was injured in the aftershock, so now we have to wait for the structural engineers to assess the building and give us the all-clear before we can continue the rescue efforts."

No. No! Tears flooded my eyes as his words sank in. I couldn't accept his explanation. Wouldn't.

"There has to be something we can do, Parker," I said, swiping his name off the patch on his uniform. "My neighbor is in bad shape. And it's not just his foot. I think he has internal injuries too. He won't make it through a building inspection, much less through the night."

Parker shook his head. "I'm sorry. I wish there was more I could do. It's just not safe."

"But..." I pointed up at the building, directing his attention to the firefighter who was currently rescuing a resident and her dog off a balcony. "But you're rescuing them."

"Yes, with the cherry picker, Miss. Our rescue efforts have to remain outside of the building at this point. With your friend being under the rubble..."

The firefighter didn't complete his sentence. There was no need to. I understood perfectly well what he was saying. RJ was on his own, and if he couldn't figure out a way to break free of the hole he was in, he would very likely die in that pocket of life that was barely sustaining him.

I dropped my head, crestfallen. "How long?"

"Captain wasn't sure, but he thought a couple of hours, maybe more, depending on what they find. I'm so sorry."

It wasn't his fault, I knew that. His remorse was real. This man-boy was used to being a hero. No doubt saving people was what he and his firefighter brothers and sisters lived for, but when it came right down to it, risking their lives to save others didn't seem like the fairest split. He deserved to go home to his family tonight too.

But what about RJ? I'd made him a promise, thinking his survival was well within my control—but it wasn't. Not at all. RJ's fate belonged to factors no one could have foreseen, and now he was about to face the worst night of his life, utterly alone. Being a teacher with extensive first aid training, I understood that injured people were especially vulnerable to hypothermia. And with nighttime approaching, RJ's body temperature could drop quickly. If that happened, his heart, nervous system, and other organs wouldn't work normally, and it could lead to heart and respiratory system failure, or even death.

My heart pounded, anxiety thrashing through my veins. I knew what needed to be done. I couldn't leave him there. My whole life I'd been searching. I'd thought before that finding my father would end the hunt, but now I understood it wasn't him I'd been searching for. What I wanted was a connection—something bigger than me, something that brought down the roof. In that parking garage, digging RJ out of the angry earth, his arm going around me, and gifting me his most profound gratitude— I'd felt it. That something bigger I'd always craved. God, he'd been in front of my face this whole time. How had I not seen it?

But my eyes were wide open now. Today, in the trenches, our connection had been forged in desperation and strengthened by devotion. We'd both sacrificed for the other. We'd put our lives on the line. We'd been adversaries before—near strangers—but now, we were more. I wasn't sure how to explain it. I just knew. And, for that reason, I would be there for him in his time of need, even if it meant dropping back into the hellish world in which he still resided. But this time, I'd come prepared with the lifesaving tools I would need to keep him, and me, alive through a hard, cold night.

I began taking inventory of supplies in my head. *Blanket, water, flashlights, first aid supplies.* But that wasn't enough, not if the couple of hours Parker predicted stretched on. What if the structural engineers never deemed the building safe? Then what? We might need to take matters into our own hands.

Hammer and chisel.

Knife.

"Miss? Can you answer the question?"

I tilted my head up, realizing Parker had been conversing with me the whole time, and I hadn't heard a word. "I... I didn't hear what you said."

"You all right? You look a bit pale."

It was only then I realized how cold I was and how unsteady I felt on my feet.

"I'm fine," I replied, waving off his concern.

"You know what? How about if we just start with a simple question?" he said, tapping the tip of his pencil to the small spiral notebook he'd extracted from one of his many pockets. "What's your name?"

"Dani Malone."

"Is Dani short for Danielle?"

"Does it matter?"

Parker blinked. This was supposed to be his easiest question, and I was making it more difficult than it needed to be... for good reason.

"Actually, it does matter. I'm going to need your full legal name."

"Why?"

"This is a large-scale disaster. We need to know who has survived. Who is missing. Who has..."

Parker stopped himself before uttering that last word, the one that followed that place where all hope was lost.

Died.

But that wouldn't be RJ. I wouldn't let it be him.

"So full name, please."

I sighed, really not wanting to disclose such personal information but having no real reason to conceal it except for the judgment that would surely follow from someone his age.

"Gladys Danielle Malone."

The firefighter glanced at me then blinked in rapid succession before mercifully dropping his stare and penning my name on his notepad.

"Gladys Danielle Malone," he repeated it to himself, the slightest smile lifting the far corner of his lip.

"I was named after my mother," I said, feeling the need to explain. "She's an asshole."

Parker's brow lifted in amusement. "How about I just call you Dani?"

"And we've come full circle," I replied, trying to remain my snappy self even in the face of a wave of dizziness that suddenly passed over me. I swayed in place.

"Whoa," the fireman grabbed hold of me before I fell.

"Bruce!" he called out.

A heavyset man with close cropped hair and a goatee rushed in to help. The two guided me toward an ambulance.

"I'm fine," I insisted. "It's nothing."

"Except for the glass protruding from your arm," Bruce said.

"This little thing? I have earrings bigger."

"Humor us," Parker replied.

"I don't have time for humor. I have things to do," I said, the list of items I needed to buy rotating through my head.

"I understand, but I still have a few more questions to ask you about your neighbor, and then you can go. But while we talk, Bruce here will patch you up, all right? That way we don't waste any time."

I rolled my eyes at his reverse psychology. I was a teacher. I employed that strategy every day of my life.

"I see what you're doing, Parker."

He displayed a 'You got me' shrug.

Sighing, I glanced between the two guys before agreeing to their idea of tender loving care. I suppose it wasn't the worst idea ever. After all, it couldn't hurt for Bruce to sop up some blood before my big rescue effort. Parker was pretty smart for his age.

Back in firefighter mode, Parker dove into questions about the conditions inside the garage and the approximate area where RJ was located. I answered everything the best I could, given I was describing an upside-down world. And as I talked, the goateed paramedic tortured me with his evil tweezers, using them to extract tiny pieces of glass from my skin before irrigating it with saline. Once the bandage was placed, he'd move onto the next, and the process would repeat. But even professionals had their limits, and for Bruce, his was met with the jagged piece of glass in my upper arm. He wasn't touching that one. Instead, he handed me a bottle of electrolytes and took my blood pressure for what seemed like the hundredth time. But I had to give the guy credit, whatever he'd done had helped clear my head, and I felt stronger now, ready to face the challenge ahead.

"Last question. I promise," my firefighter said. "I just need RJ's last name. Oh, and do you know what his initials stand for?"

I searched my memory banks for any mention of RJ's real name, but I was pretty sure I'd never heard it spoken before. "Sorry, I don't know what the initials stand for..."

I thought of RJ's instructions. *Tell them RJ Contreras is trapped in the parking garage.* And yes, this did seem the right time to name drop my celebrity crush.

"But his last name is Contreras."

"Contreras?" Parker questioned, his eyes dancing with amusement as he scribbled it into his notepad. "That can't be an easy name to go through life with—everyone thinking you're the boy band singer."

"Unless you *are* the boy band singer."

"Right." He chuckled, still not getting the hint.

"Actually my neighbor—the guy awaiting your rescue—is *the* RJ Contreras."

Parker looked up from his notepad, his disbelieving eyes scanning me for insanity.

"So, let me see if I have this straight. You're saying that RJ Contreras from *AnyDayNow* lives here?"

"Yes. I mean, he did until the earthquake."

My firefighter buddy met the eye of the paramedic who, in turn, shook his head and grinned like he just assumed I'd been sideswiped by a block of concrete to the head and the blow had rendered me a delusional groupie girl. His colleague's reaction seemed to convince Parker that I was kidding.

"Dani, come on. You can't really believe a multi-millionaire pop star lives here?"

"I know it sounds crazy, but I'm not lying. It's him. He knew all their songs."

"*I* know all their songs."

That was a good point. I was going to have to dig deeper to convince him.

"Why would I make up a story like this?"

"I don't know. Maybe you had a picture of him on your wall and were staring at it just before the building came down."

Oh, well, that did make more sense than my story except… "I was in the garage, so no wall and no poster. Try again."

"Okay, maybe you had an *AnyDayNow* air freshener hanging on your rearview mirror. I'm just being realistic. RJ Contreras does not live in this building."

"But what if he does? What if it really is RJ, and the truth is just a rescue away? Think about it, Parker. You have a chance to save a legend. And imagine how grateful RJ would be. Maybe even enough to gift his favorite firefighter with VIP backstage passes for life."

"Are you bribing me?"

"Only if it's working."

"It's not."

I sighed, long and loud. "Parker, you frustrate me. I'm trying to focus your attention on the bonuses of celebrity rescue and you're just poo-pooing it away."

"Poo-pooing?" he questioned with a lift of his brow.

"I'm a first-grade teacher."

"Ah, that explains it." Parker chuckled, shaking his head as he walked away. "I tell you what, Gladys. I'll be sure to add 'international pop sensation' next to RJ's name. Will that make you happy?"

"You'll see, Peter Parker. You'll see."

I knew he thought I was crazy, and that was okay, because as more survivors called for help from the rubble, I wanted the only thing on Parker's mind to be saving RJ Contreras and collecting his prize. And, no, I didn't feel bad about name-dropping either, because while I didn't think celebrities deserved special treatment, in this particular instance RJ had earned his spot at the top of the triage list based on peril alone.

"Alright," the paramedic said once his colleague had gone. "Blood pressure is better. And my patch up job should suffice until we get you to the hospital and a surgeon can safely remove the glass from your arm."

My head shot up. "Hospital? No."

"Hey, don't worry. The surgeon should have you fixed up in no time. It looks like you got lucky. The glass appears to have missed the brachial artery which runs down the underside of the arm."

Bruce didn't get it at all. Of course I'd prefer a safe, sterile environment for the glass extraction; but there was no way I was going to sit in some hospital, waiting my turn, while RJ was underground with the threat of hypothermia looming on the horizon.

I sighed, glancing down at the windshield sticking out of my arm, realizing I was past the point of anesthetized surgery. If, as Bruce predicted, my injury was superficial, then the end result would be the same whether it was removed in a sterile environment by a trained, board-certified surgeon or removed right here on the back of the ambulance... by yours truly, Doctor Dani.

God, my mother would be so proud.

Dragging life-saving oxygen into my lungs, I grabbed hold of the glass and tugged. This right here—this was what separated the ladies from the heroes.

———

I blinked up at the paramedic from my spot on the curb—the place I had sunk to after pain stole the breath from me.

Bruce was not happy. He'd spent the time tending to my post-surgery care listing all the things that could have gone wrong—but hadn't. I let him vent while he layered gauze and wrapped bandages around my arm. "If you'd severed the brachial artery, it would've resulted in unconsciousness in as little as fifteen seconds, and death in as little as ninety."

"Well, then, we're lucky it didn't sever the brachial artery."

"Do you think this is a joke?"

"No. But you don't understand the predicament I'm in. If I had any other choice..."

"You *did* have a choice," he squealed. "It's called a hospital."

"I know. I'm sorry, it was stupid," I replied, choosing to appease him to speed the lecture along.

Bruce stopped tending to my wound and looked me square in the eye. "What predicament are you in? What is that brain of yours planning?"

"Nothing," I lied. "I couldn't go to the hospital because... I'm afraid of needles."

"Uh-huh. This wouldn't have anything to do with saving 'RJ Contreras' would it?" He used air quotes to shame me.

"No."

"Dani, there's nothing you can do for him."

Oh, yes, there was, but I knew better than to disclose my plan to Bruce. He would tell Parker, who would then escort me out of the danger zone.

So, I lied again.

"No, but I can be here for him when the rescue personnel bring him out. I can be the first one he sees."

Bruce considered my words carefully before finally accepting them.

"Okay, but you need to stay back, away from ground zero. Do you hear me?"

"I do. And thank you Bruce. I feel better already."

The cautious expression on his face told me he really wasn't sure what to do with me, but he had more pressing issues to deal with than some silly girl with rock star fantasies.

"All right, fine. We'll play it your way. I'm going to release you now, but listen to me carefully. This bandage is just a quick fix. Once your superstar is saved from the rubble, you need to go to the hospital and get your arm stitched up. Do you understand?"

"I do," I said, getting to my feet and surprising myself with their steadiness. "And do you know why I understand this, Bruce? Because you've repeated it at least five times."

"Only because you haven't listened to even one of them."

I smiled, stretching out my good hand to shake his. "It's been fun doing business with you, and don't listen to the others who whisper behind your back. You're a decent paramedic."

He chuckled. "You're a spunky little thing, aren't you?"

I glanced around, checking for spies before whispering, "It's how I reel in the pop stars."

Bruce shook his head, clearly amazed by my ability to keep the delusion going so effortlessly. "Okay, well, give him my best wishes."

"I most certainly will."

We parted ways then, with me headed straight for the safety across the street where neighbors and looky-loos alike were gathered. It wasn't every day that an earthquake toppled a building in Los Angeles, and unluckily for those in my apartment building, we'd happened to be at the epicenter of the tragedy. But I had no interest in being a spectator. What I needed now was to borrow a phone and get just one of my forty-plus siblings to answer.

And I knew just who to call first—Donny. Sigh. If there was anyone else in the vicinity, trust me, I would've tried that person first, but Donny only lived three short blocks away, so the call went to him first. I'd done the math. Even factoring in that he would need to stop playing his video game in the basement of his parents' home, put on some pants, find his keys, and grab a snack, Donny would still be here faster than any other sibling.

"Hey!" A young woman in a trendy dress beckoned me over. Due to her impeccable wardrobe, I had to assume she'd arrived after the collapse—in order to profit off our misery. "Did you escape from that building?"

I wondered what her first clue had been—the fine particles of my apartment complex now attached to my eyelashes or the blood-soaked mess the self-surgery had made of my clothing?

"I'm Misty Swallows. You might have seen my videos? I'd really like to interview you."

I was no longer listening, having narrowed in on her phone like a ravenous vulture. Besides, there was no need for introductions. I already knew who she was: influencer Misty Swallows. And I was no fan, but nevertheless, I was about to make her superficial dreams come true.

Heading straight for her, her makeshift cameraman lifted his phone.

"Uh-uh," I shook my finger at him. "No filming."

He glanced at Misty for instruction. She gestured for him to lower it before focusing her attention back on me and repeating, "Were you in the building?"

"Yes, but not just me. There's someone else in there, and he needs your help."

"*My* help?" she asked, looking down at her high fashion Off-

White brand dress. Clearly, there was only so far this influencer was willing to go to help her fellow man.

"Not that kind of help," I said, letting her off the hook. "What would you say if I told you your next post is about to go viral?"

Her eyes widened, and I swear I saw a dollop of drool form on her painted lips. "I'd say you're my new best friend."

"Oh good, then you'll agree to my terms. Just audio. And afterward, I need to use your phone."

Misty readily agreed, pitying me with a lingering stare. No doubt she assumed my silver streaked disaster 'do and dust-up makeup job were the reason for my for not wanting those coveted fifteen minutes of fame, but vanity had nothing to do with it. I was protecting my students on the off chance I didn't make it out of the parking garage alive.

After agreeing to my rules and giving Misty Swallows the ultimate gift—a trapped RJ Contreras on a silver platter—she readily handed over her phone. Honestly, after the exclusive I'd just given her, I considered stealing it. With what Misty stood to make on her video, she could buy plenty more iPhones where this one had come from. But my mother's nagging voice was never far away, and I knew I couldn't go through with the hasty plan.

Stepping away, I dialed up Donny. Not only did his proximity to the scene make him the ideal helper but he was also the only sibling whose number I had memorized. Not out of devotion, but because Donny had once bragged that his phone number, in letter form, spelled out 'arousal,' and since then, I'd never been able to erase it from my memory.

"Hello?"

"Donny, it's me—Dani. I need your help. Can you come pick me up right now?"

"Who?"

"Dani."

"Dani," he said, elongating my name as if he were trying to place me.

"Dani, your sperm sister."

"Ah, right. Dani. Has anyone ever told you that you sound like Princess Leia?"

"Yes. You. Many times. Listen, Donny, the earthquake just toppled my building..."

"Yeah, that quake was sick, man," he interrupted.

Sick wasn't the first adjective that came to mind when describing what I'd experienced, but I didn't have time to debate vocabulary with a dimwitted gamer. "Did you hear me? My building collapsed. I lost everything. I really need your help. Oh, and can you bring your credit card? I'm going to need to borrow some money. Can you do that for me, Donny? Can you help me?"

It was a heartfelt plea, a cry for assistance.

"I don't know, Dani. It's really not a good time. I'm on level seven."

So much for asking nicely. "I don't care if you're in a galaxy far, far away. Pick me up right now or I'll come over there and cut your electricity!"

"Fine. Jesus. Princess Leia is so much nicer than you."

"Just hurry."

"I'm saving my game, geez. Chill. Do I need underwear for this?"

I growled in response. Forget cutting the electricity, I was going to murder my sperm brother in his sleep.

The sound of a man calling my name drew my attention. I whipped my head around to find Jeremy—smartly dressed for our second date—rushing toward me. I was saved! So relieved was I to see him that I threw my arms over his shoulders and buried my head in his chest. No lie, I would've burrowed into him for safekeeping if only human biology allowed such a feat.

"My god, Dani, this is just unbelievable," he said, hugging me tightly. "I saw it on the news. I came as soon as I heard that it was your apartment complex. Are you all right? Were you inside when it happened?"

I lifted my head and looked over at what was left of my building. Tears welled in my eyes as it hit me... really hit me. I had been *in there*. And so had many of my neighbors. My heart sank. Families lived in there. Children. Pets. So much suffering. I knew I couldn't save them all. But if I could save even one...

"Uh, Dani?" Donny said, interrupting my reunion with Jeremy to remind me that he was still on the line. "Was that a 'yes' or a 'no' to the underwear?"

I winced. "Never mind, weirdo. Go back to your video game."

"Sweet. Thanks."

I shook my head as I handed the phone back to Misty and wondered how our father had gotten it so wrong the day he'd created Donny.

Grabbing Jeremy by the hand, I dragged him away from the burgeoning crowd. "I need help."

He nodded unconditionally. With Jeremy, there were no levels that needed to be met and no undergarments to be slipped on. Unlike my own flesh and blood, Jeremy was eager to be of assistance to the dusty girl he barely knew.

"Where's your car?"

"I parked around the corner. Do you need me to take you to the hospital?"

"No. I need you to take me to the supercenter down the street."

"The supercenter? You want to go shopping?" he asked, his voice tipped in surprise. "*Now*?"

"I need supplies."

"For what?"

I swept my arm behind me to encompass the crumbling

mess that had once been my life. His eyes widened, realizing the stupidity of his question. But what he didn't realize was my desire to go to the store was not to buy toilet paper and tampons. No. What I was really going for was to gather the supplies necessary to keep another man alive.

Had Jeremy known that, I doubt he'd have been so eager to help.

9

RJ: AAA

I waited for Dani to disappear from sight before dropping the act. It had taken everything in me to pretend I was okay—to give Dani hope that she might be able to save me. Hell, with that steely determination of hers, she'd given *me* hope. I'd actually thought with my own personal Wonder Woman by my side that maybe, just maybe, everything would be okay. But the truth was my body was no match for the destruction that had rained down upon it. Dani had relieved most of the strain, yes, but she didn't have the healing powers to fix the damage that had already been done. And from the aching alone, I could tell it was extensive.

I didn't need x-rays to tell me that I'd probably broken every rib in my body or an ultrasound to confirm internal injuries. The pain was excruciating, and it was all I could do to keep a brave face in front of her. But now that she was gone, there was nothing to hold me back, and I let out a groan that rattled the already besieged parking garage.

To my surprise, the walls threw back an echo. Or was it a voice...? I quieted, momentarily considering that I wasn't the only trapped soul in this wasteland.

"Hello?"

Nothing, not even an echo.

"Is anybody there?"

I waited, hoping. I'd always been a fairly private guy, but even I could appreciate a little companionship at what could, very well, be the end of my life. When no reply echoed forth, I reluctantly turned toward the task at hand, which was to not sit by idly like some eternally trapped jack-in-the-box and accept my fate. I might no longer be alive when the rescuers found me, but at least they'd know I tried.

In an effort to free myself, I placed my hands at my side and attempted a backward pushup. That genius idea did nothing but bring a fresh wave of nausea and pain, making me wonder what was worse, the pain I could feel or the pain that I *couldn't*— which was anything south of my shin. My eyes tracked down, settling on my stone prison. With my left ankle crushed under a block of concrete, I understood that even if I did survive, there was a real good chance I wouldn't be leaving here with all my body parts.

With brute strength not working, I adopted Dani's approach of digging dirt out from my hole in an effort to free up some space around the concrete block and wiggle my way out. But the further down I got, the more concrete my raw, bloodied fingers met.

Frustrated by the futile effort, I slammed my fists down onto the earth and screamed at the top of my lungs.

"Fuucckk!"

What followed was a volley of F-bombs that rivaled the time Dane had thought it was a good idea for us *AnyDayNow* boys— at the height of our fame—to toilet paper Tucker Beckett's vacation house in the Hamptons without realizing he had security guards and a pack of attack dogs protecting the place.

"Please," came a muffled sound, beset with pain. "Enough."

A voice. Wait... a voice? Holy shit... it hadn't just my voice echoing; someone else was in here with me.

"Who's there?" I asked.

"Albert. The old guy in apartment 140," he said, his voice so withered I had to strain just to hear him. "Who are you?"

"RJ, the young guy in apartment 426."

"You're not the one who looks like a Manson follower, are you?"

His comment was so random, I couldn't help but chuckle... and wonder if with my wayward hair maybe I was the guy he envisioned. "Honestly, I might be."

"Wonderful."

Not to be upstaged, I asked. "You're not the old guy who smells like cat litter, are you?"

I swear I heard the faintest laugh. "I might be."

"Delightful," I mimicked.

And then there was silence. I waited. Worried. "You okay there, Albert?"

"Uh... no, not really," the man said, drawing in a gurgled breath between each word. "I'm afraid I'm not long for this world, son."

The way he said it with such certainty brought a lump to my throat.

"Don't say that. Help is coming."

A prolonged silence followed making me wonder if Albert was drifting in and out of consciousness. *Please. Don't die.* I didn't even know this man, and already I was immeasurably attached. He was my only link to the living world, and I didn't want to lose him.

"Albert, stay with me."

He grunted.

"Albert! I'll start swearing again if you don't answer me."

"I'm here."

"Good," I exhaled. "Because I can swear in eighteen different languages."

"I don't doubt it," he responded, his voice tapering off.

I waited patiently for more.

"You know, I'm eighty-two years old. I've lived a long life. Didn't think I was scared of dying. Turns out I am."

"I'm twenty-five, and I didn't think I was scared of dying either."

"You young-uns never do. So fearless. Then you get old, and suddenly you're no longer invincible."

"I don't know, Albert. I'm stuck in the same predicament you are, and right about now, I'm not feeling entirely invincible."

"No, I suppose you wouldn't be. Can I give you a survival tip?"

"Okay."

"Preserve your energy."

"My leg is crushed under concrete. I'm about as immobile as you can get."

"I meant stop swearing like a sailor. It's not going to get you out of here any sooner. Besides, it's not becoming of a young gentleman."

"I'm no gentleman."

"You might have been, had your mamma washed your mouth out with soap once in a while."

"I was raised on foaming soap. Not sure if it's as effective as the old school bars at curbing bad language."

Albert commenced a minute-long coughing fit, and by the time it was over, the old man had barely any breath left.

"Hang in there, Albert. Help is on the way."

"There's no helping me, RJ. I have a piece of rebar skewered through my gut. I'm bleeding out."

Lowering my head to the earth, I swore under my breath at

the injustice of it all. Why had I even met this man if it meant having to hear him die?

"Talk to me, son," Albert said, his voice already sounding as if it were fading. "Take my mind off this."

I could've stayed silent for my own self-preservation, but Albert needed me to step up and be the man I hadn't been in five long months. "What do you want me to say?"

"Anything. Just talk."

"Uh... I'm a singer."

"A shower singer?"

"No," I smiled. "A professional one."

"What kind of music?"

"I sing current stuff, like pop and rock."

"Oh."

In that one word, I could tell Albert was not impressed. Maybe a little more elaboration might turn him around.

"I'm in a famous band—or I was. We broke up last year. Ever heard of *AnyDayNow*?"

"Can't say I have, but then I listen to old-timer music," Albert replied, stopping to catch his breath. "My great-granddaughter might know you, though."

"How old is she?"

"Becca is sixteen."

"Then she knows us."

"So, you're in one of those bands with all the screaming girls?"

"Lots of screaming. Yes."

"What's it like, being on stage, worshipped?"

Had he asked me that question this morning, I might have responded with a cynical answer, but this morning seemed so long ago. My perspective had already shifted in the time I'd been entombed. Now I'd give anything to be up on stage performing again. Why had I walked away?

"I'm not performing anymore, but it was incredible while it lasted."

"Why aren't you performing?"

I sighed. "Because, Albert, I'm a narcissistic fool."

"Aren't we all?"

"Yeah, but I'm their king. I got tangled up in my own hype and let my ego get the best of me. I lost the joy of singing and performing. That's why I was here in apartment 426, hiding out like a goddamn coward."

"At least you figured it out while you're still young. Some of us take a lifetime."

"Yeah, well, twenty-five might be the end my lifetime."

"I surely hope not, son. You're just getting started. Me, I've lived my life... and it was a damn good one. If you remember one thing about me, let it be that I was a lucky bastard. Married my best friend. Had forty-seven years with her. We had two kids. Five grandchildren. Four great-grandchildren. I worked as a school bus driver almost my whole life. Not a glamorous job like yours, but I loved it. My name's Albert Arthur Aldrich, and them kids called me Triple A—like the insurance. The nickname stuck, and my family and friends all call me that now." Albert chuckled weakly and I just knew there was nostalgic smile on his face as he remembered. "Yep, I'm going to die a happy man."

"I wish I could say the same. I'm alone. An outsider. Always have been."

"I believe we make our own happiness. Everything is a choice. Do you want to be bitter and only look to the past, or do you want to find joy in the things right before your eyes?"

"And if I don't get out of here?"

"Then spend the time you have left remembering the good times. Surely you had some of those."

I fell silent as I tried to gather those good times into one tidy pile in my head. That way, when I needed them most, they'd be there, like Albert's had so readily been.

"Don't you give up hope, RJ. I believe you will get out of here. You'll go on with your life and probably forget all about the old guy in apartment 140."

"You? Never."

"That's the spirit. I tell you what. I'm gonna put in a good word for you with the man upstairs. Tell him you deserve a second chance."

"I'd appreciate that."

"But you gotta promise me you won't waste it. Get back on that stage. Stop living like an outsider. Make every day you're alive mean something. Like me, RJ. I got no regrets. I lived a damn good life."

I knew all this. What Albert was proposing wasn't rocket science. But saying you will do something and actually doing it are two very different things. The truth was, if I died today, I'd do so as a man who'd squandered the best years of his life because he couldn't let go of the anger and the past hurts. My career. My friends. My fans. Dani. All this time with her right next door! Why hadn't I opened my eyes and made those days with her mean something? Maybe then I would have seen her for who she truly was. Despite only knowing me as some down-on-his-luck asshole, when everything was on the line, she'd chosen kindness and compassion over her own wellness and safety. I didn't deserve her devotion, I knew that, but somehow, I sensed her act of selflessness was the stepping stone I'd needed to become a better man. A more patient man. A more loving one.

A man who would die happy.

"I hear ya, Triple A."

He didn't respond.

10

DANI: FOR A GOOD CAUSE

I LOOKED AT JEREMY. HE LOOKED AT ME. WE BOTH LOOKED BACK at the store.

Then I briefly closed my eyes, resigned to what needed to be done despite being adamantly opposed to doing it.

Thou shall not steal.

Those weren't just words to me. My first—and last—foray into theft had been as a five-year-old girl swiping a pack of gum. Mom made me take it back to the store and explain to the manager what I'd done. The mortification alone was enough to cure my thieving ways.

Until today.

Trust me, the last thing I wanted to do was to break the law and steal what wasn't mine. I was a teacher, who taught good values to her students, and this was not modeling good behavior. Under normal circumstances, I would've jumped at the chance to be a paying customer. But if the opportunists streaming out of the front entrance with big screen TVs in tow were any indication, the store was not operating under normal circumstances. The earthquake had jolted awake the looters, who had then come out in force to take what was not theirs. And sadly, if I wanted to get RJ through the night, I was going to have to join their uncouth ranks.

Jeremy turned his attention back to me, his eyes widening as he grasped the full extent of the plan formulating in my head.

"Oh, no. No way, Dani."

Shame colored my cheeks, the residual side effect of the good girl I used to be.

"I'll come back with money in a few days," I hastily explained. "And I'll repay them for everything I take."

"No, you won't, because you're not going in there," he ordered.

I jerked my head back, surprised that he thought he had any authority over me at all. His comment only made me dig in further. "I'll do what needs to be done."

Jeremy's eyes narrowed. "Then you'll do it in the grocery store down the street. I'll drive you there now."

If I hadn't already determined Jeremy wasn't for me, that decided it. "You will not do that. This is the store I want to go to. Besides, it's doubtful there's a store in a ten-mile radius of the epicenter that's going to look any different than this."

"Then I'll drive you to a store in a twenty-mile radius... or a thirty-mile radius, if that's what it takes to keep you out of prison."

Wait, was he being a mini dictator because he was worried about me? Ah. Maybe I was being too harsh? I looked his way, feeling nothing but irritation when I looked at him. I wanted to explain to him why it had to be this store in particular. That this was the only one for miles around that carried the type of survival supplies I needed to keep us alive. But I couldn't tell him that without revealing why I was stealing in the first place. The fact of the matter was, I needed Jeremy to help me save RJ.

"Just... please trust me. It has to be this one."

Jeremy rotated in his seat, staring. The tsking look on his face reminded me of my mother's. I was a naughty, insolent girl who needed correcting. And maybe, had my apartment not come down on top of me a little over an hour ago, I would have bent to his coercion. But I wasn't the same girl who had nit-picked my way through dinner last night. Today's Dani would do whatever she deemed necessary—including looting—to keep RJ breathing.

"You understand that some of those people have guns, rights? Are you really willing to get yourself killed for your favorite facewash?"

That Jeremy thought me so shallow that I'd risk my life for Aveeno was the final nail in his coffin. I no longer cared what he thought of me or if he would wait around and drive me back to the scene. I could get back to RJ without him.

My jaw tightened. "I don't have a choice."

"You do have a choice. Every single person in that store has a choice—and they're making the wrong one. Don't be like them, Dani. You're better than that."

Not today I wasn't. Today I was a soldier, going to war for the man who'd wrapped his grateful arm around me and called me his hero. As long as RJ lived, they could throw me in jail because I'd know in my heart it had all been worth it. But if I did nothing at all and RJ died, I'd never be able to look myself in the eye again.

Jeremy must have taken my moment of quiet reflection as his chance to change my mind. He put his car in gear. "I'm going to play my get-out-of-jail-free card on you," he said, rolling forward. "You can thank me later."

"Stop the car," I demanded, opening the door.

"What the hell is wrong with you?" he blasted. "Shut your door."

"No!" I unbuckled my seatbelt. "I'll jump if I have to."

"You're crazy." He slammed on the brakes. "Go, if that's what you want. Get arrested. Get shot. My god. No one needs supplies that bad."

"I do," I replied, tears of frustration threatening to fall. "I need them."

"Why? What can be so important that you risk arrest? That you risk your life? Tell me that."

I wanted to scream at him, to tell him RJ would die without me; but if he thought this was bad, what would he do if he knew I was planning to go back inside the parking garage? Jeremy had tattler written all over him.

I opened the door. "Thanks for the ride."

Jeremy shook his head, as if what little hope he still had of being able to salvage something with me had been dashed when he understood the full scope of my mental instability. I let that remain his last thought of me as I climbed out.

Jeremy was gone the second my feet hit the pavement.

————

There was nothing like a wily band of looters to speed up the shopping process. Typically, I was one of those looky-loo shoppers, who pushed my cart up and down the aisles with no big plan and no big hurry. But today was a wee bit different. Not only was I on a timeline to save RJ, but the situation inside the store was deteriorating quickly, and lawlessness was setting in.

Having a plan and knowing the layout of the store worked to my advantage. I stuck to the periphery, staying low and out of the way of the hardcore 'shoppers.' I also avoided the more sought-after areas of the store, like the electronics department and the pharmacy. Much to my surprise, the camping section had not yet been picked apart. You'd think after an earthquake, this would be the first place people would head, but obviously the looters in this store were thinking more long-term survival, like iPhones and TV's with built in apps.

Grabbing a survivalist-type backpack off the shelf, I began my shoplifting experience by shoving the most basic of supplies into its spacious openings. Lanterns, flashlights, batteries, a first aid kit, space blankets—really just anything I thought might help us get through the night. The only knife I could find was a Swiss Army one, not really going to help the cause, but I swiped it anyway... because I could. Oh, god. I was going to hell.

I'd just managed to wipe those shelves clean when another aftershock hit. Falling to the ground, I protected my head as the world around me rattled. They were getting less intense in strength, but that offered little solace given the fragile house of cards above RJ's head.

Once the shaking stopped, I watched my fellow looters pick themselves back up and continue the important work of pillaging. These were some hardy souls... But so was I, and until I got something to chip away at the concrete holding RJ down, my shopping spree wasn't over.

I arrived in the tool aisle, only to join a handful of others filling their carts.

"What do you need, hun?" one woman asked, so welcoming.

"A hammer and chisel."

"Hammers are over there, but no chisel."

It was like she'd taken inventory. Disappointed there was nothing of use to free RJ's foot, I nonetheless swiped the last two hammers off the wall and waved them in the air for her to see. "Thank you."

"No problem, hun. You have a nice day now."

I chuckled. This just proved that, when done right, shoplifting didn't have to be an unpleasant experience. Still, the longer I was here, the more danger I was in. Making my way toward the store's exit, I stayed low and plucked things off the shelves that might prove valuable while avoiding the place with the most value of all, the pharmacy. A Z-pack or a bottle of painkillers would go a long way to getting RJ through the night, but I was already pushing my luck and didn't dare head in that direction. The pharmacy was where the diehard looters came out to play.

A pang of guilt gripped me as I exited the store with the stolen contraband slung heavily over my shoulders. I pushed the shame aside, telling myself I would be back to confess my sins, just as I had all those years ago as a five-year-old gum-stealing thief. The consequences this time around would be stiffer, that much I understood, but I hoped maybe they would take into consideration the desperation that had necessitated the action. If not, I'd take my punishment knowing I'd done it to save a life. My chest clenched—*if* it wasn't already too late.

I looked around the parking lot, hoping maybe Jeremy had had a change of heart and had circled back around to get me, but he hadn't. And I didn't blame him. If the roles had been reversed, and he had asked me to risk my life for J. Lo, I wasn't sure I'd be all that eager to risk arrest either.

The pack on my back was awkward and heavy, making the nearly two-mile journey back on foot feel endless. After surviving what I had today, my body was depleted. God, I missed Jeremy's car. And it didn't help matters that I was also carrying a gallon of water in each hand, the weight of which forced me to stop and rest every fifteen minutes or so. But even as day turned to night, I forged on, arriving back at the apartment complex only to discover that rescue workers were still standing around. Even the giant crane was no longer plucking people off their balconies. It was an eerie sight, almost as if the trapped had been left for dead. And while I understood the reasoning behind the stall, I couldn't help but be horrified for those who really needed saving. I knew then that I'd made the right decision by going in search of supplies.

The flapping of signs off to my right caught my attention. The crowd behind the caution tape hadn't just doubled, it had swelled into the hundreds. And as I drew nearer, I understood why. The signs—they all had RJ's name on them.

Free RJ

I love you RJ

We want RJ out AnyDayNow

I would've relished my role in the fandom had I not been so worried about him. It had been at least three hours since I'd left. So much could have happened in that time. But I couldn't focus on that. I had to believe he was alive and waiting for rescue. What would he think about the outpouring of love? Would it make him stronger, or would he shrink further into himself? It made me wonder why he'd been in hiding in the first place. What was the reason he'd chosen to isolate himself, when clearly he was loved by so many?

Leaving the fans and their signs of hope behind, I walked the length of the barrier, trying to find a way back in. In the time I'd been gone, they'd fortified the area with concrete barriers and police officers strategically placed inside the perimeter. I understood the reasoning. For the safety of everyone, they needed to keep the onlookers out, but it just made my job harder. Not only did I need to make my way to the hole undetected, but I also had to get past the barricade.

I spotted my firefighter, Parker, among a gathering of men and women still waiting to go in. I wanted desperately to talk to him, to find out what was happening, but I had a sense if he saw me with a huge backpack on my back, he'd know instinctively what I was doing and report me to his superiors. No, this was my mission to complete, and the only way to do that was to keep it covert.

Keeping to the outer areas of the makeshift wall, I found a place to wait undetected until I was given some sign. I wasn't sure what that might be, but I was sure I would know it when I saw it. All I needed was a distraction that might allow me to duck behind the barriers and disappear down the rabbit hole.

My chest tightened at just the thought of going back in there. Since leaving RJ, I hadn't really given much thought to entombing myself once more. I'd been entirely focused on the task at hand. But now that I was lying in wait, the terror was slowly setting in. When I'd left RJ earlier, I hadn't known what I knew now. I hadn't known that our small pocket of safety had been supporting the weight of half the building. One more after-shock was perhaps all it would take to bring the rest of it down on top of us.

A popping sound, possibly from an erupting gas pipe, served as the distraction I needed. With the focus elsewhere, I darted past the barriers and ran toward the opening in the earth. Toward uncertainty. Toward danger.

I went for him.

You better be alive in there, RJ Contreras. You promised me.

11

RJ: FADING FAST

ALBERT NEVER SPOKE AGAIN. I CALLED OUT HIS NAME OVER AND over, even dropping a string of f-bombs to spark his ire, but there was nothing. No movement. No sound. Albert was gone. Suddenly the walls around me closed in. I had been left to navigate alone in this desolate underground. The pain from his loss hit hard, so much harder than it should have for an old man I barely knew. But Albert had made a mark on me, and something had changed.

The importance of our short time together could not be understated. I'd always thought I preferred solitude; even craved it after those crazy *AnyDayNow* days. I'd come back to an empty home, and the silence seemed a welcome reprieve. But there was something to be said about the power of human connection, and now that I'd had a taste of it, I couldn't imagine living without. Things I'd thought I didn't want—a wife, maybe a few kids —suddenly made perfect sense to me. I wanted what Albert had had. If this experience had taught me anything, it was that life wasn't meant to be lived alone; not when death was such a solitary endeavor.

Dusk descended on the parking garage not long after

Albert's passing. Whatever miniscule light I'd been afforded at the beginning of the ordeal was ripped from me as I was swallowed up in desolate darkness. In the pitch-black, desperation reigned supreme. My best guess was I'd been trapped inside for three, maybe four hours, and still no bulldozed walls. No first responders calling my name. No signs whatsoever of any help coming my way.

It was hard to rationalize the reason why. I knew Dani was trying—that she'd put everything she had into getting me help —but what if there was no help to be had? What if the world outside the parking garage was worse than the one inside? Visions of an apocalyptic landscape took shape with every aftershock that rattled my prison. The quakes had leveled off in intensity since the first two big ones Dani and I had ridden out together, but regardless, I braced for the impact each time another one rumbled to life, certain the rickety ceiling would take its last bow or that the ground would open up further and devour me whole.

With each bleak hour that passed, I could feel my strength wavering—my future fading away. All the things I should have said. All the things I hadn't done. What had I been waiting for? Why had I thought time would stand still long enough for me to get my shit together? It wouldn't... it hadn't. I'd been so dumb, wasting time I didn't have. All these months I'd been locked away in my apartment being a fucking baby when I should have sucked it up, swallowed my pride, and jumped right back into the game.

There was a lesson in there somewhere, but right now, with chills wracking my body, I really wasn't in the position to ponder. Instead I focused on Dani, imagining her warm skin against my shivering body. She'd heat me from the inside out like she'd been doing since the day we met.

Dani. Talk about a wasted opportunity. Come to think of it,

why had I wasted it? It wasn't like I couldn't have had her if I'd put my mind and body into it. Getting women into bed was a particular skill set of mine, right up there with knowing how to pick the tastiest watermelon. To be fair, my chances were bolstered by the fact that women loved sweaty musicians hot off the stage. I supposed that gave me a warped confidence in my abilities. Maybe as Chad Woodcock, I wouldn't be turning them on so easily. Maybe I'd actually have to try.

Not that I'd ever tested the theory. When I went off the grid, I purged myself of anything that had to do with my former life, and that included the enablers—the women who put up with my shit for the opulent benefits it afforded them. If they left me, they left the lifestyle too. So, they stayed until I'd had my fill, and then I'd kick them to the curb for a new woman and a new cycle of exploits.

But the minute I moved into this shitty apartment, all that changed. Chad Woodcock had no special privileges afforded to him. He was just an average Joe with no known gifts to speak of, and yet, Dani had seen through all that today. She'd looked inside and seen that the douche next door was worth saving. It was maybe the first time in my adult life that a woman had judged me for me and not for the lifestyle I lived.

It made me rethink every encounter with her over the past five months. She'd fascinated me from the start—that sassy-assed balcony warrior who treated me like a commoner and had zero tolerance for my shit. God, she'd been such fun to rile up; the barky Pomeranian bitch-slapping my Great Dane. She was just so over-the-top nippy that I couldn't help but turn that energy back on her, in the most negative of ways. What I should have done—what I'd wanted to do every day since seeing her sunning in a bikini on our balcony—was to pin her to her reclining chair and give those luscious lips of hers a try. But I'd been so preoccupied with my own problems that I'd abstained from creating new ones. Clearly that had been a mistake because I now understood that this girl had been placed on this earth to save me from myself.

Come on, Dani. Be my hero. I'll make it worth your while.

I believed in her. If anyone could make it out alive, it would be scrappy Dani Malone, a woman who wasn't afraid to be brave in a world that had, very recently, tried to claim her. There really was no better advocate. If Dani made it out of this parking garage, I knew she'd be tirelessly campaigning for my release, using that mouth of hers for good, not evil.

I dozed on and off, and each time I awakened, I could feel my deterioration. Weakness was setting in. I was cold. I was hot. I was in pain. I was not. The 'not' part came later as numbness set in. It was then I started really considering my fate. I was slowly dying. It wasn't the way I'd thought it would be. So sad. So lonely. The unfairness of it all. I wanted to live, but the decision was no longer up to me.

It was after one of these wakeups that the anger set in, and I raged at the world, screaming at the top of my lungs to be saved.

But no one ever came.

12

DANI: TO THE RESCUE

LIKE A SOLDIER EVADING CAPTURE, I ZIGZAGGED MY WAY TO THE hole in the ground, expecting at any moment that I'd be struck down by enemy fire. But there was no chase. No bullets ringing out through the night. No voices calling me back. The reality was that no one even saw me bolt past the barriers. Maybe I wanted the intervention; someone to talk some sense into me. But no. Jeremy had tried that, and it hadn't worked.

Arriving at the opening in the ground that I'd escaped from earlier in the day, I stood there a moment contemplating my decision. I was willingly going back into a place of death and destruction—for *him*.

This wasn't me at all. I was sensible—usually—and smart. I did not lean on men to set my world straight. So why now? Why him? Why was I risking everything to give a man I barely knew a chance at life? And RJ Contreras, of all people. He wasn't exactly known as a salt-of-the-earth kind of guy. RJ had a reputation that preceded him, one that would have pursed my mother's lips like she'd chewed and gagged down an entire lemon piece by piece.

My mother. The things I'd done today... oh, man, she could

never know. I'd never hear the end of it, in life or death. I could almost hear her speaking at my funeral. *Dani got her dumbness from her father's side of the family.*

Disappointing my mother in death seemed an acceptable way to go, so I dropped to my knees and prepared to insert myself back into the earth. First things first. I pushed the two water containers through the hole I'd climbed out of earlier and watched them slide down the dirt slope, fortunately staying intact on the way down. Easing the straps off my shoulders, I tried the same easy-does-it approach with the backpack only to discover that you can't shove a monstrously overstuffed bag through a narrow hole. After heaving and ho-ing to no avail, I tried a new approach. Getting back to my feet, I sat down heavily on the bag, my full weight enough to tip the scales and send the backpack through the hole. I didn't have time to celebrate because as my bag went through, so did I. Unlike the graceful descent the water jugs took, mine was a tumble for the comic books. Caught up in a dirt avalanche, I somersaulted head over foot all the way to the ground, landing with a thud at the bottom of a debris pile as a meteor shower of concrete and hell rained down on me.

Stunned, I took the briefest moment to gather my wits before grabbing my flashlight and directing the light upward.

I gasped. Instead of a small opening in the ground, the narrow portal was now a cavernous crater, steep and unstable. There was no ridge to climb anymore; no way for me to get out on my own. The next time I would see the light of day would be with the rescue unit, just like RJ.

I rose to my feet, shaking the dust from my hair and tried not to dwell on my own personal survival statistics because I knew they were decreasing with every passing minute. And it didn't help that it was so dark. Even with the flashlight leading the way, I was turned around, unsure which direction to go.

"RJ?" I called out.

No answer. I called again and again. Nothing. He couldn't be...? No. I refused to believe that RJ had succumbed to his injuries because everything I knew about that man said he wasn't going to let go without a fight. Unless he had already fought... and lost.

At that very moment, the silhouette of my mangled car came into view, illuminated by the beam of my flashlight, and I saw RJ right where I'd left him, only now he was slumped over, his head hanging limply and pressed into the ground.

"RJ?" I whispered, falling to my knees and lifting his heavy head with my hands. He was hot to the touch. "It's me."

He wasn't just sleeping; RJ was semi-unconscious. I shook his head from side to side, calling his name, but when that didn't wake him, I took to slapping his whiskered face.

"Wake up, RJ! Come on. Wake up."

I felt him jerk in my hands, his head bobbing around as he blinked into the bright light. "Dani?"

"Yes, it's me. I was so worried," I said, refraining from kissing him in relief as my fingers slid over his face. "You don't look good. You're burning up."

RJ pawed at his sweat drenched shirt, seeming confused. Then, without warning, he grasped the bottom hem of the shirt and pulled it right over his head.

"Oh!" I rocked back in surprise. "Okay. We're taking the shirt off."

"Hot," he mumbled, the one-word sentence appearing to be his only means of coherent speech.

"Yes, you are," I said, then stopped myself, knowing how that might have sounded. "I meant temperature-wise, not... um... never mind."

Thankfully, RJ was too miserable to follow along with the train wreck that was my mind. I placed the back of my hand to his forehead. "You have a fever. How long have you been feeling like this?"

RJ held up random fingers—for no apparent reason.

"Okay," I answered, a hint of a smile passing over my lips. "Let's try this a different way."

Nursing my injured arm, I gingerly pulled the heaving backpack off my shoulders and dropped it to the ground. Reaching inside, I pulled out a tin cup and poured some of the jug water into it before dumping it over his head.

RJ instantly revived, shaking the water droplets from his long hair. "The fuck?"

His head shot up, and he settled his gaze on me.

I waved. "Hey there. I'm back."

He blinked, wiping the liquid from his eyes. The dust mixed with water created a sort of paste on his face.

Reaching into my backpack, I pulled out a lantern and a pack of batteries. While RJ watched wordlessly, I popped the batteries into the compartment and flicked the switch, illuminating the space around us.

"There. That's better."

RJ's eyes blinked rapidly, as if his fever-ravished brain tried desperately to catch up. I had a cure for that too. From the first aid kit, I scored a sample packet of Tylenol and tore it open.

"Here, take these," I said, handing him the two tiny pills while pressing the cup of water to his lips. "Drink up."

RJ was as obedient as one of my little first graders. The only difference between them being that RJ actually knew how to swallow a pill. I refilled the cup three times before he'd had his fill. And while I took a drink for myself, I noticed him staring.

"Are you a dream?"

The way he looked at me with such wonder in his eyes made me think of my Disney princess years, when it had been me staring at the Little Mermaid. But now it was RJ Contreras from

AnyDayNow gazing upon me with the same dreamy eyes. Of course, he was delirious, so there was that.

"Yes, RJ," I replied, fingers framing my dusty face. "Behold your dream girl."

And he did, every nook and cranny. My insecurities kicked in, causing me to bite down on my lower lip and slip a wayward strand of hair behind my ear.

"You're the most beautiful thing I've ever seen."

I'd waited twenty-seven years for a compliment like that, and it just had to come from a boy stuck halfway into the earth's core. Not exactly the boost of self-esteem I was looking for.

"That's the fever talking," I said. "How about you try that line on me again when you're not hallucinating?"

"Okay," RJ replied. "I will. Because you are."

I shook my head. "I'm what?"

"Beautiful."

This time our eyes locked, and there was no mistaking the smolder in his. Was RJ really hitting on me, or was that his triple-digit core temperature talking?

Only one way to tell. Breaking the connection, I dipped my hand back into the backpack. Producing an instant ice pack, I squeezed it like a boss and slapped it onto the back of RJ's neck.

"That outta cool you down."

And I was right. The water, Tylenol, and ice worked together like synchronized swimmers, and within minutes of their life-saving performance, RJ's head seemed to have cleared enough to... berate me.

"Dammit, Dani. What're you doing here?"

"There he is." I clapped. "Glad to see you back."

But not entirely glad. I liked romantic, febrile RJ.

"You swore you wouldn't come back."

"You think I wanted to? No. But someone has to save you."

"Yes—the firefighters, with their tools and bulldozers. Not Dani with her sack of goodies."

"Hey, watch your mouth. Each and every item in that bag was carefully stolen for your benefit."

RJ's eyes widened. "Do I even want to know what you've been up to since leaving this place?"

I shook my head. "No. You do not."

"I don't understand what's happening. Last I remember, you were bringing back the cavalry."

"Things have changed."

"What do you mean, things have changed?"

I paused, trying to find the right words. "They *are* coming. It's just…"

RJ, his brain now completely unfogged, cut me off. "Just what? Does anyone even know I'm in here?"

"Oh…" I hesitated. "They know."

"What does that mean?"

"So, I got out, obviously. Then I found emergency personnel, told them you were trapped, and they were preparing for the rescue effort."

"Okay, that's good."

"Yes," I nodded. "That's the good part of the story."

He winced. "What's the bad?"

Without missing a beat, I replied, "All the rest."

"Dani," RJ protested, growing weary of the game. "Just tell me."

"Okay, here's the deal. Our building has sustained major damage. You're not the only one in this zip code trapped in the rubble."

A pained expression passed over RJ's face. He looked away.

"What?"

"Nothing," he mumbled, not meeting my eye.

I got a funny feeling that something had happened. "Are you okay?"

He nodded. "Go on."

"Okay, well, when I got out, the firefighters and police were already here. But you know that first aftershock we rode out together? Well, one of their firefighters was injured in it while trying to save someone, so now they're under orders to wait for structural engineers to come in and deem the building safe before they can allow their people back inside."

"So, let me see if I have this straight. What you're saying is I've been *waitlisted*? Like a college freshman?"

"Well, I wouldn't have put it that way, but yes. If it makes you feel any better, everyone in our building is currently being waitlisted."

"I don't feel better at all. No one ever gets off the waitlist... at least not until it's too late."

I gripped RJ's shoulder and locked eyes. "They're coming, RJ. It just might take more time than we thought. That's why I came back with supplies. I'm going to keep you alive until your name moves to the top of the list."

RJ let my words sink in before slumping over. "*If*, Dani. *If* it moves up."

"Listen to me." I grabbed his hand, feeling a steely determination fall over me. "I know it seems bleak, but I made damn sure they won't forget about you."

"Yeah? How?"

"Do you have any idea how fast a social media post travels when you add the hashtag *RJContrerasTrappedInEarthquake*? Lightning speed, I tell you! Your fans went batshit crazy. Little *Day*ers began arriving two hours ago with their buckets and shovels, ready to dig you out themselves. They're out there holding signs and chanting, 'Free RJ!' Reporters have arrived. Media barriers have been set up. And that, my vacuum-packed friend, is why no one's going to forget you are trapped in the parking garage."

A grin broke wide across my lips. "You're welcome."

RJ stared at me, the defeat in his eyes having morphed into something else... something that resembled awe. "Damn, you're good. Now I sort of wish I hadn't redirected that line of ants into your apartment last week."

I burst out laughing, smacking him with the back of my hand. "I knew that was you."

"Wait—how did you get the glass out of your arm?"

"I pulled it out."

His brows shot up. "By yourself?"

"I had to. The paramedic who was treating me threatened to send me to the hospital for surgery. I knew if I went there, I wouldn't be able to come back to you."

"So, you just ripped it out?"

"Pretty much."

RJ shook his head, clearly shocked and awed by my dedication. "You are the coolest woman I've ever met, Post-it Note Dani. I think I might actually love you."

"That's the plan. I save you. You love me forever. Easy. And just so you know, I want two kids—a boy and a girl. In that order, so don't disappoint. Oh, and, if it's not too much to ask, I'd also really like to have one of those miniature potbelly pigs. We'll name her Peggy. Are you okay with all that?"

"I... I'm not okay with any of it."

"Why not? You don't like pigs?"

"Actually, Peggy was my favorite part of your proposal. I hate kids, and I'm definitely not marriage material. You can do a whole lot better than me."

"Maybe I don't want to. Maybe I like a fixer-upper."

RJ laughed. "Dude, I'm a tear-down, not a fixer-upper."

"Let me be the judge of that."

"All right then. I tell you what. If I live through this, I'm all yours."

I smiled. "Promise?"

Studying me, the playfulness faded from his face. "I hate that you put yourself in danger. This place is death, Dani."

"Not for you, it's not. I'm your hero, remember? Have a little faith."

He studied me like I was some alien species. "I've never met anyone like you, and I've met a lot of people in my life. It pisses me off that I wasted so much time hating you."

"But did you, really? Because I seem to recall you spying on me from time to time behind the blinds, RJ."

He laughed. "You saw that, huh?"

"Oh, I saw it. I kept waiting for you to slide that door open and make all kind of sweet love to me, you coward."

"Really? Because that wasn't the vibe you were giving off."

"No?" I questioned, all innocent-like. "And what vibe was that?"

"The kind of vibe where you'd rip my nuts off if I stepped foot on the deck."

"Ah." I waved off his concern. "You men are so sensitive nowadays."

The playfulness in his eyes vanished, replaced by a smoldering sexiness. "You're right. I should've slid that door wide open and made sweet love to you."

"And I would've ripped your nuts off."

We both laughed, knowing every bit of both of our declarations were very true.

"Hey," he said, suddenly serious. "I'm sorry for everything I've ever done to make you crazy. I was... in a bad place, and I took it out on you. But if I survive this shit, I'll make it up to you, Dani. I'll be a better man. You'll see."

I believed him, every single fantastical word, wanting to be there along his path to self-discovery. Dropping my hands into the dirt, I leaned in on all fours and kissed him. It was quick and unplanned, but it was out there now, no takebacks. His eyes held mine, so heated and inviting. He was challenging me to continue the kiss, while offering no effort whatsoever on his part. RJ knew well that all he needed to do was hang back, and women would come to him.

Cocky bastard.

And yet...

Cupping his whiskered face in my hands, I pressed my lips against his lusciously parted ones and flicked his tongue with my own. And then I pulled back and waited, confident enough in my kiss that he would be back for more.

RJ smiled, understanding this game very well.

"Come here," he said, ever so gravelly.

I'd never heard anything quite so inviting. Everything in my body wanted to cave to this sexy man in the hole. But RJ needed a course correction. He needed to know who was in control.

Returning his smoldering gaze, I shook my head. "You know, I don't think I will."

Still on all fours, I hung there in lusty suspension with my lips parted and waiting. *Come on, you asshole. You know you want it.*

And then he leaned in, fingers outlining my lips and sending a fiery explosion to my core. My god, he was good. Even fastened to the earth, he could still set me ablaze. How stupid of me to think I could win this game. RJ was to seduction what Donny was to *Call of Duty*. Both were at the top of their game. I'd never had a chance.

Tangling my hand into his hair, my mouth was suddenly on his. I could feel the curve of his smile against my lips as he silently celebrated his victory. But it was short-lived as the kiss grew deeper and he plunged his tongue between my lips.

He drew back suddenly, his heavy-lidded eyes fixed on me, wrought with lust. Heat coiled in my belly. I couldn't keep away. He shouldn't make me. My lips crashed into his again, vying for possession. Every single thing about the kiss was off the charts, almost like I was only now just realizing that I'd been doing it wrong all this time. This right here was what I'd been missing; this hunger that nearly stopped my heart.

I understood now that from the moment he'd moved in next door, RJ had changed me. By challenging everything I'd thought I knew about myself, he'd awakened a fighting spirit in me that my domineering mother had shut down somewhere along the way. She wouldn't like this new me—this spark RJ had ignited. She'd blame it on my father's side of the family, but that wasn't the least bit true.

This could all be pinned on the infuriatingly sexy man next door.

13

RJ: A CLOSE SHAVE

THIS WILD GIRL, HER FINGERS WRAPPED IN MY HAIR. I WANTED everything with her, and would have taken it too, if I hadn't been sentenced to eternity in a hole not meant for two. But that kiss... It was purgatory, that frustrating place between life and death. My body screamed for Dani at the very time it was preparing for the end. Before she'd come back, I'd accepted my fate, allowing the darkness and misery to invade. But now that she was here, there was light and hope and lust. I'd gone from withering away in my grave to having it all. But this was all a mirage! No, worse, it was torture because it was a taste of what life could be like if someone were to come and save me. But they wouldn't. This was my end.

And somehow—some way—I had to let Dani go.

I pulled away. She reached for me, wanting more, but I rebuked her efforts.

So much I wanted to say, but nothing seemed right. She must have sensed my conflict.

"Hey," she said, pressing a feather-light kiss to my lips. "We'll get through this."

I nodded, not wanting to dampen her faith but also under-standing that 'we' was not part of this equation. Dani had risked everything to come back to me, and now I had to do the same for her—convince her to go. Albeit kissing her was probably not the best way to make that happen.

Cupping the back of her neck, I leaned my forehead onto hers and grazed her sweet lips with my thumb. I couldn't remember ever feeling desire like this. It was more than sexual, it was emotional, and that was what made our connection so sizzling. I'd finally found my perfect match—hours before dying.

"You have to go," I whispered.

"No," she whispered back.

"Yes."

"No."

I pulled away. This woman never listened. Ever. I both loved and hated her resolve. But this devotion she had to a lost cause... it damn near killed me.

"Dani. You'll die in here."

She leaned back in and whispered, "I don't believe that."

We stared at one another for the longest time. I wanted to shake some sense into her, but I knew it wouldn't change Dani's mind. She'd decided to believe in a fairytale where everything worked out in the end. But our story was not going to wrap up so nicely, and I think, deep down, she knew it.

Dani returned to a seated position in the dirt, dusting herself off all while keeping her eyes trained on me. It was as if she were awaiting my next move. Like I had one. If ever I'd been stripped down to the naked core, it was now, and without all the fancy packaging, I was nothing but that insecure little boy begging for love and acceptance.

Dani's loyalty to me at my most vulnerable was as remark-able as it was depressing. She barely knew me, and yet, still she had more allegiance to me than did my own parents—neither of whom would've stayed here by my side so I wouldn't have to face the end alone.

I shook my head, wanting her to remain in the rubble with me but knowing how selfish that made me. She had to go.

"You're going to make this harder on me."

"Actually, the intention is to make it easier."

"Well, you're not."

"You haven't seen what's in my bag."

"So, leave the bag and go."

"Or, I'll keep my bag and stay."

"Dani, I..."

"Stop, RJ," she blurted out. "Give it a break, okay? Leaving is not an option."

There was a quiver in her voice, and something about it gave me an uneasy feeling.

"What does that mean?"

More hesitation. What was she not telling me?

"Nothing. I just don't want to leave, and you're in no position to make me, so let's end this discussion now, or I'll go to that corner over there and enjoy my own calamity picnic while you sit here in your hole and starve."

I blinked back my surprise. There was no reasoning with her, but then, when had there ever been? She did what she wanted, and nothing I was going to say would change that. I could either spend what time I had left fighting and pleading for her to go or just accept that she would take her exit when I did.

"Okay, fine. You can stay."

"Ah, so nice of you," she replied in a cheeky tone. "Not that I need your permission."

"No, you never have," I agreed, lifting my arms to the sides. "Oh, and Dani? Welcome home."

A smile instantly brightened her pretty face. "Thank you. And let me say, I really like what you've done with the place."

I nodded, as if pleased with my efforts. "It's taken twelve aftershocks to get to this point, but I think it's really coming along nicely."

"Oh, for sure. Is that car dangling off the edge over there a new addition?"

"Why, yes. Thanks for noticing. I believe that was earthquake number six. I can't remember exactly. They've all been so much fun."

Dani giggled, rummaging through her bag. Eventually she produced a protein bar. "Here."

I refused her offering.

"Are you sure? I thought the enticement of my calamity picnic was what changed your mind about me staying."

"No. It was the fact that I don't have the strength to argue with you."

"All the more reason to eat."

I wished I could, but pain had robbed me of an appetite.

"I'm not feeling great," I admitted.

Her brows furrowed. "Just give it a try. You need the calories to get through this, RJ."

I took the bar from her, not because I was hungry but because she needed me to maintain the illusion we'd be leaving here together.

Tearing the package open, I sank my teeth into the bar and chewed through the rubbery texture. My stomach churned, but I kept it down.

"Where did you get all this stuff, anyway?" I asked.

"I told you. I stole it."

"I know, but I thought maybe you were kidding."

Her eyes flickered in amusement. "Um... no. And just FYI, I'm gonna need you to pay my bail."

"Your bail?"

"It's not like I'm a seasoned thief, RJ. My face *will* be all over the security cameras at the store."

"Okay, look. I'm not a looter, but I don't have to take a course in it to know I need to hide my face."

"I'm one of those visual learners. Next time you're stuck in a quake, I'll have it all down."

Damn, she was cool. Layers upon layers of it. "I had no idea you were such a rebel."

She laughed. "Because I'm not. You're just a really bad influence."

"Me? I never told you to steal. You could've just gone up to your apartment and filled a garbage bag of supplies."

Dani winced.

"What?"

Again, I got the distinct impression she wasn't being totally forthcoming with her information.

"Nothing. I told you—no one is allowed back into the building."

"Then why'd they let you back inside?"

That stopped her. I could almost see the wheels turning, the lies forming. But then she slumped her shoulders and sighed. "They didn't. It's dark. I slipped past the police lines."

My eyes widened. Was there nothing this woman wouldn't do to save me?

"Jesus, Dani. It's like you've been through SEAL training."

"Or maybe just dealing with your disagreeable ass for the last few months has prepared me for battle," she said, fidgeting with her hair.

Why so nervous?

"Dani, what are you not telling me?"

"I couldn't gather supplies at my apartment because..." She

started and stopped twice before finally finishing the sentence. "Because all the apartments on our end of the wing are gone."

"Gone? What do you mean? Where did they go?"

She pointed up. "They're on top of us."

And then her words registered. I sat there a moment, absorbing. Triple A hadn't been in the parking garage when the earthquake struck, he'd been in his apartment on the first floor and had fallen down to me. And if his apartment had been crushed by the ones on top of him, then... my god... the loss of life would be staggering. For the first time since this all began, I had complete clarity. I wasn't the unlucky one in this scenario. I was still alive.

Seeing my distress, Dani reached out and touched my arm. "Are you okay?"

I answered her question with one of my own. "So, there are no structural engineers assessing the building? That was a lie?"

"No, not a lie. Only part of the complex came down. The rest is still standing... for now."

"Meaning what?"

"It's unstable."

"Unstable? Like the rest of it's going to collapse?"

She hesitated before nodding.

I shook my head, shocked and horrified as the stark truth sank in. Why had I ever demanded it of her in the first place? If I'd had even a sliver of hope before, it was all dashed now. Closing my eyes, I dropped my forehead to the earth. A shiver racked my body, but before I even had time to address the chill, Dani draped a blanket over my shoulders and wrapped her comforting arms around me, burying her head into my neck.

"That's why I didn't tell you, RJ. I'm so sorry."

"They're not coming, are they?"

"They haven't done the assessment yet. For all we know, it will be deemed safe and they can renew their efforts by morning. That's why I came back bearing the fruits of my labors," she said, dragging the bag of wonders to her side. "I have another space blanket if you need it."

Realizing we were in for a long night, I replied. "No. You need it. What else do you have in that backpack?"

Dani unfolded from me and began removing items. "Mostly camping supplies, but I did take a pass through the personal care aisle *and* the grocery aisle. I pretty much shoved everything I could fit in here."

Something in the forming pile of stolen contraband caught my eye. "You've got to be shitting me," I said, holding up a three pack of razors. "What the hell is this?"

"I can understand your confusion. It's this thing that's used to shave hair off men's faces. It's called a razor. Would you like to say it with me, RJ? R...a...z...o...r."

"I know what it is, Dani," I said, eyeing the handheld mirror, shaving cream, and sensitive skin after-shave she'd also stolen. "I just for the life of me can't imagine why it would be needed in our particular survival situation."

"I thought maybe you might want a clean shave for your big moment when rescuers pull you out. Your face will be splashed across every headline in the world. I was just being forward-thinking... thoughtful."

"No, you just hate my beard."

"That too."

I gathered up all her shaving paraphernalia and dropped it back in the bag. "The last thing I'm worried about is my vanity."

"Good for you. High self-esteem."

I couldn't help but laugh through my misery. "Can you please use that brain of yours for good? Figure out a way to get me out of here. Everything I've tried has failed."

"What have you tried?" she asked. "Napping?"

"No. I tried pulling my leg out from under the concrete...
then I took a nap."

"Ah. Okay. So, I do have one thing we can try."

Dani pulled out two pink hammers with *Do it herself* written
along the handle.

"You couldn't find anything more gender neutral?"

"Enough with the judgment, RJ. When you're looting, you
don't get to be choosy."

"Sorry. I just didn't know hammers were such high-ticket
items. What are we going to do with them?"

"Bang the shit out of the concrete and free your foot."

Rather simplistic, but it was as good a plan as any, so I picked
up the hammer and got started. Using the claw end, Dani and I
banged the hell out of the unforgiving surface. It was maybe
fifteen minutes in that we realized the futility of the mission. A
few small, insignificant chips had broken free, but it didn't even
come close to freeing my foot. Dani's stolen seven-dollar
hammers were a flop.

Frustration mounting, I'd finally had enough and flung the
hammer at Dani's car.

"Hey, watch it. That's my ride."

Her ride was now just a pile of junk, but that didn't stop a
thought from forming in my brain. "Do you have a car jack?"

Dani jumped up. "I'm on it."

She tried opening her trunk first, but that was a no-go, so she
began searching other demolished cars with her flashlight until
she was finally able to pop a trunk and pull out a car jack.

Our enthusiasm quickly faded, however, when there was no
way to even get it under the concrete to lift the block off my foot.
She kept trying, though, salvaging anything that might help my
cause, but in the end, our efforts were for nothing. I was still
frustratingly and painfully stuck.

Dani plopped into the dust beside me, her face flushed with

exertion. There was a feeling of finality. We'd done all we could do.

"I'm sorry," she said.

"Don't be. They were all long shots to begin with."

"I know. But I really thought the nail file was going to work."

I forced a smile at the levity she was trying to bring to the hopeless situation. "We tried... maybe if you'd stolen a jackhammer."

"A jackhammer without electricity holds no value down here."

She was right. I felt defeated. Bending over, I closed my eyes and rested my head in the dirt.

"Hey." She rubbed my back. "You have to stay awake."

"I'm trying. I'm just so tired. It's getting harder to breathe, and my whole body feels like it's shutting down."

"Head up, RJ. Come on."

"Just let me sleep for a little while."

"No," she said, trying to pull my head up. "You slept while I was gone. Now it's time to stay alert and be here with me."

"Because you think I'm going to die if I fall asleep."

Her eyes filled with tears. "Okay, yes. I worry about that."

"What do you think is going to happen here, Dani? Nobody's coming. The only way you can avoid watching me die is to leave."

She looked down, brushing away the tears that were rolling down her cheeks. "And I already told you, I'm not going to leave you."

"Why do you care what happens to me?"

"What kind of a question is that? Why wouldn't I care?"

"Because no one else does."

The words, they just slipped out, and I instantly regretted them. Dani would never let a statement like that lie.

"That's not true," she said. "You're loved by millions."

"That's not love. At least not the kind that counts."

"What's the kind that counts?"

"The mom who tucks you in at night. The dad who coaches the Little League team. The brother who sticks up for you when others are being mean. The woman who sneaks back inside a collapsed building to try and keep a dying man alive. That's the kind that counts."

"And you didn't have that growing up?"

We were stumbling into forbidden territory, a place I rarely ventured. It had happened only once before—with Bodhi. He'd confessed things about his controlling father and I'd unexpectedly reciprocated, giving him a glimpse inside. He'd climbed my walls only to discover the insecure boy who hid behind sarcastic wit and a biting tongue. He knew I was unwanted; unloved. That knowledge was power, and now I was considering giving it to another—a woman I barely knew, but one I could easily love if given the chance.

"No." Just one word said it all.

Dani reached out and touched me. "I'm sorry your family wasn't there for you.

I drew in a breath, shallow at best, and nodded. I was grateful she didn't press for more.

"I'll try to stay awake for you," I sighed, feeling such affection for Dani that I wanted to see the smile return to her face. "You didn't steal anything fun, did you?"

"Funny you should ask," she said, dipping her hand in the bag and pulling out a deck of cards. "You wanna go fish?"

———

Somewhere midway through our first game of Go Fish, Dani equated fish to tadpoles and tadpoles to sperm and then suddenly she was balls deep in an incredible story of her father and his one hundred and eleven children. At first, I thought she was kidding, but her story was too out there not to be true. The Lucky Swimmers Club. Donny. She'd reeled me in. I was no longer tired. I was no longer waiting for death, so fascinated by this woman I could almost forget about the pain. I wanted to live, if only to meet the dozens of Donor 649's offspring. It went to show you *could* make your own family, like I'd done with the boys. Like I could do with Dani if given the chance.

"I'm just speechless..." I shook my head.

"I know. It's a lot to take in. My *situation*," she said through air quotes, "isn't for everyone."

"I don't know about that. You could make a documentary or film about this. Your brother Landry alone is worth the price of admission. Dude's got some major Batesy vibes going on."

"I think Landry is pretty harmless," Dani said, grabbing another card from the deck and rearranging her hand. "Do you have any nines?"

"Go fish."

"He's more emotionally immature than anything else."

"Dani, he has a clipping of her hair in a little container he wears around his neck. And she's *not* dead. Next thing you know, he'll be draped in her skin and wearing her as a fashion statement."

She unraveled her legs in order to stretch one out and tapped me with her dirty shoe. "Be nice."

"I'm never nice," I said, pushing her foot away. "Stop kicking me. You do realize I have major injuries, right?"

"You do realize you insulted my brother, right?"

"He's your sperm brother, Dani," I corrected. "It's not like you took baths together as kids."

"First, ew. And second, why are you never nice?"

"Because no one requires me to be."

"That's such a celebrity thing. You people think you can act however you want."

"Hey, I don't make the rules." I shrugged, checking my hand before calling out, "Do you have any fours?"

Dani made a face and handed over two cards.

I laid four fours down.

"So, what if you *had* to be nice?"

"Like if someone was torturing me or something?"

Dani rolled her eyes. "Sure."

"I fake it."

"You fake it?"

"Yeah. Like at concerts, I smile and pretend that I like the fans. But the truth is, I barely tolerate them."

"RJ," she complained. "They're kids."

"I know, and that's why I pretend."

Her eyes were wide with surprise. "My god. You need to be socialized with other humans. As soon as we get out of here, I'm going to set up playdates and teach you how to play nice with others.

"Good luck with that. Do you have any jacks?"

"No. Go fish."

I picked a card. "And you're socialized? You've never dropped the f-bomb in class before?"

"Of course not. They're six and seven years old.

"So?"

"So, they're impressionable. Last thing I want is a bunch of potty-mouthed RJs running around."

"You're telling me you've never sworn once around them."

"Nope. Not even when Ardavan accidentally shit on me."

The things she said. I shook my head, laughing under my breath as I passed over a two of hearts.

"You wanna know, don't you?" she asked, looking up from

her cards with mischief in her eyes. "Let me shave off your beard and I'll tell you."

No way did I need to hear her story *that* bad, but I liked having something she wanted, and if shearing my face made her happy, maybe my act of kindness might be the difference between heaven and hell.

"Say pretty please." I smiled. "And I might just let you."

14

DANI: MAKING CONTACT

IT TOOK ONE PAIR OF SCISSORS, TWO RAZORS, AND THREE BAND-Aids to get the nastiness off RJ's face, but it was all worth it when I watched him examine his smooth face in the small handheld mirror under the warm lights of the camp lantern.

"Damn. I look good."

The understatement of the year. Shaving that face of his, revealing it one stroke of the razor at a time, had been like a religious experience. The way he pursed his lips when I shaved up his neck. The way his eyes watched me with a mix of both trust and terror. The way he cursed me under his breath when he felt the nick of the blade. Oh lord, I needed a shower.

But any animosity he might have been harboring during the weed-whacking was forgotten when the hunk of a man saw his reflection in the mirror.

"I forgot how fucking handsome I am."

"And you wonder why I didn't recognize you, Chad Woodcock."

Surrounded by mounds of coarse stubble, I bent down and blew them in the opposite direction.

"Whoa, do you have any idea how much that's worth? You

should gather it up and sell it on eBay. If I die, you'll make a small fortune."

I really hated when he referred to his death like it was a forgone conclusion. He might not have had any faith, but I still did. Granted, I didn't know what was going on inside of him, but I knew he was injured just by the way he flinched at the slightest movement or the way his breathing was becoming shallower. Despite the brave face he was putting on, I knew he was struggling. That was why I played card games with him and even shaved him. It was my way of keeping him focused on something other than death. And what could refocus a man's attention like a woman with a blade to his throat?

"You know I don't like it when you talk like that," I said.

His gaze shifted from his reflection to me. He wanted to say something but refrained. It was almost like he was pitying me. And maybe, yes, I was in denial; but until I had no more hope, I would do everything I could to keep this boy alive.

"Sorry."

I nodded, fighting the tears that had flowed easily all day. I desperately didn't want him to die. There was just so much more I wanted from him. On my walk back from the store, I'd manifested our post-quake life together, and it was a glorious one. I wasn't about to give up on it without a fight.

"Actually, instead of eBay, maybe you could donate it to some hairless dude who can't grow his own beard."

"I like that," I said. "Pay it forward."

"Exactly."

Our eyes locked.

"You really are a beautiful man—beard or no beard."

"And you're a beautiful woman." He reached out and touched a strand of my hair that had fallen from the elastic band. "Did you know I have a thing for your hair?"

"You do?"

"The way it bounces in those high ponytails. It's like every time you walk away, your hair flips me off. I love it."

I laughed, because that was exactly what I'd intended it to do. I tossed my hair in his face.

He grabbed the ponytail and tugged me toward him, whispering in my ear,

"If I wasn't tethered to the earth, you'd already be on your back."

"No, RJ. *You'd* be the one on *your* back."

His eyes flickered with lust. He wanted me, and I had no doubt that, if he'd been of sound body and mind, RJ would've taken me on a ride. But he wasn't okay. *We* weren't okay, because if that building came down on our heads, neither of us would ever long for the other again.

Perhaps reading my mind, RJ let go of my hair and leaned back. His eyes closed. He was so tired. Was it right to keep him from sleep? Maybe it would help his body recover... or maybe he'd never wake up. I couldn't take the chance.

"Do you want to play some more card games?"

"I want to, but I'm winding down," RJ replied. "Can we just talk?"

"You're asking Dani Malone if she wants to talk?"

"Tell me about your job. Your students."

I launched into a day in the life of a first grade teacher, and despite having lived life at its highest caliber, RJ seemed enthralled and, dare I say, charmed by my simple stories and the sweet gems that came from the mouth of the innocents.

"It seems like you have involved parents at your school," RJ said, sounding almost envious.

"Really high, like 70% parent participation. I actually have to have a lottery on field trips because so many of them want to chaperone."

"Do you ever wonder how that happens?"

"How what happens?"

"How some parents are so invested in their kids and some aren't. It's like what determines that, you know? How does a kid hit that jackpot?"

Reaching up, I ran my fingers along his shoulder. So comfortable. In some ways, it felt like I'd known him forever, but when he said things like that, I realized how very little I knew about him.

"I take it you didn't."

"No."

So much I wanted to ask him, but by the clenching of his jaw, RJ seemed to not want to emote.

"My mom was a seventy-percenter. Over-involved—a helicopter parent," I admitted. "It was overwhelming. I never really got to choose my own path. She was always there, bubbling in the blanks of my life. That can be damaging too. I let her decide everything, even my major in college. It wasn't until I got some space away from her that I was able to explore who I was as a person, and finally I was able to take my life into my own hands."

"And then you have the thirty-percenters."

"Your parents?"

He nodded. "Only with a twist, because they were seventy percenters with my two older brothers. I got the leftovers."

"I see parents sometimes that clearly favor one child over another. It's infuriating to watch."

"It wasn't just favoritism, Dani. It was straight-up neglect. I didn't understand it as a kid. I couldn't wrap my brain around the fact that they loved my brothers and not me. I thought it was me; that I was somehow unworthy. No matter how hard I tried to be good, to be better than my brothers, I never managed to win their favor, and it wasn't until I got older that I understood why."

It was then that RJ told me about his mother's affair, about his father's rejection, and how he became a second-class citizen in his own home. My heart broke for him. I couldn't imagine bringing an innocent child into the world, only to blame him for the sins of the mother.

"Is that why you took up singing? To get their attention?"

"Not in the beginning. My real father was a musician, so I already had a natural affinity for music. I could sing from the time I was a toddler and had taught myself how to play multiple instruments from YouTube. But my early talents went unnoticed. It wasn't until middle school, when a teacher heard me singing at the lunch tables, that I realized I had something special. Then I dove in full throttle, thinking maybe if I could achieve enough, I'd be worthy of my parents' love. When you try so hard to get attention and still no one cares, it's crushing. But it pushed me to be bigger and better until I was on top of the world and they could no longer look away."

"They have to be proud of you now."

"You'd think. But you know what my mother said to me when I returned home after my first worldwide tour? She said, 'Sure, you're famous, but you're not Bodhi.' Since then, I've compared myself to him. I love the dude, but he's also my competition. When our band broke up, I had to get the jump on him; release my album before him. Be more famous than him to prove to her that I *am* better than Bodhi. But then my first album was a huge flop, and I couldn't face them. I couldn't face the world feeling like such a failure."

"And that was when you moved in next door to me," I said, the mystery of my famous neighbor finally solved.

He nodded, swinging his arms around. "Now all this. I couldn't die in a more high-profile way, and yet my mother will still find some way to discredit it. '*The guy in apartment 411 survived, why couldn't RJ?*'"

"God, RJ, I'm so sorry. No child should ever have to feel unloved. That breaks my heart."

"And the worst part is, I don't have a will. She and my dad and brothers stand to inherit my fortune, and they don't deserve it. Not one penny of it. But the irony is, I'll only prove my worth after I die."

The injustice infuriated me. My mother might have been domineering and opinionated, but she would never do what RJ's family had done to him—never make our relationship contingent on what I could provide to her. I had a newfound appreciation for the woman. I wanted to hug her—tell her I loved her and to thank her for the opportunities she'd given me in life. We might never see eye to eye, but I knew, without any doubt, that if it came down to it, she'd lay her life down for me. RJ couldn't say the same.

"I don't remember ever reading about this part of your life. How did you manage to keep this out of the press?"

"Hold up." RJ chuckled in amusement. "You *are* a Dayer! I knew it. Who was your favorite? And if you say Bodhi, I will destroy you."

"Hunter."

"Hunter? Your favorite Dayer was *the choir boy*?"

"Yes, RJ. I have a sweet spot for nice, sweater-wearing guys. So sue me. Now, back to you. How did you manage to keep this information out of the press?"

"I pay handsomely for my family to keep their mouths shut."

Seriously? Blackmail, even? I was pissed for him.

"Not long after graduating high school, I was summoned to Los Angeles to audition for some secret project. They'd seen some of my performances on YouTube. Before I knew it, I was one of five unknown singers in a band with some stupid-ass name. I figured it would be a stepping-stone, a way to get my name out there. None of us thought *AnyDayNow* would take off, least of all my family, who were relentless in their ridicule of me joining a boy band. But their smug smiles disappeared when the band exploded and the money started pouring in. I might not have impressed them with my singing, but money talks, and pretty soon they wanted a cut of it. Given the shit they put me through, I wasn't inclined to share."

"I don't blame you."

"Anyway, it caused a huge rift. My mother went on a talk show, where she accused me of being selfish. My oldest brother, Luis, threatened to write a tell all. It was getting messy enough that the *AnyDayNow* handlers stepped in and muzzled them with a nice cash payout from my bank account. As part of the shakedown, I also agreed to buy them a house in our hometown with enough room for everyone to squat in on my dime. But here's the thing about bribes—t's never enough. They always want more."

"So, your relationship with them is purely financial now?"

"Pretty much. Yes. You can only take so much."

Emotion played out over RJ's face. He'd been reluctant to share at first, but as the truth trickled out, his wasn't the success story I'd imagined. Behind his confidence, behind his swaggering smile, behind his exceptional talent was a little boy begging to be loved. It was heartbreaking, really. How little children require! A hug. A kind word. A kiss on the forehead before bed. How hard was that? But in a testament to his strength of will, RJ had not only endured, he'd soared.

"I just can't understand why they'd sell your story in the first place. It only makes them look awful."

"You'd be surprised what people will do for a payout. You realize, Dani, if you wanted to, you could buy ten Broncos with the amount of money you could get for this story. My god, can you imagine how the media will eat this up?"

"I'd never sell you out. Ever. No amount of money would ever entice me to hurt the ones I love."

RJ's brows lifted and I froze, realizing too late what had slipped out of my mouth.

"I mean... I didn't..." I tried stumbling through some ridiculous explanation before giving up mid-sentence.

"Hey, relax. It was a slip of the tongue."

Actually, it wasn't. As strange as it seemed, going through this with RJ, I'd never felt closer to anyone in my life. If what I was feeling toward him wasn't love, then it was at the very least a strong infatuation.

"I just meant you deserve better."

"Hey, come here," he said, pulling me into his arms. "I know what you meant, and I feel the same way. You've changed me, Dani."

In the glow of the lantern, I tipped my head up and accepted his grateful kiss. There was a change in us, a newfound closeness. He'd opened up about his difficult childhood, something I was sure he rarely did. That he trusted me like that made me feel like there was more to us than a one-night-disaster.

Wrapped into a space blanket, RJ and I talked until I heard his speech begin to slur and his body grow heavy beside me.

"RJ." I sat up, cupping his face in my hands. His eyelids drooped, and he shed his blanket as fever encroached on him once again. I watched in horror as he weakened before my eyes. His breathing at times sounded as if it were being passed through a filter. He was hot then cold, alternating, and as the night wore on, it became more difficult for him to maintain his body temperature.

"Oh god, I'm miserable," he groaned. "I don't know how much more I can take."

"Just give the Tylenol a little bit more time to work," I said, dosing him way more than the recommended amount and giving him more every time his fever spiked. But the longer we remained in here, the less effective the pain medication became. It was like fighting a war with a toothpick.

"I know you're trying, but I'm way past Tylenol, Dani. I crossed into the fentanyl category a few hours ago."

I slid my fingers over his face. "I know. You just have to hang in there. Help is coming."

I said the words, but as the hours passed, I wasn't so sure anymore. In addition to losing feeling in his left foot, RJ's skin was tacky and his stomach bloated. His pain, at times, was intense. There was something going on inside him, something unseen causing the inflammation and fever. The truth was RJ was in bad enough shape that, even if help were to come, they still might not be able to save his life. I had to do something besides just sit here and watch him die.

My head popped up, remembering one of the first items I'd shoved in my bag. I hadn't really thought much about its usefulness, and still wasn't sure, but anything was worth a try. I dug deep into the unexplored depths of my backpack.

"Do you know how this thing works?" I asked, holding up a long-range walkie-talkie for RJ to see.

He perked right up. "You have a *walkie-talkie* and you're just showing me that now?"

"Sorry." I shrugged. "I forgot I stole it."

"My god, Dani. This could be our ticket out of here."

RJ was so excited by the find I refrained from pointing out that rescue workers already knew where we were and still hadn't come to get us. But I understood his need to connect with the outside world. Down here, in the depths of despair, any small word from above was encouraging.

———

"Hello, can you hear me?" RJ said into the receiver.

We waited for the reply with bated breath. Seconds earlier, we'd heard chatter on the line.

"You don't sound like Hector," said the very young sounding voice on the other side.

"Because I'm not Hector," RJ responded.

"What did you do to Hector?"

"Kid, Hector's not here. Do you not understand the concept of a walkie-talkie? Other people can be on the same frequency."

I nudged RJ. "Be nice. He's just a kid."

"I am being nice."

"No. You're being Chad Woodcock."

Groaning, he said, 'Fine' before pressing the button once more. "Hey, little dude. Can you bring that walkie-talkie to your dad or mom... pretty please?"

"You killed him, didn't you?" the kid said, his voice rising to a higher pitch. "You killed Hector."

Just as RJ had lowered the button to respond I leaned into the receiver and said. "Hector's fine."

RJ released the button and glared at me. "Dani. We don't know if Hector's fine because we don't have Hector. Now he's going to think we're holding Hector hostage."

"Oh, right."

"Let me do the talking," he insisted. "I have more walkie-talkie experience."

"Is experience really that important when all you do is push a button and talk?"

RJ put a finger to his lips to silence me before resuming his long-distance conversation. "Look, kid. We don't have a lot of time. We're trapped in the parking garage of our apartment complex, and..."

"I'm calling the cops," the boy blurted out.

"Good, call them. That's what I want."

"And I'm gonna tell them you chopped up Hector."

"Whoa, Jesus Christ. Where in the conversation did you get that conclusion from?"

"RJ." I tugged on his hand. "He's scared. Just speak calmly to him."

"He's not scared. He's a little shit who watches too much *Law & Order*."

"Look, I get it—you're the expert with walkie-talkies—but I'm the expert with kids. Just be patient with him."

RJ rolled his eyes before pressing back down on the button. "All right, Sherlock. Let's try this a different way. How'd you like to make some money?"

"I'm listening."

"I'll give you twenty bucks to let me talk to your mom or dad."

"Fifty."

"Fifty? You literally have to walk down the hallway!"

"Fifty." He held firm. "And I want you to Venmo me *before* I hand it over."

Through clenched teeth, RJ replied, "How about you hand it over right now or I put you in the microwave when I get out of here?"

I grabbed the walkie-talkie out of RJ's hand and pushed down the button. "One hundred dollars. But you've got thirty seconds to get this into your mom's hand. Go!"

———

Twelve-year-old Burton woke his mother at five in the morning and passed over the walkie-talkie. She hopped in her car and drove the mile distance to the collapsed building on Waterbury Rd. Holding onto her son's walkie-talkie, she found the closest fireman and asked for Parker, who, it turned out, was still on shift. And within fifteen minutes of RJ threatening to shove Burton into a microwave, I heard a familiar voice.

"Gladys, is that you?"

I smiled with relief. "We talked about this, Parker. The name's Dani."

"Ah, man, Dani. Tell me I heard wrong. You didn't go back in, did you?"

"You met me, Parker. What do you think?"

He didn't snicker like before when he'd found me frustratingly entertaining.

In fact, Parker didn't say a word. That couldn't be good.

"When are you guys coming?" I asked.

"Listen, Dani," he said, his voice barely more than a whisper. I could tell by the way he was breathing that he was on the move. "If you can get out, you need to do it right now."

"Why? What's going on?"

"I shouldn't be telling you this, because it hasn't been made public yet, but the engineers have deemed it too unstable for us to go back in. The building is swaying. The rest of it can come down on top of you at any minute. You have to get out of there."

Tears rushed to my eyes. "I can't."

"Look, I know you don't want to leave your neighbor, but you can't save him. You have to think about yourself. You'll die in there."

"Well, then I'm going to die," I said, my words wrought with emotion. "Because I have no way out of here."

RJ blinked in rapid succession. "What do you mean?"

"When I was shoving the backpack through the hole, it caused a cave in. I fell through like freakin' Alice in Wonderland. And now there's no mountain of debris for me to climb anymore."

The look of horror on RJ's face said it all. This whole time he'd thought I was free to go; that when things got really bad for him, or if he died, I'd make my way out into the land of the living. But now he knew the truth. There was no way out. We were both going to die in here together.

15

RJ: TIME'S UP

MAYBE IT HAD BEEN THE FEVER TALKING, BUT I HADN'T FULLY understood the sacrifice Dani had made for me. This whole time, she'd known what was going to happen to her if the rescue team didn't arrive, yet she'd stayed immeasurably calm, playing card games with me and shaving my damn face. But I wasn't the only one who needed comfort in this storm. Dani needed it too and had never said a word. What sort of super-human strength did this woman have?

I felt sick. This was all wrong. It couldn't end this way. At least not for her. Just the thought of Dani's bright light going out spurred me to action. I didn't know who this Parker guy was, but it was clear by his instructions to her that he cared about her well-being, and that meant he and I were on the same page.

Taking the walkie-talkie from Dani's hand, I raised it to my mouth and pushed the button. "Parker, this is RJ Contreras."

Silence.

I added. "You heard right."

"From *AnyDayNow*."

"Yes."

"Did Dani put you up to this?"

"Dude, I'm about to die. Does it sound like I'm playing games with you?"

"Oh, shit. No. Sorry, I just... I thought Dani was making it up to get me to come rescue you... I mean there've been unconfirmed reports on the news, but it's all based on the podcast Dani did with Misty Swallows."

I turned to Dani. "You had time for a podcast?"

"How else do you think I got your fans out here?"

"I don't know. Maybe a tweet?"

"I have fifty-eight followers, RJ. Nothing I have to say is going to go far."

Shaking off the surprise, I redirected my attention to what was most important.

"Listen, Parker, you and I have the same goal. Dani needs to get out of here. I know it's too unsafe for you to come down here and get her, but can you leave a ladder in the hole so she can climb out herself?"

Parker cut out long enough that I worried we'd lost the connection.

"Parker?"

"I'm here. Sorry. Most of our trucks have already moved out. I'm looking to see if any unit might have an extension ladder. Hold on."

The sound of Dani's crying tore at my heart. I pulled her to me and she buried her head in my neck while we waited to see who lived and who died.

Static preceded Parker's voice on the walkie-talkie. "I got one. Bringing it over. But she needs to come out *now*. We've pushed everyone back and are evacuating the buildings in the vicinity. Listen, I can't stress this enough—a collapse is imminent."

"I hear you. Just have the ladder in place. I'll get her there."

"No," Dani sobbed, grabbed hold of my face and staring me straight in the eye. "I told you. I'm not leaving without you."

"And I'm not leaving here...ever. Don't you get it, Dani? I'm going to die here, but you don't have to." My voice broke into a thousand pieces. I was a man facing my own mortality, and the last thing I needed was more regrets. "Please don't put your death on me."

Dani's jaw tightened, her eyes blazing with anger. "Then don't put your death on me."

"Without you, I'd probably already be gone. I know what you've done for me. You sacrificed everything to come back in here and help me. You gave me hope. You made me laugh in this hopeless situation, and I can't possibly be more grateful to you. But it's time. There's nothing more you can do for me. Please, if you care about me at all, you'll go."

Dani was a mess of emotions, and my heart hurt watching her struggle. I knew what I was asking her to do. I was sentencing this beautiful, caring, loving woman to a lifetime of guilt. But there was no other option because Dani Malone's light needed to stay on.

Parker interjected. "Are you still there?"

I tipped Dani's chin up and kissed her lips. "Do this for me?"

Her eyes met mine and there was a resolve in them. With tears streaming down her cheeks, she nodded.

I pushed the button. "We're still here. Get the ladder ready. Dani's coming out."

———

We spent the next few horrible minutes saying goodbye.

"Hey," I said, cradling her neck. "It's okay."

I'd never been a crier—barely showed any emotion at all half the time—but there was no reason for restraint now. This was it. The end of the road. Once Dani left, I'd be alone, waiting to die. And that moment couldn't come fast enough, because once she left, I'd already be dead.

"No, it's not okay," Dani cried. "None of this is okay."

With my thumb, I swiped at her tears, placing a tender kiss upon her lips.

"I need you to do me a favor."

Dani tipped her head up, her eyes red and swollen. "For you, RJ, I'll do anything. Always."

Her response took me apart piece by piece. My whole life, that level of devotion from a woman was all I'd ever wanted. A loyalty my mother had never been willing to extend to her youngest child. Sure, I'd gotten it from my fans, but none of that was real. They didn't love me. They loved the idea of me. And now there was Dani, the woman who'd risked it all. In these last moments with her, I felt her heart beating against mine, and I knew I was loved.

"I need you to get in contact with Bodhi Beckett and tell him you're my gale force wind."

"Your gale force wind? What does that even mean?"

"He'll understand. And tell him to check inside the curtain rod."

"RJ, you're not making any sense."

"It'll make sense to him."

"But how am I going to contact him? Bodhi's famous. He's not just going to accept my friend request."

"You worked your way into a podcast yesterday. I think you can figure out how to contact one celebrity."

Dani threw her arms over my shoulders and buried her head into the nook of my neck. I held her, wishing, wanting. But it was selfish. She had to go.

Into her ear, I whispered, "Now go, Post-it Note girl. Make me proud."

"I will, and RJ, I promise you this. I'll make sure the world never forgets you. Everyone will know the man you really are."

She kissed my cheek then pulled free of my arms, sobbing the words, "I love you. Don't forget it."

My heart ripped from my chest as I watched her hurry away, her cries echoing through the hallowed space.

Dani Malone never looked back.

16

DANI: SIGN FROM ABOVE

I'D NEVER EXPERIENCED SUCH SORROW. THE PAIN BURNED through me like licks of fire from the inside. I wanted to turn back, to take my chances, but I understood that RJ didn't just want me to go for me but for him as well.

How I was going to process this once he was gone, I didn't know. All I knew was that I would keep my promise to him. I would make him the hero he was in the eyes of the world. I would never let anyone forget his name or the sacrifice he'd made to save my life. If that wasn't love, then I didn't understand the meaning.

Before I even got to the hole in the ground that was now a crater, I saw the ladder gleaming in the early morning sun. It was like a mirage, beckoning me forward and promising me a future it would not afford to RJ. I slowed as I drew closer, wanting to embrace its saving graces but at the same time throttle it.

I placed my hand on a rung and looked up to the sky. My freedom was but a climb away. I knew Parker was out there somewhere, waiting. He'd told us he would be fired if he disobeyed orders, so he'd lowered the ladder and left, leaving it up to me to save myself. But as I was about to take the first step, I noticed a bag on the ground. Bending down, I turned it over, only to see my name written in black Sharpie and a message scrawled over the canvas.

Give this to RJ.

I don't know how I knew what was in the bag before even opening it, but I did. I swallowed back the horror of what was inside. Parker was giving him a chance—but at what cost?

A few feet from the bag was a single crutch, with *Bruce* scrawled in Sharpie on the side. I picked it up and sprinted back the way I'd come.

17

RJ: AT WHAT COST?

ONCE DANI LEFT, I WRAPPED MYSELF IN THE BLANKET AND prepared to die. There was nothing else I could do. In that entire vast expanse of items she'd shoved into the backpack, she'd forgotten the one thing that would have made leaving this earth easier—a pencil.

I didn't have a will; never thought I needed one. I was twenty-five. I wasn't going to die. But here I was at the end, and the only thing I could think of was that the ones who would benefit most from my death were the ones who would miss me least.

There was some solace in knowing that Dani would pass my message along to Bodhi. He'd connect the dots and use that knowledge to carry out my wishes. It might not keep my family from grabbing my fortune, but it might help Dani rebuild her life, even if Bodhi had to take money out of his own pocket to make it happen.

I thought back to our conversation after our last *AnyDayNow* concert. Despite the sweet sorrow of our breakup, Bodhi was on a high. He couldn't stop talking about his girl, Breeze.

She's the one, he'd said.

How do you know? I'd asked.

You just know. I can't explain it, RJ, but I promise you, when your Breeze comes along, she'll knock you on your ass.

I'd laughed at that. *No light Breeze will knock me on my ass. I'd need a gale force wind.*

————

I heard her coming before I saw her turn the corner. She was back. I wanted to scream. Now I'd have to say goodbye all over again.

"Dani! Dammit!"

"I know." She dropped to her knees, cupped my face, and placed a breathless kiss on me. "But Parker left this for you."

She dropped the bag beside me. I opened the top and looked inside, lingering there as my brain caught up to what it was seeing. Slowly, my eyes tracked up from the bag and landed on Dani's. No words passed between us. We both understood. And then I reached into the bag and pulled out the knife.

————

It was hard to describe the moments leading up to the act itself. I'd heard about animals chewing off their own feet to free themselves from traps and the mountain climber who'd cut his own arm off to survive. I'd wondered what sort of desperation you'd have to be feeling in the moment to resort to such horrifying measures. Now I knew.

And while Dani prepared the area just above the concrete slab with the supplies provided in the bag by her buddies topside, I readied myself by getting into the headspace I'd need to get the job done. I'd grown up a victim of circumstance—the bastard child of a manipulative, selfish woman who tried to fool a man who wasn't my father into loving me. It hadn't worked, setting me up for a lifetime of having to prove my self-worth. If I sang well enough. If I looked good enough. If I had the most fans. On the cover of popular magazines. Top of the charts. *Maybe then.* But none of that was sustainable. And none of it made me feel deserving. So, it wasn't that surprising that when my value to society was tested, I'd fallen completely apart.

How had I not seen it before? Inner strength did not come from the adoration of others. It came from within. And as I sat there, knife in hand, prepared to do whatever it took to defend my life, I finally understood what it took to be a man.

I was not a victim anymore.

And if I lived through this, I'd never be a victim again.

18

DANI: THE CLIMB

QUITTING WAS NOT IN MY VOCABULARY. EVEN WHEN LIFE THREW curve balls at me. Like the time I failed to get accepted into medical school after a lifetime of preparing; I'd quickly readjusted my aim and swung for a different field. Even when this earthquake sent my world into chaos, I'd kept my focus, doing what needed to be done. But this...

I'd hit my limit. I was done.

Dropping heavily to the ground, I pulled the walkie-talkie from my pocket and pressed the button.

"Parker, are you there?"

I waited, wiping the blood, sweat, and tears from my eyes.

"I know you've already done so much for me today—above and beyond in every sense of the word—but I need you now more than I've ever needed anything in my life. I know you could lose your job if you disobey orders, and I promise you, I wouldn't be asking you this if I had any other choice. But please, Parker. Please, help me."

There was a crackling on the other end like he was there, listening, and had chosen to remain silent because there was nothing more to be said. How could I blame him? What I was asking for was too much. Tears streaked across my face as I bent down and kissed RJ's fever-ravished forehead. He was unconscious now, the pain, the exertion, the loss of blood all working together to create the perfect storm.

I looked down at the gauze wrapped tight just below his lower calf. His foot was gone, left crushed under all that concrete. I watched him do it, horrified but in awe of his strength, his desire to live. The screams. The blood. They would haunt me to the day I died. But I stayed there by his side, even taking over when the knife fell from his hand. We'd come that far. I had to set him free.

And when it was done, RJ had wrapped his appreciative arms around me once more. His foot was gone, yet his resolved remained. He wanted to live; we both did.

But neither one of us had been prepared for the trek that followed. Using the crutch Bruce had provided and me as support on the other side, RJ and I began the arduous journey across a wasteland of destruction and fallen debris. When it had just been me climbing over crushed cars and mangled rebar, the trip had seemed manageable but RJ, fresh out of self-surgery and with only one foot to navigate on, was quickly beginning to fade.

Yet I kept pushing him past what should be expected of any human body. And when he finally fell, there was no getting him back up. RJ was out cold, his skin so pale it was streaked in shades of light blue. Still I didn't give up, calling on whatever reserves I had left inside me to drag him through the debris and over mounds of crumbling concrete until I dropped to the ground in sheer exhaustion with his near lifeless body draped over me. We'd made it to the crater. But that was the furthest the two of us would go because that ladder was my breaking point.

"Parker, if you can hear me... I tried. I really tried. I got RJ to the base of the ladder, but he's unconscious and too heavy for me to get him out of here. His pulse is so low. I don't think he has much longer. I'm going to stay with him until the end, and then once he's gone..." I swallowed back a sob. "I'll come out."

I stroked RJ's handsome face, pressing kisses along the smooth skin and smiling at the memory of shaving him grave-side. When he'd been at his most vulnerable, RJ's spirit had shown. And while he would not be able to make the grand, heroic exit we'd both planned, I would never let anyone forget his name. RJ Contreras would live on as a shining star.

"That's my last promise to you," I whispered in his ear.

The walkie-talkie crackled.

Hold on, Gladys. I'm coming.

———

Parker descended the ladder with a stretcher strapped to his back. But he was not the only hero to climb down those stairs. His captain, Marcel, was already on the ground, checking RJ's vital signs and calling orders to those who stood above the hole, waiting to hoist him up on the stretcher.

I stood off to the side, watching. In shock. Emotional. RJ was lifted onto the stretcher and strapped in. And, as Parker cushioned his leg for the trip out of the parking garage, the firefighter who I knew after this would be my friend for life turned to me.

"It's time to go."

Everything was taking place in slow motion. I heard his words but couldn't reply.

"Dani," Parker's voice shook me out of my trance. "You've done enough. Let us do the rest. Go."

I began to cry. Yes, I'd done enough. It was time. Looking up,

I saw a firefighter at the top of the ladder, holding a hand out to me. I lifted my foot onto the bottom rung and began the climb.

19

DANI: IN THE NICK OF TIME

IT WASN'T UNTIL RJ HAD BEEN LOADED INTO THE BACK OF AN ambulance and whisked away in a swirl of lights and sirens that the weight of the trauma I'd experienced finally hit me. My heart began to race, and my blood-stained hands turned clammy. Then came the weakness and dizziness that brought me to the ground. Before I even knew what was happening, I was on my back, blinking up at the morning sun.

Rapid, weak pulse, I heard them say. *Blood pressure's low.*

I wanted to let them know I was fine, not to worry about me, but an oxygen mask was placed over my nose and mouth before I could get the words out, and I was honestly just too exhausted to fight another battle. So, minutes after RJ was taken away, I also found myself on a stretcher in the back of an ambulance being whisked away in a swirl of lights and sirens. I closed my eyes, letting the movement of the vehicle lull me to sleep... until someone stuck a needle into my vein.

"Ouch," I complained, trying to draw my hand away.

"Don't pull it out or I'll have to stick you again."

My eyes were slow to identify who'd spoken, but when they

cleared, I saw Bruce, the opinionated paramedic, staring back at me.

I lifted the oxygen mask off my face. "Hey, I know you."

"Oh, I know you too. You've made today very eventful."

"Really not my fault. Please blame Mother Nature."

"I don't know, Dani. I feel like you're not giving yourself enough credit."

I managed to form the barest of smiles. "You're mean. You wanna be my friend?"

"If what you did for RJ is your idea of being a good friend, then yes, I would very much like to be added to that list."

"Consider it done," I replied, happy to expand my network for this big teddy bear of a man. "And I think we both know I didn't keep RJ alive on my own. I had a little help from my friends."

Bruce caught my eye, knowing exactly what I was talking about.

"That moment when I saw the bag, the crutch..." I drew in a breath to keep from crying. "We couldn't have done it without you, without Parker. Without the supplies..."

Placing a finger to his lips, Bruce looked around before saying, "How about we keep that part of it to ourselves?"

My eyes rounded. Oh, shit. The last thing I wanted was for anyone to be penalized for helping us bring an end to the nightmare. I mimed zipping my mouth shut only to unzip it a second later to add, "And about that friend request. I feel obligated to disclose that I have one hundred and ten siblings."

"Of course you do."

The fact that Bruce didn't even blink at the news told me he was getting used to my particular brand of crazy.

I tapped the IV in my hand. "Please tell me that's straight up vodka going into my blood stream."

He smiled, shaking his head. "Oh, so close, but no. Saline.

You were showing signs of dehydration, but I haven't ruled out shock due to infection. I mean, considering that I watched you pull a piece of glass out of your arm with dirty fingers, it's certainly a plausible scenario."

"What hospital are you taking me to?"

"The closest one."

"Is that where they're taking RJ?"

"I can't tell you that."

"Can you at least tell me if he's going to be okay?"

"I can't tell you that either."

"Seriously, Bruce. It's me. I thought we were past these formalities."

He chuckled, securing the oxygen mask back over my nose and mouth. "All I can say is he's going to the nearest hospital. And I don't know his condition—that's the truth. But I can tell you he wouldn't have survived very long in the parking garage, so at least you gave him a chance."

A chance. Yes. I'd done my best. I'd kept him alive long enough for the experts to take over. What more could I ask of myself? Yet still, a chill skipped over my skin. What if, after everything, he didn't make it? Or what if he survived only to go back to his world and me to mine? I drew in a series of deep breaths to calm my nerves. I'd given him a chance. And in the end, that was all that mattered.

I unzipped my lips again to say, "We, Bruce. We gave him a chance."

Bruce pretended to ignore me as he checked the saline bag for flow, but when he turned back his eyes had softened. "We."

Smiling, I closed my fake zipper. *We.*

————

The remainder of the building collapsed forty-five minutes after RJ was pulled from the rubble.

I'd just arrived at the emergency room and had been hooked up to monitors when a collective gasp could be heard throughout the unit. For a split second, all activity came to a standstill. Because this was the closest hospital to the apartments, its rooms were filled with victims and their families. Some were quietly affected, while others wailed, but most just stood there looking stunned. I lay in my bed numb, unable to wrap my brain around any of it. Parker had warned me—he'd said it was swaying and about to come down—but it hadn't been real to me then. The risk those men had taken to save our lives... I had no words.

Forty-five minutes was all that had separated RJ and me from a certain death. Others hadn't been so lucky. No one knew how many people had still been trapped inside when the building came down. Whether they were alive or dead at the time made no difference now. No one could have survived the collapse. All those unlucky souls who'd been waitlisted right alongside RJ were gone. As the full scope of the tragedy hit me, I let go of the stress and sadness of this unfathomable day. But, as with widescale catastrophes like these, I was far from the only one suffering, and I took solace in my sobs joining in chorus with those around me.

Once I'd gotten my emotions back in check, I asked the earthquake victim beside me being treated for a possible wrist fracture if I could use her phone. There was no hesitation as she handed it over to me in a fog, mumbling the code to unlock it. Her zombie-like reaction told me everything I needed to know about her—she'd been one of my neighbors.

The first person I called from the borrowed phone was my mother, who nearly collapsed at the sound of my voice. She'd seen the news and knew it was my building. Not having heard any word from me since after the quake, she'd assumed the worst. Uncharacteristic babblings of love followed. From her. From me. As I rattled off an outline of my day from hell, my mother was there for me—holding strong and keeping me sane. In true helicopter mom fashion, she immediately went to work trying to fix the problem, making lists of everything we'd need to do to get me back on my feet again.

We. There was that word again. I liked the sound of that. So much of today had been *me* and making decisions I wasn't sure were right. Going back inside the garage. Leaving RJ to die. Helping free him from his prison by picking up the knife. I blinked the nasty image from my mind. Mom was here now. She'd make everything right. I'd never been so grateful to be raised by such a capable and determined woman.

My thoughts returned to RJ and his messy origin story. If only he'd had such support growing up. No one should ever have to worry that their death will be a benefit to others. How lonely his big, flashy life must have been if he had no one to truly trust.

The second call I made was to Donny. Again, not my first choice, but his was still the only number I remembered. Thankfully Donny seemed to have finished his video game sometime between my last call and now, and he was more attentive to me this time around. But, as I learned in the course of our conversation, his newfound focus was because he'd been scolded in a group chat with other members of the Lucky Swimmers Club after letting it slip that he'd received a distress call from me and had done jack shit to help. Maybe this was just his way of getting back into their good graces, but I didn't care. The dude was now fully clothed and willing to do just about anything I asked.

His mission was simple—inform the sibs that I was being treated for dehydration and would be released from the hospital in a few hours. He was also tasked with putting out the word that I needed a place to crash until I could secure myself new housing. My mother, of course, had insisted on me coming home, and I'd given the idea some serious thought, but my childhood home was a good two hours away, and I couldn't be that far from RJ, not until I knew he was going to be okay.

Just after returning the phone, I saw Parker walking toward me like some mirage. My lips began to quiver, and I opened my arms to him. I knew it was probably against some rule of the firefighter code to hug the clientele, but we were past protocol.

His arms wrapped around me and I had another good cry on his shoulder before any words were exchanged between us. Parker's uniform soaked up my tears, and once I'd gained control again, he let me go.

"Better?" he asked, looking a little less prepubescent with a five o'clock shadow dusting his jawline after what had to have been a very long shift for him, no thanks to me.

"Better," I confirmed. "What do you know about RJ?"

"He's in surgery. The paramedics were able to stabilize him on the way over. I saw RJ just before they took him back to the operating room. He was somewhat awake, and moving his head around. He's in good hands."

I absorbed everything he said, while nodding my approval. "I never should have forced you to make that decision. On the walkie-talkie... I was just distraught. I'm sorry I put you in the position I did. I hope you aren't going to lose your job over this."

"I won't. My captain was down there too."

"You could've died."

Parker didn't respond, probably because he knew I'd spoken the truth and didn't want to make me feel worse than I already did. I grabbed his hand and squeezed my gratitude.

Clearing his throat, he said. "I've got to get home. Haven't slept in almost forty-eight hours. You're one tough chick, Gladys. I don't regret a thing."

"Neither do I. And Parker? Thank you. It doesn't feel like a strong enough word, but it's all I got."

"It's all I need... well, that and some backstage passes."

————

I felt better after Parker's visit. He'd taken one less worry off the roster. He'd absolved me of the guilt of putting him and his fellow firefighters in harm's way. And with the slow drip of fluids returning my body to its normal functioning state, I could focus on the other nagging items on my list. Where would I live? Was my classroom still standing? And would I even still have a job once a snapshot of my grainy face on the store's security camera was placed on the principal's desk?

But there was more. What was going to happen between RJ and me? We had, after all, exchanged some pretty heavy words in those final moments together, just before all hope was lost. I'd even uttered the big L, and meant it from the deepest depths of my soul. But what now? There was no doubt in my mind what we'd experienced together in that garage—what we'd said to each other—was real, but who was to say it wasn't merely situational and that our connection had been forged out of desperation by a man who had no options left?

"You've run dry," a nurse said, startling me out of my thoughts as she checked the saline bag hanging to my side. "Vitals look good. How are you feeling, hun?"

"Better. Will I be released soon?"

"You're all stitched up and the blood work is back. There's no infection. The doctor will be by in a few minutes, and as long as she doesn't have any further concerns, you should be free to go."

I let out the breath I'd been holding onto since being informed an infection might land me in the hospital for a week, maybe two. What good would I be to RJ tethered to an IV in a hospital bed?

"That's a relief," I said, and without really thinking I asked. "Have you heard any word on RJ? Is he still in surgery?"

The woman looked up from the IV drip, her utter surprise telling me I wouldn't be getting any insider information from her. "RJ Contreras? He's here? At this hospital? So the rumors are true?"

Her answer surprised me. I just figured she'd know the goings-on of her own hospital, but apparently not. And what did she mean by rumors? What exactly was circulating out there? What if my interview had unleashed something entirely unintended?

"Oh, I... I don't know." I stumbled over the words. "I just thought..."

"Wait—you're not the girl everyone's talking about, are you?"

Jerking my head up, I caught her curious stare. *The girl?* Oh, shit. Had I become part of the save RJ campaign? That had never been the intention. I'd kept my face and identity hidden in order to keep the focus on him.

I looked to my left. Broken wrist woman was blinking at me with wide, interested eyes. I looked to my right. More of the same. They were leaving me no doubt—*the girl* in RJ's story was trending.

"Me? No. I heard it on Twitter."

The nurse's face fell in disappointment. The wrist lady looked away. In a matter of seconds, I'd gone back to the nobody I'd always been comfortable being.

Not long after that odd encounter, the doctor came and officially discharged me—but not before word arrived from hospital staff that my mother had called and that she could not get to me due to road closures that had turned her back around on the two-hour drive. And so, I exited the emergency room minutes later utterly alone. It was a weird feeling, being on my own in this new world order. I wasn't sure what to do or where to go. I was a wilted ghost, wandering the halls. How strange a feeling it was to move from operating on the highest level of octane the body could sustain to this, a deflated balloon with nothing left but its withered remains. And, without a phone, I was even more disconnected from the world. I needed to know what was happening around me, though at the same time, I dreaded the news.

I followed signs toward the exit, though I had no intention of leaving the hospital. The plan—my only plan—was to find the waiting room for surgery patients and settle myself down on a plastic chair until I got some word on RJ. It wasn't like I had anywhere else to go. I was homeless, penniless, and scared out of my wits for a man I might possibly love. Until I learned his fate, I would not leave this place.

As I turned the corner, the corridor opened up into a large, brightly lit waiting room, and that was where I saw them, taking up a whole wall of the waiting room. There were at least two dozen of them.

"There she is!" Simone called out. "Thank god."

My shoulders slumped and tears of relief burst from my eyes as my siblings rushed toward me. Reese got there first, her pregnant belly bumping into my stomach before her arms wrapped tightly around me. Kimber was close behind. Ross and Charlie were joined by Otis as they formed a tight circle around me. But more kept squeezing in. Tim, Simone, Conrad, Kaia. My siblings had heard the cry for help and had dropped everything to be by my side. I sobbed, not from sadness this time but from the relief of knowing I had their unconditional support, which would enable me to come out of this disaster fully intact.

Almost as amazing as being there for me emotionally, my brothers and sisters had also planned several steps ahead so I wouldn't have to. Having taken up a collection, they'd gathered enough money that I didn't need to worry about how I would get through the next few weeks.

Slipping an arm around my waist, my sister Cleo announced, "And you'll be staying with me, Sis."

"Are you sure?"

"Of course. We have a spare room and have de-slobbered it just for you."

Cleo's baby, a six-year-old bulldog named Bubba, a drooling, farting, bad-breath machine, was giving up his nap room just for me.

"Thank you." I hugged her tight.

RJ's pick for the Norman Bates of my sibling unit, Landry, stepped up and thrust a phone in my hand.

"Here. It's yours to keep."

"Are you sure?" I asked, shocked by his generosity. "This is expensive."

He shrugged. "My mom gets me the newest model every birthday."

"Oh, wow," I said, trying not to judge him too harshly with last year's iPhone model in my hand. Regardless of how he'd come by it, I was still unbelievably grateful to have my connection to the world restored.

"And don't worry, I erased anything that could get you in trouble with the law."

I caught Ross in the background, with those wide disbelieving eyes of his, and I knew what he was thinking. If any of Landry's search history remained, I could one day expect a visit from the FBI. But I ignored Ross because I needed this phone, and I would risk the consequences down the road.

"Ah, Landry. Look at you, coming in clutch," I said, hugging his totally stiff body before letting him go. "Thank you for this."

He blushed, looking more uncomfortable with my affection than charmed. "I have my computer with me. When you're ready, you can sign into your cloud and download your contacts."

"You're the best. Thanks."

"Story time," Otis declared, taking my hand and leading me back to a row of chairs. "Tell us exactly what happened. And don't leave out any part where the scrumptious RJ Contreras stars."

And so, as my siblings gathered around, I told them the events of the day, leaving out one detail—that the final cut that had amputated RJ's foot came from my shaky hand. I would've preferred not to bring up the amputation at all, believing it was RJ's choice to reveal that information, but my siblings already knew, since word of his dramatic rescue was spreading across the globe. Yet despite not giving my brothers and sisters every gory detail, I gave them enough that there wasn't a closed mouth in the group when I was finished.

From the back, Conrad raised his hand. I pointed to him. "Yeah, how did RJ Contreras end up in your parking garage?"

"RJ is Chad."

The twins both rocked back in their seats in unison. "Chad Woodcock?"

"Yep."

"Wait—are you talking about that douchey neighbor?" Simone asked.

"Yes. Chad was RJ in disguise."

Otis looked about ready to explode. "So you're telling me you've been living next door to RJ Contreras and didn't know it?"

I nodded.

"Not only that," Charlie said, "but she's been having daily

face-to-face arguments with him for five months and still didn't recognize him."

"He had a beard," I feebly defended myself.

"I told you it was an alias, didn't I?" Conrad replied, folding his arms over his chest and adopting a smug expression.

Ross high-fived Charlie. "Chad Woodcock rocks!"

"I'm so confused," Reese said. "Who did you save? RJ or Chad?"

"They're one in the same," Otis replied. "Try to follow along, Octomom."

"I have two babies in here. I'm not incubating an army."

Kaia, the shyest Swimmer in the group, spoke up from her spot in the corner. "What are you going to do now?"

I shrugged. "Wait here at the hospital until he wakes up. It's really all I can do."

"Do you think he'll want to see you when he wakes up?" She asked.

The thought hadn't crossed my mind, but now that it had been asked, I wasn't so sure myself. Would he need me now? Would I matter in his big, important life? But I thought I knew RJ well enough to answer her question with confidence. "Yes, Kaia, I think I'll be the first person he'll want to see."

"Ah, you're so lucky," she said, stars twinkling in her eyes.

"Lucky and unlucky," Otis said, weighing the two options with his hands. "She did have to nearly die to get his attention, and that's never a recommended first date ice-breaker."

"You want my advice?" Conrad asked, staring at me with his characteristic intensity.

"Always."

"With a high-profile celebrity in the hospital, there's going to be extra security on his floor. If you don't want to get kicked out of here, sit back, stay silent, and blend. And keep that wristband on."

I nodded, filing away his suggestions. After securing assurance from my siblings that they wouldn't repeat the story I'd told them, they trickled out of the hospital one by one until only Simone remained. "Are you sure I can't stay with you?"

"No. I have a better chance of getting past security alone."

"I know, but I hate to leave you after what you've been through."

I held up my phone, newly updated with my contacts. "But now I have a phone and can reach you."

"That's true. Here." She pressed cash into my hand. "Take this for food."

I hugged her. "You're the best."

"I know." She winked, swatting my butt before walking away. "Now we're adjourned."

———

I found myself a nice little cubby in the ICU waiting room, a spot where I could watch everyone coming and going. The goal was to find, and then introduce myself, to RJ's family. It seemed the only way into his inner circle, even if, according to RJ, they hadn't been a part of it for many years. But I understood that family ties could be a tricky thing, and I reminded myself to keep an open mind. There were always two sides to every story, and maybe RJ was just too close to his to see clearly.

An hour passed, maybe two, which I spent most of googling RJ and his family on my new phone. What surprised me most was that for the high-volume public figure that RJ was, as well as the sheer number of pictures of him on the internet, I couldn't find even one image of them together as a family. The other *AnyDayNow* boys were photographed beside their next of kin, but not RJ. Never RJ.

Murmuring in the waiting room caught my attention. I looked

up to see a press conference commencing on the TV overhead. I moved closer, wanting to hear what was being said. With the backdrop of our apartment building, now a pile of rubble, the police chief went on to describe the state of things after the 7.1 magnitude monster earthquake had roared through her city. Lasting just over twenty seconds, the temblor and its many aftershocks had caused widespread damage. Sections of major freeways had collapsed. Buildings had fallen, although none as dramatically as ours. Roads had spilt in two. Even a tsunami warning had been issued, putting the entire coastline on alert. And the loss of life... there was no doubt in anyone's mind it would be staggering.

"As far as the reports circulating about popular boy band member RJ Contreras," the police chief continued, "we can confirm that he was in the parking garage of the building behind me when the earthquake struck and subsequently became trapped inside. We can also confirm that he was pulled free from the rubble by another survivor less than an hour before the building collapsed. RJ was taken to the hospital, where he has undergone surgery for a range of injuries. He's currently in the intensive care unit. I have no further information on his condition at this time."

One by one, major players stepped up to the microphone to discuss disaster relief plans, road closures, the Red Cross. I lost interest then, secure in the knowledge that my siblings had provided me with all the assistance I needed. It wasn't until reporters started firing questions that my interest was piqued once more.

My sources tell me that RJ was forced to amputate his own leg to escape the wreckage because rescue workers were not allowed in the building to rescue those trapped inside?

RJ was the only survivor pulled from the rubble. Did he receive preferential treatment because he's a celebrity?

"I'm not authorized to speak to RJ's medical condition. I will say that the decision to not allow the rescue efforts to continue was a heavy blow for our brave first responders, who were ready and willing to step inside the building and save whoever they could. As hard as it was, we believe we prevented further loss of life with the difficult decision. And there was no preferential treatment. RJ was not rescued by our first responders. He was rescued by a young woman who was with him at the time of the collapse."

That piece of information sent the crowd into a frenzy, with questions coming from all corners.

What do we know about this woman?

Can we get a name?

"The young woman is not a public figure and has not consented to her name being distributed to news outlets. But I would like to commend her. This woman showed an incredible amount of bravery, risking her own safety to help RJ escape the building. That's all for now. I'll update you when we have further details."

I watched the police chief walk away, spellbound by what he'd said. They were protecting me, maybe even protecting the firefighters, if they knew about their involvement at all. This story was bigger than I ever could have imagined, and I was sure the quake would set off a ripple effect that could very well alter my life for good. Was I ready for that? Maybe on RJ's arm I'd be okay, but on my own, I wasn't so sure the frenzied press wouldn't eat me alive.

Giving up on the news, I went back to my row of chairs and lay down. With my head resting on my hands and my feet tucked up under me on the hard, unforgiving seat, the events of the day finally caught up to me, and I fell fast asleep. How long I slept I couldn't say, but I was jerked awake by an aftershock that sent startled gasps around the waiting room. I shot upright, smacking my head on the armrest.

"Ow," I whined, rubbing my skull while taking a glance around at my fellow waiters. Most looked as startled as me, but there was one...

I narrowed in on her, my eyes popping open when I realized who it was sitting by herself in a row of seats opposite mine: Heather Contreras. Two things immediately stood out about her. One, she seemed not to be affected by the trembler at all, going about her business like nothing was wrong. And two, she did not look like the monster RJ had described her to be. But then, the worst ones never did.

With her head down, Heather was fixated on the screen of her phone as her thumb scrolled. I wondered what she was looking for. Did I have the answers she was seeking? For one fleeting moment, I wondered if she might be googling me, like I'd googled her earlier in the day. From that search, I knew certain facts about her. She was fifty-two years old, a Scorpio, and listed her occupation as 'RJ Contreras's mom,' which according to her son was a fairly accurate job description, given she was on his payroll. With tight blonde curls that reached to her shoulders and skin tanned to rawhide, Heather gave off the impression of a woman who'd been wild in her youth but had since come into a wad of cash and was now on the board of directors at the local country club. Damn, I could smell the judgment wafting off me. I had to get that negativity in check or I wouldn't be able to gain her trust. And without Heather's trust, I'd never get an invitation to her son's bedside.

I stood up and crossed the room, stopping a few feet away.

"Mrs. Contreras?"

She lifted her eyes for a split second then went back to scrolling on her phone.

"I'm a friend of RJ's."

Heather lowered her glasses a smudge to peer at me over the rims. "Aren't you all. Who let you in here?"

"Oh... I... let myself..."

"Only immediate family of ICU patients are allowed. You never should have been let through the doors. I'll have a talk with security about this," she replied, with the haughty awareness of a woman who got what she wanted all of the time.

Holy crap, she was intimidating, and that came from someone who had grown up with an intimidating mother. But at least mine pretended to be nice to strangers, only talking behind their backs when they weren't around. Heather was all front-end intimidation.

"Mrs. Contreras, I was admitted to the hospital earlier in the day," I tried again, offering up my wristband as proof. "With RJ."

Now Heather raised her head, removing her reading glasses to get a better look at me. "Please tell me you're not the one who cut my son's foot off."

I rocked back, shocked by the stark accusation.

At my silence, her eyes widened. "Oh, my god, you are!"

"I was with him in the parking garage, yes. But RJ made the decision."

"RJ? He made the decision? To cut his own foot off? Listen to yourself. Do you think I'm dumb? Do you think I don't know my own son?"

Her anger fueled my own. "I think maybe you don't know what it feels like to be desperate and about to die."

You would've thought I'd stabbed a knife into her gut the way her expression turned murderous. But years now dealing with mamma bears protecting their young had insulated me from such attacks.

"We were told to evacuate; that the building was about to come down. RJ was trapped, his foot crushed under concrete. He did what he had to do to survive."

"No," she snarled. "*You* did what you wanted to. Not him. My son would rather die than live his life as a cripple."

"I took over, but only after the pain got too much for RJ. Don't you understand? I couldn't let him suffer like that. Someone had to get him free."

"Oh, and you're that someone?" she scoffed. "What a savior you are."

Wow, this was not going according to plan. Now I knew where Chad Woodcock got his fighting spirit. But if I hadn't backed down from him, I sure as hell wasn't going to back down from his unreasonable mother.

"Maybe if I explained to you what happened in..."

"I don't need to know," she cut me off. "According to the doctors, you made such a mess of his ankle, they had to amputate it even further up."

I winced at the memory of that moment cutting through tendons and bone. Did she really think that was something I'd wanted to do?

"And you understand the alternative would've been a dead son, right?" I questioned, pointing to the television with images of our collapsed building. "Because if I'd left RJ in there with a partially amputated foot, you'd be burying him."

Heather's eyes lasered into mine as she dropped her voice to a low growl. "Watch your tone with me. You don't think I haven't dealt with your kind before? There's nothing special about you. You're not even that pretty. If you think RJ's going to fall madly in love with you, then you're sadly mistaken. I know my son, and RJ doesn't love anyone. Never has. So don't think you have some direct line, you little tart. *I* have the direct line."

What in the living hell? Had Heather just made this some warped competition? And to disrespect RJ like that, implying he wasn't capable of love! In a perfect world, I would have let her insult go unchallenged. I would have held my head high and walked away. But after the events of today, there was no perfect world, and I had no obligation to keep my mouth shut.

Leaning forward, I spoke for her ears only. "Have you ever thought that maybe he just doesn't love you?"

It was dangerous, cutting, and the second the words left my mouth, I regretted them. Not because I didn't think them true, but because I'd just made a powerful enemy. I'd secured my place at the back of the line. Heather would never allow me to see her son now.

Her eyes locked on mine, Heather stood up. "You just picked a fight with the wrong person."

As I watched her walk away, I knew without a doubt that Heather would make me pay.

Minutes later, I was being escorted out of the hospital doors.

20

RJ: PATIENT PRIVILEGE

I CAME TO BEHIND A LONG WHITE CURTAIN. I WASN'T SURE HOW long I lay there, blinking up at the ceiling and trying to figure out where the hell I was, but it seemed a long damn while. Was I dead? Was this Albert's heaven? If so, I was decidedly under-whelmed. Where was my halo? And my dead dog, Bobo? And what the hell was that moaning going on behind the curtain to my right?

As my mind cleared of the drugs, I realized that the beeping of machines, accompanied by the dull, aching pain in my ribs, meant I was very much alive. And then I remembered. My foot! Jerking my head off the pillow, I looked down at my drastically shortened, and heavily bandaged, leg and let out a curse that would've made Triple A cringe.

A nurse rushed in.

"Hey, relax. Just lie back," he said, shoving the oxygen tubes back in my nose. "If you take these out, the doctor might be forced to intubate you again."

I pointed down at my leg and forced the words out of my raw, swollen throat. "What happened to the rest of it?"

"You don't remember cutting it off?" he asked incredulously.

Of course I remembered. It wasn't like the severing of it wouldn't live on in my memory forever. That shit was what nightmares were made of. No, I wasn't surprised my foot was gone; I was surprised that it was considerably shorter than where Dani had hacked it off for me.

"There's like two extra inches gone." The accusatory tone of my voice somehow transferred all the responsibility for those extra missing inches onto the mild-mannered ICU nurse tasked with caring for me.

"Let me get the doctor for you," he said, hurrying out of the curtain room.

"You better run, dude," I mumbled under my breath, wishing I had something to chuck at his retreating frame.

"Try to be a little nicer," the moaner on the other side of the curtain said. "Julio is just doing his job."

What the...? She sounded old as fuck, and normally I'd humor her just for the fact that she was old as fuck, but not today. I had no humanity left for the before-dusk dinner crowd.

"Try to mind your own business," I grumbled through gritted teeth. "And if you wouldn't mind keeping that moaning to a minimum, Myrtle, that would be just swell. Feel like I'm in some fucking porno."

Silence ensued. Even the beeping machines seemed to take a momentary break, no doubt fearing my wrath. And then the strangest sound came from the curtain room on my right. Laughter. Then moaning. Then more laughter. And more moaning. I wasn't sure if she was having an orgasm or dying.

"Oh my," she said, through a spattering of giggles. "You're a chip off the old block, aren't you?"

That got my attention right away. Just exactly which block was she referring to? "What does that mean?"

"Let me put it this way. If your mamma is Satan, you're the spawn."

My eyes widened. Well, shit. She was definitely speaking from experience, which meant dear old gold-digging mom had been here. Who'd let that woman in?

"How do you know my mother?" I asked, a cast of suspicion now settling into my words.

"I don't *know* her. I just know *of* her. She's a little hard to ignore. Has the entire staff terrified."

"Yeah, well, I'm not her," I grumbled, although I could see how she might have assumed that, based on performance. "I'm just having a bad day. Not that you care, but my foot's gone."

"Not that you care, but my breast is gone."

How was that for evening the score? I had no rebuttal. Dammit, what was wrong with me? The first chance I had to prove myself a whole new man and I'd spent it being a jerk. If I wanted to rise above the noise of my former life, I had to first meet people where they stood.

"Cancer?" I asked.

"Yes," she replied. "Earthquake?"

"Yes. How'd you guess?"

"Most everyone in here was injured in the quake. I picked the wrong day for a mastectomy."

The way she said it, with just the tiniest bit of snark, beckoned a smile from my lips. Maybe she wasn't so bad after all.

"I'm sorry for being a jerk," I said, taking those first few steps toward humility. "I shouldn't have snapped at you... or Julio."

"Eh, you're fine. You've had a rough few days. Besides, I was somewhat flattered. No one's mistaken me for a porn star in forty years."

I laughed, the effort of which caused sweeping pain to extend outward to every extremity. Even my missing foot ached.

"Oh god," I groaned. "Was I hit by a freight train?"

"From what I hear, close. Want my advice? Tell them it hurts before you feel pain. Make 'em keep on top of the morphine regime."

"You seem to speak from experience."

"I was a teenager in the 60's."

This woman's spunk reminded me of another: Dani, my unsung hero.

"Hey, has there been a woman in here with me? I mean not the bitchy one... someone nice."

"Nice?" she replied. "No, nothing nice had been on that side of the curtain, that I've heard."

So, where was she? A moment of panic gripped me. Had she even made it out of the parking garage? I struggled to recall the details of those final minutes. The tourniquet Dani had tied around my shin. She'd grabbed my hand, the one with the knife. Our eyes locked. We both understood the gravity of what was about to happen, and we went into it with the naivety of first-time surgeons. It would be rough—that much we knew—but because my foot was already numb after hours of being crushed under a concrete block, I'd figured that would act as a sort of anesthesia.

Those first cuts proved me oh, so wrong. I wasn't numb; not even close. The pain was unreal, cutting through cartilage and bone. Torture, pure torture. I'd made it nearly the entire way through before my hand began to shake and my vision to blur. Just a few more cuts, but I couldn't go on. The knife dropped to the ground. Dani picked it up and tried wrapping it back into my fingers. But I was too far gone. My head swimming from the pain. I implored her to finish the job. Dani. So brave. So beautiful and so brave. She didn't want to, of course, but she did it anyway. For me.

I remembered being cut free and her wrapping the stump. I even remembered her helping me walk with the crutch... and then there was a complete black out. How had I gotten out of there? And where the hell was Dani? After what she had done for me, there was no way that woman was sitting idly by, waiting for an invitation.

Something wasn't right. What could possibly be the reason Dani wasn't here? She'd made it clear by her actions that she'd stop at nothing to be there for me, so why wasn't she? I tapped into the rising panic. Could she be lying in a hospital bed herself? Had Dani been hiding her injuries from me, just as I done to her?

But then I realized there was a far simpler explanation for why Dani hadn't breached ICU protocol to be by my side; an explanation that even the curtain lady had called.

If your mom is Satan...

It all became clear. The reason Dani wasn't here was because the Grim Reaper had gotten to her first.

"Are you the singer everyone's talking about?" the woman next door asked, clearly already knowing the answer to that.

Her question barely fazed me. I was used to being the singer everyone was talking about... or at least I had been before I'd disappeared from the public eye five months ago. But usually when someone asked me that question, it was with stars in their eyes and was referring to some kickass accomplishment of mine... not for being stuck like a roly-poly in a crack in the sidewalk.

By keeping me relevant in the eyes of the internet, Dani had essentially guaranteed an interest in my plight. Why wouldn't the media jump all over this story? It had everything they salivated over: fame, pain, and an arrogant celebrity being knocked down to size.

"Probably," I replied. "What are they saying?"

"Pretty much the same thing over and over and over."

"That sounds about right. Do they know about the amputation?"

"People in the far corners of Antarctica know about the amputation. It's all over the news. I had surgery two days after you'd been brought into the ICU, so I was fairly surprised to be wheeled up right next to you. Even more surprised that you were still intubated and unconscious—three days after the quake. From what I heard, it was a bit touch and go for a while there."

"Because of my foot?"

"No. That's the least of your problems. The pressure on your ribs from the concrete actually partially collapsed your lung, and they had to artificially inflate it, or something like that. You're also being treating for a possible infection. Doctors haven't ruled out pneumonia yet."

All of this information was new to me, told to me by the faceless cancer patient next door. "You sure have an ear for detail."

"Thank you. I try to stay crisp in the mind by playing sudoku."

How nice for her.

"While I appreciate the insider information," I replied, "isn't it like a federal offense to listen in on someone's medical history?"

"No. What you're talking about is doctor-patient privilege. But what we've got going on here is called patient-to-patient privilege."

"Ah, got it."

"And I wasn't eavesdropping. I just have good hearing."

"Great. I get the one senior citizen with supersonic hearing."

"And a good memory," she added.

"Because of the sudoku?"

"That's right. Do you want to hear about the rest of your injuries?"

"There's more?"

"Oh yes. Much more," she replied, with an almost gleeful

undertone. "In addition to the partially collapsed lung, you have multiple rib fractures, an amputated foot that they shaped in surgery for a future prosthetics, various crush injuries, and because you bled into your lungs, you had to have a transfusion."

I sat there a moment, taking it all in. With all that going on inside me, how had I survived in there as long as I did?

"You're lucky to be alive," the busybody next door said. "But I don't think I have to tell you that."

"No," I agreed. "You don't. Hey, what's your name?"

"Sue."

"Sue? Isn't that appropriate? I figure I have a pretty good case against you for listening in on my personal medical history."

"Again—not a crime to have good hearing. Besides, it's not my fault your life plays like a soap opera."

No, she was right about that. I'd been doused in drama my whole life. My eyes began to feel heavy.

"Is there anything else I need to know, Sue, or can I take a nap now?"

Silence. Okay, that was weird.

"Sue?"

"Uh, nope. Nothing else."

The way she said it indicated that there was, indeed, something else she wasn't telling me.

"I know you're lying to me. What is it?"

There was a long pause before she replied. "I shouldn't say. It's not my place."

"None of my business has been your place, but that hasn't stopped you before."

"Okay, look. Just a little piece of advice from an old gal with plenty of life experience: Get yourself a better support system."

"What do you mean by that?"

"It wasn't just the doctors I overheard. I also listened in on your mother talking on the phone. Your father and brothers are on their way from Idaho. Apparently, your mom flew out first, and there was some..."

She hesitated.

"Some what?"

"Some debate over whether the others would follow."

"What was the debate about?"

"Well, your dad—I could hear him talking through the phone—he wanted to... um... he... um..."

My face fell flat. Whatever she had to say I wasn't going to like. "Spit it out, Sue."

"He wanted to take a wait and see approach," she blurted out.

A twitch formed in one eye. "Wait for what?"

"To see if you were going to survive first, because he didn't want to fly out to California twice—you know, like once to say goodbye and again for the funeral. Kill two birds with one stone, he'd said."

Two birds with one stone? My jaw dropped.

"It's an hour and forty-eight-minute flight!" I screeched, my voice taking on the squeakiness of a prepubescent boy. "He's waited longer in the line to get gas at Costco."

"It gets worse."

The monitor beside my head started beeping faster. "How can it get worse than my own father skipping straight to the memorial service?"

"Uh... your brothers only agreeing to come if your mom threw in a trip to Six Flags?"

What the ever-loving fuck? I dropped back into my bed, hurt and confused. I mean, I knew they'd never liked me, but I hadn't realized the extent of the animosity between us. I suppose I'd figured paying their way for six years and giving them a roof over their heads would buy me some favor with them, but no.

When I'd needed their support most, my brothers had traded my life for the Drop of fucking Doom.

Sue's voice cut through the silence. "I don't understand how they can be so cruel."

Her and me both.

"I'm sorry, RJ. I should never have said anything. The pain meds they have me on are like a truth serum."

"No. You should have. At least now I know what I'm up against."

"Don't let them get you down. I can tell just by talking to you that you're better than that family of yours."

"I don't know about that."

"You're special, RJ. You were spared when a whole lot of others weren't. Did you know that the building collapsed less than an hour after you were pulled out?"

The shock of her words rendered me speechless.

"You were the last one to get out alive. If you ask me, you've got an angel on your shoulder."

No. I didn't have an angel on my shoulder. I had Dani Malone.

I owed my life to her. Unlike my father, Dani hadn't taken a 'wait and see' approach to my survival. She'd come back for me when no one else did. She'd cut me free, wrapping her arm around my waist and helping me hobble toward the exit. And then, when I collapsed to the ground, Dani had somehow gotten me to the exit. That was devotion. That was family. That was the woman I wanted to create a whole new life with.

I remembered the promise I'd made to myself in the garage just before I took the knife to my ankle: no more playing the victim. I'd get through this and I'd come out stronger on the other side. Suddenly those extra two inches of leg lost didn't matter anymore. It would be a rough road ahead, but nothing I couldn't handle. My family might not think so, but I'd proved my worth to myself, and nothing they said or did from this point forward would ever change that.

If they wanted war, then I'd give them war.

"Are you all right?" Sue asked. "Now I feel bad."

"Don't. You've given me the clarity I needed."

"You know... I have a big, loving family. We always have room for one more."

I smiled at Sue's offer. A stranger was offering me refuge, something my own family refused to give. And that only solidified my resolve. Oh, yeah—my next of kin were going down.

"I might just take you up on that, Sue."

———

I was somewhat disappointed that my own personal secretary hadn't warned me about the trip down to radiology to get a CT scan of my lungs. Nor did she give me a heads up on the phlebotomist, who took some of that precious borrowed blood that had been pumped back into my veins. By the time I returned to my curtain room, I was eager to get any new intel from my neighbor.

"You awake?" I asked.

There was no response. I tried again. "Sue?"

Julio entered the room. "She's gone."

The blood drained from my face. I did not have a good track record with my elderly best friends lately. "She died?"

"No. She was moved to a room."

"Oh." I actually gripped my chest in relief. "Jesus. You scared me. Did she leave anything for me?"

"Why would she leave anything for you?"

Good question. What exactly could she leave me, other than a parting medical diagnosis or another backstabbing story about my shitty family?

"No reason," I said. "Hey, what's her last name?"

"I can't give you that information. It's patient..."

"Confidentiality... Yeah, I know."

Where was that discretion when the bat-eared next-door neighbor was getting her material for a tell-all exposé? Not that I was upset our paths had crossed. Like Albert, I was convinced Sue had been dropped into my life for a reason. It was like having two geriatric angels to guide me through my very own whacked-out version of *It's A Wonderful Life*.

"I tell you what," Julio said in the cheeky way of a dude with some game. "If I see her, I'll tell her to call you."

I laughed. "You do that."

Is he here?

I could hear the shrieking bouncing off the sterile ICU walls. It was my mother and she sounded pissed.

Julio's brows rose. He glanced at me, looking terrified.

I gave him a curt nod. "Welcome to my world, dude."

21

RJ: MOMMY DEAREST

Sometimes the best approach was to go in full throttle. Take the opposition by surprise. So when my mother flung the white curtain aside like some C-list actress, I was ready to pounce.

"Oh, thank goodness," she said, playing the doting mother role. "They said you were awake."

She was met by my blank stare. "What did you do to Dani?"

My mother blinked. "Dani? I don't know any Dani."

"Sure you do. She'd be the one all up in your face demanding to see me."

Her expression shifted and hardened.

"Where is she?"

"This is an ICU, RJ. Only family is allowed."

"Says who?"

"The hospital."

"Then let me speak to someone in charge. If they knew what she's done for me, they'll let her in."

Mom was silent.

"Fine. I'll ask Julio to contact management for me."

"They won't come."

"I'm a freakin' celebrity, Mom. Trust me, they'll come."

My mother looked down at her phone, appearing almost bored with my boastful declaration. "Maybe they would come if you called the shots, but you don't, so they won't."

"What are you talking about? If I don't call the shots, who does?"

"Remember way back when you were eighteen years old and heading off on your first *AnyDayNow* tour? The band handlers wanted all of you to assign someone medical power of attorney, just in case something were to happen on the road like a bus accident or something. Do you remember who you granted that power to?"

"No. But I'm assuming by that greedy look on you face that it was you."

"That's right."

"So what? I'm an adult now."

"Eighteen is an adult, RJ. You signed that legally binding document as an adult and never rescinded it. I still have medical power of attorney, and I say Dani can't come in to see you. Period."

My eyes narrowed in on her. "You really want to play this game with me?"

"It's no game. I'm looking out for your best interest, and Dani is not it."

"And you are? Renato is? Luis and Manny are?"

"That's right, RJ. We're your family. She's not."

"Uh-huh. Tell me... where are they?"

I saw the slightest flinch in her poker face. "They're on their way."

"It's been three days. What's the holdup? From what the doc said, it was touch and go there for a while. Weren't they worried I'd be dead before they could get here?"

"What exactly are you asking me?"

"You know exactly what I'm asking. Why couldn't my father and brothers be bothered to come when I was teetering on the edge? I mean, I do finance their existence, so it would seem to their benefit to make an appearance... unless, of course, they were waiting for me to die."

"Stop being an arrogant jerk. They work, and can't just drop everything last minute to rush to your side."

"They don't work for pay!"

She glared at me. "Is it such a burden for you to provide for your family when you have millions to spare? How selfish are you?"

"That house you live in? I pay for it. That car you drive? Came from me. Hell, even your haircut came from my bankroll, so don't you dare talk to me about being selfish."

"And you always make us feel guilty, don't you, RJ?"

"Maybe if you'd treated me like a human being growing up, I wouldn't feel it was such a burden to support people who hate me."

"We don't hate you."

"Really? How stupid do you think I am? Get out!"

She stood and stomped out of the room.

I called to her retreating frame. "And I want Dani in here by the end of the hour."

Dani never showed, and now my mother and I were beyond rational conversation. We'd each picked our side, and it was all-out war. Even the doctors got involved, pleading with her to keep from agitating me in my fragile state, but it was no use. Just seeing her face was enough to raise my blood pressure. Had she conceded defeat, maybe; but since our argument, she'd doubled down on her authority, going so far as forbidding me from even accessing a phone to call a lawyer who could whip me up a new contract and get me out of this mess. I was literally a prisoner of my own stupidity. How could I not have foreseen a massive earthquake crushing me to an inch of my life the day I'd signed that contract as an eighteen-year-old idiot?

I needed help—someone who'd come to my rescue, like Bodhi or Hunter. Or a goddamn exorcist. Actually, never mind. None of those were powerful enough to take on Heather. What I really needed was someone like Tucker Beckett—who wasn't actually Tucker Beckett. Because I hated that dude. Maybe I should rehire Roland Akers. Yeah, Roland. Now that guy was awesome; would do anything I asked. Although maybe that was the problem, and partially why I'd ended up at the apartment in the first place. I needed someone to rein me in—tell me to slow down and confront me when I was wrong. That was not Roland Akers. As a Hollywood player, sure, he was one of the best, but he wasn't right for this particular challenge. No way could Roland take on my mother and live to talk about it.

No, I needed a warrior, someone who'd come in with weapons raised, prepared to defend me with his life. Someone who could tie up every loose end, get me walking again, and maybe even get me back up on the stage where I'd always belonged.

I shook my head.

"God dammit," I grumbled to myself. There was only one person I knew capable of such wizardry.

Tucker Fucking Beckett.

———

Julio and I exchanged eye rolls.

Heather was at it again. Making a giant scene. Pitching a fit.

It was her third one in under an hour, impressive even by her standards.

"He's going to be hospitalized for at least another week. Under no circumstances are you putting him in there!"

I wanted to remind her that we were in the ICU and that people were literally dying around her, but I couldn't get a word in edgewise.

"We want the VIP room."

"Ma'am, it's occupied right now," the meeker-by-the-minute hospital coordinator tried to explain. "We can't just kick the woman out."

"Is she Taylor Swift? Beyoncé? Because those are the only two VIPs that have a higher status than my RJ! I demand to speak to your superior!"

I cringed, wanting to crawl under the covers and be reborn again, to someone with the slightest bit of humility and grace. I honestly didn't know what she thought was going to happen here. She'd tied my hands, made me a prisoner in her power-hungry game, but she had to realize I'd eventually heal, get out of this hospital, and make her fucking pay.

"Stop it!" I shouted. "Just shut up. No one cares what you have to say. They just want to get rid of you."

You could hear a pin drop. Actually, that wasn't true. You could also hear the faintest spattering of murmurs from the hospital staff who'd been dealing with her tantrums for four days now, all too afraid to stand up to her. I was actually disappointed I didn't get a round of applause.

I turned my head to address the hospital coordinator. "What's your name?"

"Laura."

"Laura, any room is fine as long as it has a padlock to keep that woman out."

Laura looked to my mother for confirmation.

"Don't look at her, Laura," I demanded. "Listen to me. I'm being held hostage by this medical power of attorney bullshit that I signed when I was eighteen and which I no longer authorize. I want an attorney... and an executioner... ASAP."

"Stop being dramatic, RJ," my mother scoffed. "Everything I'm doing is for you."

"Oh, I doubt that very much."

My mother addressed Laura in a quieter, more conciliatory tone. "Just get him the finest room you have available, and as soon as the VIP room comes up, then you can move him."

"Actually, Laura. I'd prefer the shittiest room possible. Maybe then she won't visit."

Poor Laura, standing there in the middle of our feud with no conceivable idea how to end it or even if she wanted to. I had to assume she was deriving at least some satisfaction in watching my mother squirm.

"Okay, well. I can see there is some discrepancy here, so..."

"There's no discrepancy," I said. "I'm an adult. I pay my own bills. Hell, I pay *her* bills. I demand full control over all medical decisions pertaining to me, and if someone can't make that happen, pronto, I'll be forced to get on social media and let my followers know that I'm being Britney Spearsed over here."

22

DANI: THE COMMAND CENTER

OKAY, I WASN'T PROUD OF WHAT I WAS DOING. I WAS A TWENTY-six-year-old woman. I'd outgrown celebrity stalking eight years ago. But I just kept telling myself it was for a good cause. Actually, it was for the best cause—RJ.

Blacklisted after my run-in with Heather, I couldn't even get past the front doors of the hospital. It was like they had a poster with my face on it right inside with a list of my crimes. Of course, whatever she'd told them were all lies, but the security guards didn't know that. RJ didn't, either. And if he believed even one of them...

So I'd resorted to this, fan-girling in front of Bodhi Beckett's mansion. He was RJ's best friend; surely he'd be able to deliver a message to him. All I had to do was get him to stop his car, and then, armed with RJ's cryptic clues, somehow get Bodhi on my side. That was the plan, anyway. But I was on day two of my creepy vigil, and while vehicles had come and gone through the giant security gates, none had Bodhi in them, and none had stopped.

A car pulled up and I quickly rose from the curb, holding up my cardboard sign. *Please be Bodhi*, I thought, my face falling when I saw the familiar face.

"Hey, Stalker. Sorry to be such a letdown," Simone said, passing me a coffee drink through the window. "Thought you'd like this."

"Is this with sugar-free vanilla and extra foam?"

"Of course."

"And half a bag of sweet and low?"

"Do I look like a loser?"

"No, you do not. That wouldn't happen to be my favorite bacon gouda sandwich on your passenger seat, would it?"

She picked it up and dangled it in front of me. "Can't be operating on an empty stomach if you really want to creep out the guy."

"Ah, I take back everything I ever said about you and your tiny gavel."

Simone rolled her eyes. "Wish I could stay, but I have a job... and dignity."

Setting my goodies aside, I made a finger heart and blew a kiss through it as she drove away.

I wasn't sure what I would've done without my LSC siblings. They'd come in clutch for me in the days after the earthquake, providing food, shelter, and boxes and boxes of supplies that filled up Cleo's living room. If she regretted opening her doors to me, she didn't show it. No one did. They'd been there for me when I'd come out of the emergency room and again when I'd called them crying after Heather cast me from the hospital. Ross and Charlie even helped me make my sign. Although they did take creative license by making an alternate sign for me to use, which read, *Love me, Bodhi. I'm so desperate.*

It was actually the LSC support that kept me from leaving town to go stay with my mother. And it had been a surprisingly tough decision. Once my mother had finally been able to find a route around the destruction, she'd arrived at my side with a blueprint of plans. First thing on the agenda was getting me home, and man, had she ever painted a beautiful picture of what life would be like if I succumbed to her tender loving care. It would be all chicken noodle soup and pedicures and naps in the sun. I'd never seen my mother so concerned or so loving. It made me wonder how much of our mother-daughter struggles had been made up in my mind. That was until she took one look at my makeup-free face and said, 'Oh, honey, we need to do something about that.'

Yep, that yanked me back from my make-believe world and made me decide to stay put in LA and fight for my right to see RJ. Heather thought she'd won, but had she known anything about me, she'd realize I didn't take shit from members of her bloodline. I would stop at nothing to disrupt her reign.

An hour had passed since Simone rolled away. My drink was gone, and my butt was going numb on the curb. I had just stood up to stretch my legs when a car came down the road and turned into the long driveway. The same car had exited the gate thirty minutes before, and the woman behind the wheel hadn't even glanced my way. Chances that she'd see me now and read my sign were probably slim to none, but I had to try, because this woman was my quickest path to Bodhi. She was his newly wedded wife.

I held up my sign and called out to her, "Please—'m a friend of RJ's."

The car drove right on by. My heart sank. This was useless; such a waste of time. But then, to my utter surprise, the car stopped abruptly and rolled back in reverse. The window slid down.

"Let me see your sign," she said.

I held it up. It read, *I'm RJ's gale force wind.*

"Gale force wind? Who told you that?"

"RJ."

Breeze scanned the length of me before asking, "Are you her?"

By *her*, I assumed she meant the woman from the news. I'd been outed two days earlier, my name out there for the picking. But that was also the day I'd begun stalking Bodhi, so I'd managed to avoid the media onslaught simply because no one seemed to be able to find me out in front of a pop star's house.

"Yes, I'm Dani. RJ told me to tell Bodhi I was his gale force wind. I have no idea what it means, but he said Bodhi would know."

The woman slowly nodded, seemingly stunned by my revelation. "I'm Bodhi's breeze."

We stared at one another. Breeze? I'd known that was her name, from my online research, but I'd never pieced together the significance of it until now. Was RJ trying to tell Bodhi that I was his Breeze?

She leaned over and opened her door. "Get in."

After I slipped into the passenger seat, she reached her hand out. "Nice to finally meet you."

"Nice to meet you too. I'm so sorry I had to stalk around outside your house, but I didn't know what else to do. Heather booted me from the hospital and threatened to end me after I asked to see RJ."

"Ah, yes. *Heather.*" She spoke the name like it left a particularly sour taste in her mouth. "Don't take it personally. She's done the same to all of us."

"How is that possible? Is he so sick that he can't speak for himself?"

"It's not that. From what we know, he's steadily improving, but..." Breeze went on to explain how Heather had wrangled control of RJ's life by way of a piece of paper he'd signed years ago.

"So, what do we do?" I asked, already inserting myself in the fight.

"Bodhi's father, Tucker, is working on liberating him as we speak. Heather isn't afraid of too many people, but Tucker... he's one of them."

I drew in a deep, comforting breath, relieved to finally be in like company with people who seemed to care about RJ as much as I did.

Breeze pulled up to the house and hopped out of the car. Still a bit stunned by what was happening, I remained seated.

She popped her head in. "You coming?"

"I... am I invited?"

"Any type of wind is welcome in our house, Dani. Oh, and bring the sign."

Heaving two big bags of KFC from her trunk, we climbed the stairs in front of her mansion, and she opened the door.

"After you," she said. I stepped into the foyer of the most beautiful house I'd ever seen. My eyes widened at the wonder of it all. Was this how RJ lived when he wasn't residing in squalor next door to me?

"Jesus," I muttered.

"I know." Breeze smiled. "That was my first thought too. In there."

I'd only known her for a matter of minutes, and I was already charmed. There wasn't an ounce of pretension in her. She felt like a kindred spirit. I followed after her until we came into an expansive kitchen. Gathered around a dining table was a group of guys, and not just any guys. These were the other members of *AnyDayNow*, and suddenly I didn't feel worthy of being included in RJ's inner circle.

Breeze opened her arms wide. "Welcome to the Save RJ Contreras Command Center."

The band members all looked up from their plotting to observe me.

"Guys. This is Dani."

"Hey," my boy-bander crush Hunter Roy said. "You're the girl hanging around outside with the sign."

He noticed me. Was it wrong to squeal?

"The sign?" Bodhi questioned, locking eyes on Breeze. Clearly he hadn't left the house in two days, or he would've known about the stalker outside his gate.

Breeze poked me in the side. "Show him the sign."

I held it up and watched as his face morphed from one of confusion to surprise.

"Gale force wind?" boy-bander number three, Shawn Barber, scratched his head. "What am I missing here?"

Bodhi ignored Shawn's question. He was now focused solely on me. "Where did you hear that from, Dani?"

"From RJ. In the parking garage...just before he thought he was going to die."

Breeze helped clarify. "RJ sent her to you to deliver this message. Bodhi, she's Dani Malone, from the news."

That seemed to do the trick. Bodhi crossed the room, stopping right in front of me, and I could feel my cheeks heat up. It's not every day you come face-to-face with Bodhi Beckett. He was almost as good-looking as a freshly shaved RJ Contreras.

"Wait—you're the one who saved him?" Dane Makati, boy-bander number four, spoke up. "The mystery girl?"

I was still trying to wrap my brain around the idea that people knew who I was, even famous people like Bodhi and Hunter and Shawn and Dane. "I was with RJ in the earthquake, yes."

"And he called you his gale force wind?"

"*Which is?*" Shawn tried for clarity again.

This time I ignored Shawn.

"No. He told me to tell *you* that I was his gale force wind. But he didn't tell me what it meant."

"Vague as shit, if you ask me," Shawn grumbled. "Am I the only one who doesn't know what the fuck is going on?"

Shawn wasn't even a blip on Bodhi's radar. He was singularly focused on me.

"Did he say anything else?"

"He said something about looking inside the curtain rods."

The other band members seemed baffled by the cryptic message, but Bodhi did not. Something shifted in his eyes as he narrowed in on me. He understood exactly what RJ had been trying to convey.

"Curtain rods?" Shawn whined. "Is everyone speaking in tongues?"

"Jesus Christ. Would someone please slap a gag on Shawn?"

"You think I'm going to stop." Shawn was ornery in his reply. "But I'm going to keep asking until I get answers."

"Fine," Bodhi huffed. "RJ used to joke about how he was going to keep an emergency stash of money in the curtain rods —so his family couldn't find it. Understand now?"

Shawn thought for a second before shaking his head. "Nope. I still don't understand what that has to do with Dani."

"Think," Bodhi replied, his eyes on me while he addressed Shawn. "RJ wanted his emergency money to go to Dani—his girl. His gale force wind. Get it now?"

Bodhi's explanation might have been directed to Shawn, but it hit me squarely in the heart. In those final moments, when all hope was lost, RJ's last thoughts were of taking care of me. His girl. His gale force wind. Yes, I belonged here in his inner circle.

And as I took a spot at the table, Shawn smirked and grabbed some keys off the counter. "Uh, guys? Don't wait up. I'm going to RJ's house."

23

RJ: ON THE DOTTED LINE

WHILE WAITING TO BE TRANSFERRED TO A PRIVATE ROOM LATER IN the day, I borrowed Julio's phone after my mother had slipped out of my curtain room to maybe ruin someone else's day for a change. Julio hadn't really wanted to hand it over, fearing Heather's wrath, but after I explained the benefits of being friends with me, he relented.

I dialed up Bodhi. There was no answer. Had he seen my name popping up on his phone, I had no doubt he'd have been more responsive, but as it was, he probably assumed the incoming call from an unknown number was an extended warranty company giving him his 'very last' warning.

The voicemail kicked in, and with my voice barely more than a whisper, I left a message. "Dude, it's RJ. I need Tucker, and no I haven't taken a blow to the head."

I went on to describe the situation to him before hanging up and handing the phone back to Julio.

"Thanks, man. I owe you one."

We exchanged a handshake.

"You owe me two," he winked, no doubt referring to the

'groupies backstage experience' I'd offered him in order to gain access to his phone.

"Hey, I can only get you in." I laughed. "The rest is all up to you, and let's be honest, it's going to be an uphill battle."

Julio took no offense, laughing at the diss.

Still gripping his hand, I pulled him in close so as not to get him in trouble. "If Bodhi Beckett calls you back, you have my permission to tell him what room I'm in."

His eyes widened. "Bodhi Beckett is going to call my phone?"

"He will if he checks his messages."

Julio stared down at his phone as if it had suddenly turned to gold. "Bodhi. Wow. Okay, then. That's exciting and unexpected."

"What the hell, Julio," I said. "I'm as famous as he is."

"I know, but I've been changing your catheter for a few days. You've lost your shine."

The distant sound of my mother's voice caught our attention.

Julio peeked through the opening in the curtains. "She's baacckk."

"Watch it, Julio, that's my mother you're talking about."

We both laughed.

Julio returned to my side, dropping his voice. "Oh, and if I don't see you again, her name is Susan Peri."

It took me a second to connect the dots. Julio was referring to none other than Sue, my favorite Sudoku-playing, senior citizen informant.

———

The problem with residing in the ICU for long periods of time, aside from the obvious health perils, was that they adhered to a strict 'close family only' visitors rule. Because it was against policy to allow outsiders in, the staff were more inclined to side with my mother when it came to Dani. But now that I'd been transferred into a private room and visitors were allowed, I thought the isolation would finally end. I was wrong. Even after providing my new nurse with a list of the people I wanted to see, no one came. *No one.* Not Dani. Not Bodhi. Not Tucker. Not even one of my so-called 'blood' brothers.

Still without a cell phone, I used the bedside one to call Bodhi again, and as with every other time I'd tried to call today, it just rang and rang. Cursing, I returned the phone to the receiver and lay back in my bed. Where was everyone? Why weren't they answering? With no connection to the outside world, it felt like I was trapped all over again, waiting to die. At least now I had morphine to numb the pain of their betrayal.

Renato and my brothers showed up toward the end of visiting hours on my first day in the private room. Luis was wearing a Magic Mountain Six Flags t-shirt, so I had to assume they'd taken a detour to the amusement park before finally making their way to the hospital—five days late.

My mother fussed over me when they arrived, playing the dutiful mother by smoothing down my wild, unruly hair.

"Doesn't he look wonderful?" she said.

So ridiculously doting was she, I half expected her to lick her finger and wipe a smudge of dirt from my face.

"Dude, you're rockin' the girly hair," Luis said, tousling my overgrown tresses.

I knocked his hand away. "And you're rockin' the cotton candy gut."

His smile faded. If he thought he could walk all over me in my weakened state, he was dead wrong. I'd never been one to back down from a duel, and it was more so now that I knew he'd chosen Batman the Ride over me.

"Fuckin' dick," he mumbled, pulling his phone out and leaning against the window, ignoring me.

Renato walked up and slapped me on the shoulder in greet-ing. "You had us all worried there, kid."

Uh-huh, sure I did. Worried I would live and he'd have to continue kissing my ass so he could be home during the days to watch Judge Judy.

"Renato," my mother tsked. "Don't jostle him. He's got a punctured lung."

"Did I slap him on the chest, Heather? No, I don't think I did. Last time I checked, shoulders weren't connected to lungs, so I think we're good. Besides, RJ's tough. Always has been, right, bud?"

Bud? Since when had he assigned me a nickname?

"Anyway." Renato slapped me again on the shoulder. "Happy to see you up and breathing on your own."

"He still has the oxygen for a few more days. He just had a CT scan of his chest, and the lungs look better," mom said in a strange educational voice, like she was explaining a rotary phone to minors.

That was when everyone began discussing my health over the top of me. I didn't bother joining in because I didn't appear to be needed. Manny settled into the chair at the end of the bed, his eyes trained on my bandaged leg like he wanted to say something but didn't have the guts. That was the sort of relationship we had. He'd always been a follower; Luis's shadow. Growing up, we'd hung out and had fun, but as soon as Luis came around, he'd fall right back in line like the rest of them. I'd come to despise him most because I knew he had a good heart, yet Manny openly denied it for fear of joining me at the tray table for dinner.

Chewing on his nails, his eyes traveled the length of my body until they unexpectedly met mine. His widened before swiftly looking away.

"Just say it," I challenged, already feeling defensive after what Sue had revealed.

"No, I..." He dragged his eyes back to mine but there was something different in them—genuine concern. "Are you going to be able to walk again?"

I wasn't sure why his question hit me like it did. It wasn't so much what he asked... but how he asked it. Manny just wanted to know if I'd be okay.

"Yeah, I'll walk again."

"How long do they think it will take?"

That was a good question, and one I'd been asking of the long line of medical personnel that came to my bedside near daily to prepare me for what was to come. And the main take-away was that there was no quick fix on my road to recovery; no strapping on a new foot and going on my way. There would be wound healing and leg shaping and prosthetic fitting and physical therapy.

And if Heather got her way, I'd be undergoing weekly sessions with the exceedingly calm psychotherapist, who'd described in detail the emotional aspects of losing a limb. I nodded, pretending to care but, truthfully, I was relieved it was gone. It had had to go so I could live—so Dani could live. Maybe down the road I'd feel its loss, but right now all I cared about was being alive. So, I played along with the charade knowing that once I got control of my medical decisions, Heather and the psychotherapist would be the first ones gone.

"Depends on how fast my wound heals. Usually young, healthy people who lose limbs in accidents heal faster."

"Accident?" Luis scoffed. "You cut it off yourself."

"Because it was trapped between two concrete slabs, asshole!" Manny blasted our brother. The two glared at each other, making me wonder what was happening behind the scenes, a place I'd never been allowed. "You think you have the balls to do what RJ did? I don't think so."

"I never would've been living in that piece of shit building in the first place. He's got millions of dollars. Why the hell would he be hiding out there anyway?"

"Maybe because you're squatting in my house."

The room fell silent. Shards of fear could be seen on every face that wasn't mine. If I pulled the plug, they'd have nothing. Not that Luis seemed to care in the heat of the moment.

"I'm so sick of you always making us feel bad. You're just so much better than the rest of us, aren't you?"

"He *is* better than us," Manny exploded.

"Speak for yourself, lapdog! You just don't wanna get cut off —admit it."

"Shut up!" Manny rose from his chair and rushed Luis. "I've had enough of your shit."

"That's enough," Mom said through gritted teeth. "People are going to hear."

But no one was listening to Heather. Contentious words were exchanged, followed by fists and a disgruntled Renato stepping in to referee. It was around that point that security was called. I watched as the male members of my family were escorted out, with my mother hot on their heels, calling for someone's head.

"That went well," I said to no one.

A nurse rushed in, cursing my family under her breath for making her job harder. I lay back on my pillow and closed my eyes, trying to settle my racing heart. I thought of Albert and his dying words. He'd been scared but at peace. How was I ever going to achieve such solace at the end, with all this chaos in my life? The answer, I knew, was I couldn't. Not in its current state of disarray. I had to purge myself of what was weighing me down, and there was no better time to cut the strings than now. I'd give them the house and the cars and the all shiny things that went with the life I'd financed for them for the last six years, but that was where it would have to end. It had taken me awhile to come to the realization, but now I finally understood—no matter how enticing it seemed, love could not be bought.

———

I awoke to a commotion just outside my door. For a moment I was hopeful it was someone else's drama, but then I heard my mother's voice and knew it was mine, yet again.

"You can't do that!" she insisted.

Oh, god. I hit my call button. I'd need an extra helping of pain killer to get me through this latest performance.

Then came a familiar voice from out in the hall. "It's already done."

I shot up in bed, my ribs howling in protest. But the pain was welcome because, for the first time in days, there was an end in sight. I'd been saved. Tucker Beckett was in the house!

"I have a signed contract," Mom said. "I demand you force this man to leave. And take the rest of his posse with him."

"Ma'am, you need to keep your voice down. There are sick patients in this ward."

"Yes, Heather, please keep it down," Tucker replied, in that smug tone that always made me want to punch him in the face. But not today. Tucker could be as condescending as he wanted to be because he was here to end the insanity.

"No!" my mother said as the door rattled. I pictured her grabbing whoever was trying to enter. "You are not allowed in."

"Mrs. Contreras, we're RJ's legal counsel. You need to step aside."

Lawyers, even? Damn, Sue would've loved this episode of my soap opera life.

A man and woman in matching navy blue suits entered my room.

"RJ," the woman said, smiling as she approached. "I hear you called."

"I did. What took you so long?"

"Oh, no, you don't," my mother said, stomping her way in and stepping between them and me. I might have been touched by her devotion had it not been so self-serving.

The lawyer pointed in her direction. "That's what took me so long."

"RJ is not well enough to make decisions at this time. I demand you leave right now." But her words were hollow. She'd been defeated, and she knew it. All she was doing now was holding onto the last little bit of hope.

The woman in the suit ignored her as she addressed me. "I'm Mariyah George, and this is my partner Barry. We work for your former manager, Tucker Beckett. He's informed us that you'd like to dissolve your current Advanced Directive and relinquish Heather Contreras as your designated decision maker in medical matters. Is that correct?"

"Yes. That's correct."

"RJ, listen to me. You don't understand. I'm doing this for your health. For your future. Once they release you, I'm going to bring you home to Idaho and nurse you back to health. Why do you always have to be so stubborn? You just fight, fight, fight. It's exhausting. I'm doing everything I can to hold on. I know it's a big ask, but if you just give us a chance, we can be a family again."

She could not be serious. *Now?* She wanted to be a family *now?* "You're about two decades too late, but nice try there, Heather."

"Don't call me that!"

"Why? It's your name."

Her eyes filled with tears. "I'm your mom."

"That title needs to be earned."

She winced. "Listen, I recognize that you were treated poorly at times. I own that. And I know you probably don't believe me when I say I'm sorry."

"See, that's the thing. You haven't said it. You've never apologized."

"I'm sorry, okay? I was a bad mother. Is that what you want to hear? I'm sorry. I failed you, but there are things you don't know. Things even Renato doesn't know."

Now she had my full attention. "Then tell me."

She shrank back. "I can't."

"You're asking me to go home with you when you can't even tell me the truth? That's rich," I said, angry I'd even given her the opportunity to explain herself. "Give me the contract."

Mariyah set it down on the tray and handed me a pen. She pointed to the line I would need to sign to sever ties with this woman forever.

"Go ahead," my mother said, slumping against the wall. "Sign it. But please don't cut me out of your life. Please."

Setting the pen back down, I stared up at her. "Why? Why do you even care? Is this about the money? The house? The gym membership? What is it? I don't understand."

"It not about any of that. It's about you and me."

Now I knew she was manipulating me. "There is no you and me. There never was."

Picking the pen back up, I signed my name.

Mom's lip quivered, and she whispered, "He didn't want me."

"What?"

This time she said it louder. "He didn't want me."

"Who?"

"Dalton."

"Who's Dalton?"

"Your real father. He didn't want me."

"You knew him?" Anger exploded in me. "You knew who he was this whole time?"

Tears rolled down her cheeks. "I lied about everything, RJ. Your father wasn't some random traveling musician. I did know him. Since elementary school. I had such a crush on him from the time I was little. But he was beautiful and popular and everyone loved him. Like you. And I was scrawny and poor and wore dirty clothes to school. I thought he would save me. My prince. For years I tried to get him to notice me. And finally, one time he did. Took my virginity in my friend's parents' bed at a party when we were sixteen. He never talked to me again.

"Fast forward ten years. I saw a flyer with his picture on it and knew he'd be at the bar performing that night. When I went up to talk to him after the show, he had no idea who I was. But one thing led to another, and... well, you know that part of the story. I told him I was protected, but I wasn't. Anyway, I contacted him after becoming pregnant. In my warped mind, I thought he'd be happy. That he'd finally want me. I had my bags packed and everything. I was all set to leave Renato and the boys and ride off into the sunset. You. Me. Dalton. One little happy family."

"But he didn't want you..." I finished the unhappy tale for her. "Or me."

"No. He didn't. Dalton accused me of trying to trap him. And he was right. I thought he'd finally *see* me, you know? But he didn't. He sent some money and demanded I get an abortion. And I was going to do it, too, but Renato figured out I was pregnant, and he was so excited. I thought maybe it would all work out. I could pass you off as his and have a lasting reminder of Dalton to love and cherish forever."

"Sounds awesome, Mom, but something went tragically

wrong, because I don't ever recall any love or cherishing going on."

"Because Renato never accepted you. And because he didn't, your brothers didn't. I could either stand by your side outside of the circle... or reject you and be loved."

Her words. Did she not realize how much they stung? What she'd done was the equivalent of dumping a box of unwanted kittens on the side of the road. She'd forced me to fend for myself, and for what?

"We could've made our own circle, you and me."

"Yes." She choked up. "I know."

My mother reached out to me, sliding her fingers over my face. I jerked away. "Don't."

"I'm sorry. I'm so sorry, RJ. I was selfish and bitter. I hated your father for what he'd done to me. And you... you looked and acted so much like him. Strong. Beautiful. Talented. You've always stood out in a crowd. Everything that attracted me to Dalton in the first place—that was you. But, like him, you also have that same arrogance. That air of being better than everyone else. Dalton made me feel small and insignificant. Just like you've always done."

There it was again. The accusation that I thought I was better than them. If that was true, it was only because they'd forced me to compete, Hunger Games style, for their attention. I had to be the best—for my survival.

"*I* make *you* feel small?" I gaped. "Are you hearing yourself? I was a kid! I would've done anything to be accepted by you and the others... to be part of your tribe. Anything. *You* pushed *me* away, not the other way around. And not only that, you turned Luis and Manny against me. Ruined any chance of us ever being real brothers."

"Your brothers don't hate you. They're intimidated by you. Even Renato. I think he always knew you were destined for greatness. It's just... people like you, RJ, people like your father... you can never understand what it's like to always need polishing."

I shook my head, pissed. She was putting this whole thing on me. A quick glance at our lawyer audience told me they thought the same thing. Both of them stood glaring at my mother.

"I know it sounds like I'm blaming you," Mom said, breaking the silence. "But I'm not. I know this is all on me. I did this. I'm just trying to get you to see."

"See what?" I exploded. "All I see is that you condemned me for the sins of my father. You know how you could have mitigated that—made sure I didn't turn out like him? You could've raised me with humility and love. You could've taught me values and respect. You could've been my *mother*."

"I know. I know." Again she reached for me. Again I shunned her. "I'm so sorry for all the hurt I've caused you. I truly am. When you were feared dead, I was devastated. I guess I always thought I'd have time to make it up to you. And then when they pulled you out alive, I realized I'd been given a second chance. But I knew you wouldn't allow me to nurse you back to health, so I used the medical directive to try and make it up to you."

"Make it up to me? You took the hospital to its knees. You blocked my friends from coming to see me. *And* you insulted Beyoncé. How could you ever think any of this would go your way?"

Her shoulders slumped. "I don't know. Sometimes I don't think. Look. I'll leave. Give you the space you obviously need. But please don't cut me out of your life. Please, RJ. I'll do anything."

"Why? Why do you care now?"

"Losing you..."

"No. Why? Tell me the truth. If I lived in your town and was a gas station attendant or a grocery clerk, would you be begging for my forgiveness? Be honest, Mom. If I wasn't famous, would you even be here right now?"

Our eyes met, and in that moment, we both knew she wouldn't. There was nothing left to salvage between us. Maybe someday I'd have a family, but it wouldn't be this one.

"Just go."

"RJ..."

"I'll pay off the house and give you a one-time severance payment. But I'm not supporting you anymore. It's time the four of you got jobs."

She dropped her head, resigned.

"And I swear to god, if you've screwed anything up with Dani..."

"I haven't. That woman is like a boomerang. You fling her away and she just comes right on back. There's no getting rid of her."

The moment was so tense, but I nearly burst out laughing. Boomerang. Yep, that was Dani.

"I'll let myself out," she said, already walking toward the door.

"Before you go..."

She didn't let me finish. "His name is Dalton Krause."

"Does he know who I am?"

Her step faltered. "Yes. I sent an email to his business after you hit it big in *AnyDayNow*."

"And?"

"And what, RJ?" she asked, pivoting to face me.

"What does he think?"

"You tell me. Have you heard from him?"

"No."

"Then that's your answer," she sighed. "He doesn't care, RJ. He never has."

Fresh pain swept through me, knowing I was zero for two in the parenthood trap. I offered up a curt nod. "You can go now."

Her head drooping, my mother turned her back to me and opened the door. "For what it's worth, RJ, I'm sorry."

"For what it's worth, Heather, I would've loved you."

24

DANI: SOME LIKE IT ROUGH

TALK ABOUT A REVERSAL IN FORTUNE. AFTER DAYS OF TRYING TO work my way back into the hospital, I was now entering through the electronic doors with my head held high and in the company of some very powerful allies. Heads turned, mouths dropped open, and cell phones were extracted from pockets as our formidable parade of boy-banders came strolling in with all the confidence in the world.

Lead by our commander in chief, Tucker Beckett, the rest of us fell in line, walking two-by-two like animals preparing to board the Ark. Just behind the mighty Hollywood manager was a pair of crisp-suited lawyers. Following them were the *AnyDayNow* boys, Bodhi and Hunter, and then behind them, Shawn and Dane. And bringing up the rear, linked arm and arm and propelled by our very own tailwind, were Breeze and me.

You know when you meet that one person who just gets you? Well, that was Breeze. In the few hours it took to draw up the documents needed for the rescue effort, I'd already gone shopping in her closet; gotten a haircut, highlight, and blow-dry from my new hairstylist best friend; and watched half of the first episode of *Gilmore Girls* before Bodhi popped his head in and informed us that Operation Save RJ was a go.

And now here I was, walking down a long corridor, preparing to see RJ for the first time since the parking garage.

Breeze leaned into me. "You excited?"

"Yes," I replied. "But the kind of excited where I'm more terrified than excited."

"Ah. Like amusement park ride excited?"

"Uh-huh, but like that feeling you get after the ride has been closed for a while due to someone falling out of their harness, dangling upside down, and screaming for their life. That kind of amusement park ride excited."

"Very specific," she mused. "Thank you for clarifying your level of excitement. I can see why RJ likes you."

"But does he? His infatuation could be purely disaster-related."

"Or he can see in you what I see in you. Girl, I'd date you."

"Oh, my god." I squeezed her arm tighter. "I'd date you too."

"We'd be so good together," she agreed. "If only we didn't have the earth's most desirable guys getting in the way."

"Yes," I sighed. "If only."

We giggled, but insecurities piled on top of me faster than I could flick them off. *Earth's most desirable guys.* Holy freakin' shit. What was I thinking? I couldn't hold on to RJ the pop star. I couldn't even hold onto Jeremy the accountant.

"Dani," Breeze said, sensing my anxiety levels rising. "Breathe."

"I can't," I replied, slowly unraveling. "I did a thing."

"You did a thing? What did you do?"

"I googled the words *RJ* and *girlfriend*."

"Uh-oh," she gasped. "Don't do that."

"I already did," I snipped. "And now I can't take it back. Guess what? I'm not his type."

"What is his type?"

"Not five-foot-two elementary school teachers."

Breeze stopped and grasped my face. "Who cares if he dated gorgeous models and actresses? They didn't last, now, did they?"

"No, and I'm pretty sure I won't either."

"Look, shrimp, I get your fears. I had the same ones. What would someone like Bodhi want with a regular girl like me? I know if we'd met in the conventional way, like at a bar or something, he wouldn't have given me a second glance. But listen to me, Dani. The first time I saw Bodhi Beckett, he was covered in ashes and nearly ran me down with his car. We didn't meet in a conventional way, and neither did you and RJ. What you have is different than what he's had with other women. You know that. So, stop letting those nasty insecurities fill your head with doubt. A five-foot-two elementary school teacher is just what he needs."

I drew in a soothing breath. She was right. Our connection was stronger than sky-high legs and perfect cheekbones.

"Thank you." I hugged her. "If it wasn't for you, I would've become one of those romance book heroines who talks herself out of being with the perfect guy for no apparent reason."

"I know. I saw you headed in that direction, so I rewrote the ending. I got your back, girl. We're besties now."

Stars glittered in my eyes. "We are?"

"Of course. I don't share deodorant with just anyone."

"And I'd let you drink out of my straw."

She slapped a hand to her chest theatrically.

We giggled. We were just fun like that.

"Hey, can I ask you something?"

"Sure," she said.

"How well do you know RJ?"

"Not that well. I came into the picture just before *AnyDayNow* broke up and the boys went their separate ways."

"But he and Bodhi remained close, right?"

Breeze's brows furrowed. "Yes, but..."

My eyes widened. The plot was thickening. Despite spending the most intense hours of my life with RJ, he was still a mystery to me, and I was counting on Breeze to help solve him.

"RJ distanced himself after the breakup. Maybe because he was working on the album, I don't know. But Bodhi was worried about him and wouldn't tell me why. He tells me everything, so don't think I didn't try. Anyway, about five months ago, right after launching his solo album, RJ disappeared. All his shows were cancelled. Fired his manager. He wouldn't answer his phone."

"That's when I met him. Total recluse. Barely left his place. Didn't work. Looked like the Taliban."

"Huh. RJ's always been so put together. So polished. Never a hair out of place."

"That's not the RJ I knew. Mine looked like an unclipped Goldendoodle."

"He must've really been struggling then. Here's the thing about RJ. He talks a big game, but he's actually a really sensitive guy. I get the feeling he didn't have the easiest childhood. He has this need to be loved at all costs, and when he didn't get that affirmation with his solo album, it messed him all up."

I nodded, remembering our conversation in the parking garage. "It did."

Breeze studied me, curious. "I imagine the two of you talked about some heavy things in there."

"We did. I just hope he doesn't regret the things he said."

"The two of you survived something horrific together, like Bodhi and I did. Believe me, Dani, an experience like that changes you," Breeze said. "That bond... it never goes away."

. . .

Our group had come as far as we could. Until RJ signed the papers, we were not welcome on his floor. Armed with documents to prove their purpose, Tucker and the lawyers were the only ones allowed on the ward.

The rest of us waited outside the double doors. At first, the guys were patient and respectful, like good little choir boys, but as the wait stretched on, one by one the *AnyDayNow* boys disintegrated into chaos.

First an off-color joke. Then an insult. Then a push against a wall. I watched in amusement. This was clearly a four-man bromance, and I hoped, for RJ's sake, he made it five. You'd think with all the success these guys had they'd be more guarded in their play. People were watching, after all.

Bodhi shoved Shawn back. "Get off me, dude."

Seconds earlier Shawn had been trying to lick the remnants of a Snicker's bar off Bodhi's cheek.

"In some cultures, grooming each other is a sign of affection," Shawn said.

"Not cultures—that's orangutans, you idiot."

"Hey, Dane," Shawn called to him, while continuing to taunt Bodhi with his tongue from a safer distance. "Does finding another man attractive mean I'm gay?"

"Yes, it's the first step on the journey."

Hunter rolled his eyes. "I'm sorry, Dani. I wish I could say they aren't always like this, but..."

"Oh, no, you don't." Bodhi stopped him. "Dani, he might look like he's from the land of Care Bears, but he's not as innocent as you might think."

"Compared to the rest of you, I'm a saint."

"A saint?" Dane challenged, pulling up his pant leg to reveal a sketch from *The Jungle Book*. "You paid the tattoo artist a thousand dollars extra to give me a tattoo of Mowgli. I asked for wolf eyes."

Hunter grinned as if the memory was a good one.

I'd been so thoroughly enjoying the show that I didn't see who was headed our way until I heard Breeze's hushed voice say, "Guys, she's coming."

Silence fell over our group as Heather rapidly approached. Her head was held high, but this was not the same woman who'd expelled me from the hospital days ago. This one had been knocked down to size, making me wonder what had happened in the room when the lawyers brought RJ the papers.

And as she drew closer, Heather headed straight for me. My instinct was to take a step back, but Breeze stopped me from cowering. She was right. I couldn't take a backseat to the mom, not if I wanted to earn the respect of the son.

Heather came to a halt mere inches from my face. A silence fell over our entire group. I tipped my chin and steadied my gaze. *Bring it on.*

But Heather hadn't come to rumble.

She leaned in and whispered in my ear, "I hope, for his sake, you're worth it."

And then she walked away.

———

Of all the people RJ had to choose from, he picked me to be first in line to see him. I thought I was ready, prepared, but the further away I got from Breeze's pep talk, the more worried I became. RJ and I had shared something profound and life-changing together, but I had no idea what he'd been through since I'd watched Parker close the ambulance doors. Nor did I know what influence Heather could have had on him in his weakened state. It was entirely possible he was calling me in first to cut me loose now that I was no longer needed for his immediate safety.

I winced at my own totally unfair thoughts. He'd sacrificed for me too, willing to die alone so I could live. I truly believed I'd met the real RJ Contreras in the parking garage. Not the superstar. Not the playboy. Not the friend or the foe. I'd met the man, stripped down to his core, all flesh and bone. He'd shown who he was, and I had fallen hard. If that same man was on the other side of this door, then I had nothing to worry about at all.

I couldn't make myself go in. Why was this so hard? Maybe it had something to do with the fact that I'd confessed my love for him after only really knowing him for what, like fifteen hours? My god, the timing.

Dani, why? This is why you can't have nice things.

Maybe he'd forgotten. Yes, that was highly possible. He'd been delirious after all. And if he did have memories, I'd just gaslight the hell out of him and convince him he was mistaken. Yes. Perfect plan. Gaslight. Okay. I was ready.

My feet wouldn't move.

Just go in, I told myself. *He wants to see you.*

I knocked lightly on the door.

"Come in."

My heart did a happy somersault upon hearing his voice. It was raspier than I remembered, but unmistakably RJ's.

I pushed the door open ever so slightly and peeked around it.

RJ took in my turtle-emerging-from-its-shell antics, and his eyes flashed with amusement. "Whatcha doing over there, Dani?"

I curved around the door and nudged it shut with my butt.

"Gathering the courage to talk to you," I replied. Taking a step back, I rested my back against the now closed door.

"Huh. What do you need courage for? I thought we were past all that."

"Right, except last time I saw you, I told you I loved you and then I proceeded to cut your foot off. So now I'm feeling a bit awkward."

"Ah," he replied, the corner of his lip turning up. "I see where that might be a deal breaker for some guys. But I like it rough."

My cackle could be heard down in the cafeteria, but with that one quick-witted reply, he'd managed to ease my anxious mind.

RJ beckoned me forward with a finger. "Come here."

Tucking a strand of hair behind my ear, I tiptoed toward him.

"Why so bashful? The Dani I know is never shy."

"Right but that was before, when I thought you were turd-sniffing Chad Woodcock," I replied, chasing his smile with my own. "But now that you're RJ Contreras, superstar—well, that's just slightly more intimidating."

"Okay, first, I never sniffed turds as Chad Woodcock, and second, I'm a very humbled version of that superstar you're referring to. Really, if anyone should be intimidated, it's me."

"Oh okay, sure."

"I'm not joking. I'm in the presence of greatness."

"The only thing I'm great at is talking lots and lots."

RJ's playful expression faded. "I don't know how you did it, Dani. I really don't. You're bite-sized. How did you drag my six-foot-two body through the rubble?"

The memory of it flashed through my skull, and I had to shake it off to answer him.

"I don't know," I said, taking the final steps to his side. I took his hand in mine. "I wanted you to live so bad. I was like one of those moms who lifts a car off her kid. I just... made it happen."

"Well, I'm your biggest fan." RJ grabbed my neck and pulled me down, planting a soft, sweet kiss to my lips. I sank into him, the relief making my knees weak. There had been no need for worry. This was the same the guy who'd called me *hero* and who'd let me shave his face while stuck in a hole. And now I knew he was also a guy who didn't run away when the going got tough.

I peppered his face with kisses. "Just know, I tried so hard to get to you. Your mother proved harder to move than a mountain."

"I know. I'm sorry she was such a pain in the ass. She's been dealt with accordingly."

"Uh-oh. I hope it wasn't too bad. She looked upset in the hall."

"We've decided to go our separate ways."

I gaped, needing more clarity. "Like permanently?"

"Yes, or at least until my memory fades. When does Alzheimer's set in again?"

"Forty-five, fifty more years."

"That long?"

"Are you sure this is what you want?"

"No. But it's what I need. I've been angry for so long. The negativity drags me down. I just want to be happy, with you."

I pulled my salon-smelling hair to one side and leisurely kissed him. "That's a plan I can get behind."

"You think maybe the Lucky Swimmers Club might take me in, given that I too have a donor dad?"

Tapping into my greatest fear, my extremities drained of blood. "If you're one of my sperm brothers, I give up. I'm never dating again."

"Relax." He laughed. "My father's donation location was in the back of a seedy van. Yours was in a nice, sterile facility... over and over and over again."

I smacked him, giggling.

"I missed you," I said, settling against his side. "Like really, really missed you. Is that weird?"

"It should be, right?" he replied, wrapping his arms around me. "But I feel the same."

"Breeze said experiencing what we did together bonded us. I like that theory."

"Me too." With his sleepy expression, RJ leaned in. I parted my lips in invitation, expecting him to dive right in but he had other plans, ones I was ill-prepared to understand. His sensuous lips hovered around my lower lip, kissing and tugging on it lazily. I waited, anticipating his next move would be conquering my wanting mouth and kissing me like he'd just stepped into a boxing ring. But he didn't. He stayed calm, and somehow that made the kiss all that much hotter. His touch. His breath. I could feel it everywhere in my body, and my heart rate quickened at just the anticipation. I could have stayed like that forever, locked in this slow-moving torture. To be sure, if we hadn't been in his hospital room, that kiss would've ended very differently.

This was what I'd been after, the secret sauce I'd been searching for with the Jeremys—*desire* was the missing ingredient. And when he finally pulled back and our lips sensually disengaged, we lingered there in the overcharged space between us, gazing into each other's eyes. It hit me then. I was no underdog. I had his heart in my hands—this man who'd grown up feeling unloved. He was trusting me to heal him in ways that only love could provide. And in return, he was offering me... everything.

25

DANI: POST-APOCALYPTIC FAIRYTALE

The first day back at school was a rough one. The kids were unusually emotional, breaking down over the slightest things, no doubt the residual effects of the disruption to their lives. None of my kids had lost family members or their homes, but trauma was a tricky thing and could not always be measured in tangible ways. For many of these little six- and seven-year-olds, it was the first time they'd ever really known fear or that the world was not as safe as had once been promised.

I'd debated whether to go back when school resumed a week and a half after the quake. I'd only been reunited with RJ for few days and didn't like the idea of being away from him for large chunks of time. Plus I was feeling strange; prone to impromptu weeping spells and not sleeping well, the horrible fate of those who died in my building keeping me awake at night. But my kids needed their teacher and reassurance that life would get back to normal soon. And so, I went back for them.

Still, it was a struggle walking into the school—literally. RJ's fame was suddenly in my backyard. Cameras snapped pictures of me as nervous parents shielded their kids from harm's way.

Honestly, I was surprised I wasn't sent home by the principal the minute I arrived. But once we were all tucked behind the gates and school was in session, I could almost fool myself into thinking everything was back to normal and I was living my former life with one small caveat—my brand spankin' new celebrity boyfriend.

Once I had all my students settled into their seats, I opened my lesson plan and began to teach.

"Miss Malone?"

Seriously? Was it potty time already? I looked up from my rudimentary lecture. "Yes, Raja?"

"Are you famous?"

My students scooted up in their seats, excitement evident in their wiggly bodies.

"Um... no, I'm not."

"How come everyone is taking your picture and calling your name?"

"Well, I helped a man in the earthquake who *is* famous, so that's why the news people want to ask me questions."

There. Nice and neutral. I was proud of myself for keeping it both private and G-rated.

"Your boyfriend is RJ Contreras," Nelle stated as fact.

"Well..."

"Do you live with him?" Benji asked.

What the heck? Why would he ask me that?

Flustered, I shook my head. "That's not... no."

"Do you kiss?" Maverick made kissing sounds, and some of the other boys joined in the fun.

"Maverick, that's not appropriate. Don't make me give you a warning on the first day back."

"I heard you cut off his foot," Escott blurted out from the back of the room. Other students nodded their heads.

"And you stole stuff from a store."

I gulped back the horror. What were these parents letting their kids watch? My bottom lip began to quiver.

"Where..." I stuttered. "Where did you hear that?"

"On the playground."

"Me too."

Gripping the desk, I watched my knuckles blanch white. Why did this suddenly feel like the end of my career? How could I be a good influence on these impressionable children when I was the talk of the blacktop water fountain? I stumbled away from my desk.

"Miss Malone?"

I held my hand up to the class as I struggled for air. "I'll be right back." Going through the back passageway that connected all the first-grade classes, I opened the door to the adjacent room. Trina, my fellow first grade teacher, must've seen the distress on my face and rushed to my side.

"Dani?"

"I can't... someone needs to..."

I slid down the wall, dazed and gasping for breath. Burying my face in my hands, I sobbed right there on Mrs. Abbott's classroom floor. The principal was called in, and I was lifted off the ground and escorted to the office, where I slowly but surely regained control. Embarrassment set in, followed by profuse apologies for a whole array of things. My unprofessionalism. Leaving my students unattended. Bringing drama to the school's front entrance. Looting. Cutting a guy's foot off. And when I finished purging my sins, I looked up to find Principal Gomez's horrified face. Basically, I'd just outlined all the reasons she should absolutely fire me. *Way to go, Dani.*

But did I stop there? Nope. Instead, I started backtracking, blaming my behavior on lack of sleep and stress from my newfound infamy. Principal Gomez observed me with the neutral face that you just knew was masking her true feelings, which no doubt were *This chick is crazy.*

And she was probably right. There was something off with me. I'd been feeling different ever since collapsing in front of Bruce after just escaping the garage. But because all my focus was on reconnecting with RJ, the symptoms had been masked. Now that we were back together, and my new, altered life was taking shape, I wasn't sure if I was fully on board with the changes. Ten days ago, I'd been an ordinary girl living a routine life when suddenly the earth shook and—BAM—I was homeless, thingless, and dating a pop star.

I couldn't shake the feeling that I'd woken up in an alternate universe, where I was living RJ's paparazzi-fueled life. At first, the media seemed interested in me simply because I was the closest thing to RJ they could get their hands on. But then someone leaked my role in the amputation to the press and I became a hunted woman, with people digging into my past. That brought the Lucky Swimmers Club into the limelight, and all my brothers and sisters too. Things only got worse from there, when grainy footage of me stealing Dingdongs off the store shelf started circulating around the internet. RJ's lawyers got involved. So did the store. Basically, a huge mess that subsequently got me branded as a thief *and* a serial mutilator. It was a lot to take in for anyone, but then add to that the sadness I felt for those who'd perished in my apartment building and you had a recipe for disaster.

I played back the conversation with Principal Gomez in my head.

You need time to heal, Dani. Go home. Rest. We'll reevaluate in a week.

In my mind, she was saying, *You're flippin' crazy, Dani. Go home. Strap on that straight jacket. You're never coming back.*

Even if I was cleared of homicidal mania, theft, and an

unhealthy Hostess addiction, there was no way to repair my reputation or erase the images of me doing wrong in my students' heads. And although Principal Gomez assured me that my employment with the district was secure, how accommodating would she be in two weeks? A month? When I was on trial for first-degree burglary?

I needed a break; a place to hide and rest my weary head. I now fully understood why RJ had run away from his life. It sucked, living under such a punishing spotlight, and made me seriously question whether RJ and I could really make it as a couple. One thing was for sure: if I didn't put some serious focus on my mental health, we'd never get this relationship off the ground.

Getting my head back on straight had to be my number one focus, but it couldn't be done in my current digs. Poor Chloe needed her life back. She couldn't even take her pup out to pee without having to muscle her way through media. It was time to go, and I knew just where. A place away from the public eye, where I could get a piping hot bowl of chicken noodle soup and snuggle under a pile of cozy blankets.

With nostalgic tears in my eyes, I dialed home.

————

My mother was thrilled. Almost too thrilled—like witch-in-Hansel-and-Gretel thrilled. So much for sentiment. I hadn't even started the drive yet, and already I was sabotaging the homecoming. If I was going to work on myself, I had to stop villainizing the poor woman. After experiencing RJ's horror story of a mother, I should feel lucky that her focus was on nursing me back to health and not fattening me up for the oven.

I made my way to Chloe's house first, to pack what few possessions I had and leave her a thank-you note before heading to the hospital to say goodbye. Wait, no. *Goodbye* seemed too final, and this wasn't forever. It was only until I felt better. I hoped RJ would understand that. No doubt this would come as a surprise to him since I hadn't mentioned any issues. Maybe if he'd known that today's breakdown in the classroom was not the first of its kind, he might've been more prepared for what was coming. But I'd hidden those early signs of depression from him, maybe not even recognizing them myself until it became quite clear when I was on the floor of my school bawling.

Still, leaving RJ while he was in the hospital felt like a betrayal on my part. I should be stronger. But the last thing RJ needed while he was healing from his own injuries was his brand-new gal pal snotting all over him and bringing him down. Besides, according to his doctor, RJ would probably be headed home in a few days, once the course of antibiotics had reached its end. And, hopefully by then, I'd be back, and then we'd take up right where we'd left off.

I was several doors down when I heard the laughter coming from RJ's room. From the sound of it, he and his buds were definitely not following the hospital's two-visitor rule, but then maybe it didn't apply to celebrities. I pushed the door open to find the entire band plus Tucker and a teenager I didn't know all crammed into the small space.

"Dani!" My name exploded from the gathered crowd.

"Um... awkward," I said. "Did you throw a party and not invite me?"

Dane tossed an arm over my shoulder. "You caught us. We throw a party every time you leave."

Normally I would've laughed at his obvious joke, but the most I could offer today was a courtesy giggle.

"Don't listen to him," RJ replied, laughing. "You'll always be at the top of my VIP list."

He held his hand out to me and I took it. I was pulled in

for a kiss, which earned me another round of applause. The vibe in the room was festive, and it made me sad that I couldn't share their joy. Still, I put on a brave face and took a bow.

RJ studied me a moment, the space above his nose creasing, and I could tell he was reading something into my stiff demeanor.

Speaking to me in a low voice so the others couldn't hear, he asked, "What are you doing here? Why aren't you in class?"

"What are *you* doing here? I leave you alone one time and you organize a rave."

"If six people is your idea of a rave, we're going to need to get you out more, babe."

Babe? He called me *babe?* The flutters came at me full force. It was that same feeling I got back in middle school when the boy I'd liked for two years walked by my desk and said, "'Sup, Malone?" Oh, the joy I'd felt that day! But this was different. RJ Contreras had called me *babe.* That was like being drafted to the big leagues. This beautiful, successful, universally known man liked me. He wanted me. And I could have him too, yet I was choosing... *to leave?* Maybe I hadn't thought this plan through enough.

"Why aren't you in class?" he repeated, but this time his serious expression did not leave room for wiggle.

"I was sent home. Turns out six-year-olds are surprisingly up-to-date on world affairs."

It took a moment for my words to sink in, but when they did, he winced. "Oh, no."

"Oh, yes."

"Wait—they sent you home because the kids are well informed?"

"No, they sent me home because I threw myself onto the ground crying."

RJ pursed his lips, finding nothing humorous in my attempt to spin the story in a light-hearted way.

I leaned down and whispered, "I'll tell you later."

He hesitated a second, obviously wanting more, but relenting for my sake as well as the sake of those he was currently entertaining. His body loosened.

"Hey, come here." RJ gathered me in his arms and gave me a tight hug. "You want me to kiss it and make it better?"

Before I could give him a definitive answer, his lips were already smothering my face in kisses, covering every square inch before moving on to the hollows of my neck. I twisted in his arms, giggling, the endorphins released lighting me up from the inside. I did feel better. Maybe. Maybe I didn't need to go. Maybe all I needed was RJ and his endearing method of stress control. Maybe.

Disengaging from his lips, I returned to my feet and spoke more loudly, to include the rest of the room. "So, how are you guys getting away with having this many people in the room?"

"Shawn?" RJ grinned. "Care to explain?"

"Sure. See, I found out yesterday that the charge nurse has been harboring a crush on me since the early days of *AnyDayNow*."

"Not important," Bodhi said, waving his hand. "Get to the point."

"Hey, dick. RJ asked me to tell a story, and I'm telling it," Shawn snapped, before redirecting his attention on me and instantly returning to his pleasant demeanor. "Anyway, Dani, let's just say she'll never look at the break room the same way again."

My eyes rounded as I squeaked my reply, "You slept with her?"

"Ew. God, no. She's like fifty. No, I put in a special order at Voodoo Donuts—fifty made-to-order doughy, Bavarian cream-filled nurses in tiny little icing uniforms. Cutest shit ever. You can only imagine the joy I've spread through the unit. At this point, I could pretty much scrub in for surgery and no one would say a thing."

"You're a genius," I said, settling one butt cheek on the bed next to RJ. He promptly wrapped a protective arm around my waist.

"You okay?" he mouthed, his head still clearly in my drama.

I wanted to say yes—to smile with my whole being—but I just couldn't.

"No." I shook my head. "Later."

"How about now? I'll ask everyone to leave."

"No, RJ. It's fine. I like the distraction."

"Or I could be your only distraction," he whispered, his hot breath on my ear unleashing the butterflies again. Even broken and bruised, he was a sexy man. RJ had a presence about him, a confidence that bordered on arrogance. Add to that his reputation as the bad boy of *AnyDayNow,* complete with drunken escapades and women dangling off both arms, and you pretty much had any woman's worst nightmare. And now, somehow, he was mine—every troublemaking inch of him.

What was I getting myself into? RJ felt like a whole lot of man for woman like me, one who set her alarm *to go to bed.* I shouldn't want him. Practical me knew that. I should stick to what was familiar; play it safe, like my mother taught me. The Jeremys of the world were the guys I was supposed to like—the mom-approved, sweater-wearing nice guys of the dating realm. With a Jeremy by my side, I could expect a quiet, stable, productive life. But with RJ? It wouldn't be quiet because he lived his life in the wide open. It wouldn't be stable because there would always be women waiting in the wings trying to lure him away. And it certainly wouldn't be productive because... I mean... look at him. My god, I'd never get anything done.

RJ was like taking a bite out of the forbidden. And once I got a taste, I just knew I'd never be able to go back to the Jeremys. They didn't make my insides tingle. They weren't brave and daring. And when shit got real, they ran away. Last week's Jeremy had proved as much, leaving me in the parking lot to pillage and plunder alone. RJ wouldn't have left me. In fact, he probably would've been in the store looting right alongside me.

"Hey guys," RJ gave an exaggerated yawn. "I'm getting tired. Pain meds are kicking in."

"Ah, man, you're so lucky," Dane wistfully replied. "I wish I could get me a reserve supply of Norco."

"Cut your foot off and then you can."

Bodhi's eyes widened at RJ's playful reply, not finding it as humorous as the others. He shifted uncomfortably and looked away. It wasn't the first time I'd seen that look from him, either. There was something up; something that remained unspoken between the two of them.

RJ seemed oblivious to the friction.

"Speaking of that," RJ continued, "am I the only one who sees a disturbing pattern forming here? First Bodhi and the fire. Then me and the earthquake. What's next? Hunter in an avalanche? Shawn in a tornado? Dane and his damn sinkhole?"

"Why does everyone shit on my sinkhole?" Dane huffed. "It's a legitimate means of death."

Bodhi returned to the conversation. "No doubt. We just all agree that it's a far less dramatic way to go, that's all. No need to get testy."

Dane's eyes bugged. "Dude, you need to educate yourself on sinkholes. The earth's surface literally collapses in on itself and swallows you whole. You cannot tell me that Hunter surviving under a snow cap drinking his own piss Slurpees or Shawn getting decapitated by a flying cow is more dramatic than me falling in a goddamn sinkhole. Fuck you, man."

"My god," Tucker groaned. "We're arguing about sinkholes. This is why I'm out of the boy band business. RJ, Dani—good to see you again. Evan, let's go—before I pummel Dane into the ground."

The room cleared quickly, with everyone following Tucker out the door, still debating Dane's sinkhole.

"Are they always like that?" I asked.

"Have you seen any group interview with us, *ever*? That'll be your answer."

"Hey, I didn't know Tucker had another son."

"He doesn't."

"Then who's Evan?"

"Bodhi's brother."

"So... Tucker's son?"

"No." RJ chuckled. "Long story. And one I'd be willing to tell. But first, I need to hear yours."

I was about to spill when a nurse poked her head in. "Oh good, they're gone. The doctor is coming by in a few minutes, so your lady friend will need to leave. Sorry, hun."

"Give us five minutes," RJ said, not so much as a question but a command.

She checked her watch. "I can give you two."

"Three."

She considered his counteroffer before accepting. "Three minutes, RJ, and then I'm calling your mother."

He snickered, turning his attention back to me. "Now tell me what happened."

I gave him a quick run-down of events and admitted to struggling with both the emotional outbursts and the glare of the media before coming to the inevitable conclusion.

"Listen RJ, I don't have a place to live, and..."

"You can stay at my place. It's totally secure. My backyard is like a frickin' luxury resort. I'll even send in the masseuses. One after the other, just for you. I should be home in four or five days, and then I can be there—be your rock—just like you've been for me. I promise you Dani, we'll get through this together."

"I'm leaving." I blurted out the remainder of the sentence he hadn't allowed me to finish.

RJ blinked. More than once. "Okay. Where to?"

"My mom's place. This has nothing to do with how I feel about you. And it's just for a while... until I get my head on right. If I felt there was any other way..."

"There is. Dani... let me help you. I can get you a therapist. I can get you anything you want."

"Right now what I want is my mom."

That shut down the discussion. RJ had no rebuttal, no bargaining chip that trumped a mother's love.

"For how long?" he asked, resigned.

"As long as it takes. I'm sorry. I just need a breather. Everything is just bearing down on me, and I... I can't."

"I don't like the way you're talking. It sounds so permanent."

"It's not. I promise. I'll be back. Just don't forget about me while I'm gone."

"I'm not going to forget you. You're all I think about. There has to be another way to do this without you just up and leaving."

I took his hand and gazed into his worried eyes. I desperately wanted to give him what he desired—to put him first. But my life was also hanging in the balance, and I needed to safeguard that too.

"There's not."

———

Bodhi was waiting for me on the other side of the door. We'd never had a conversation where Breeze wasn't riding shotgun, and I had no idea what to say to him. Bodhi's fame terrified me in unexplained ways. Sure, RJ was famous too, but because I hadn't recognized him for the first five months of our rocky relationship, his celebrity just sort of crept up on me little by little. But Bodhi... he came at me as a fully formed star.

Catching sight of my wary expression, he asked, "Do I scare you?"

"What? No."

"Okay, because you always look like you're going to vomit whenever I try to talk to you."

I laughed because his take on my behavior was totally accurate. Spacing my fingers slightly apart, I held them up for show and tell. "I'm maybe just a little bit scared of you."

"Well, don't be. In comparison to RJ, I'm harmless. Hey listen, I've been meaning to talk to you. Have you noticed anything, um... unusual about RJ?"

"Unusual? What do you mean?"

"He's taking this really well, don't you think? Almost too well. I mean, he lost his foot, and he's acting like it's no big deal."

"It's not that it's no big deal, but he escaped death. It changes you."

"Don't you think I know that? I woke up in a fully engulfed building and had to fight my way out. I looked death in the face. I promise you, I know what it feels like."

His stark response stunned me. Of course I'd read all about his near-death experience in the news, but I supposed you never fully understand what another person has been through.

"I didn't mean to insinuate anything. Sorry. But you have to understand RJ knew exactly what he was doing in that parking garage. He knew it was his foot or his life. He was very rational about it. I think he's just grateful to be alive."

"Sure." Bodhi nodded, not looking convinced. "But rational and RJ have never gone hand in hand. All I'm saying is, something feels off. The guy I know would not be okay with this."

The first tiny prickles of concern crept over my skin. "So what are you saying?"

"I'm saying we should probably board up the windows and batten down the hatches because Hurricane RJ is swirling out in the Atlantic waiting to come ashore."

"I think you're not giving him enough credit. You didn't see the guy in the parking garage. He was calm. Level-headed." I pointed to the hospital door. "Just like the guy lying in that bed right now."

A conflicted-looking Bodhi glanced my way. He was biting down on his lower lip. Clearly, he didn't agree with my take on things. Either Bodhi was a crappy friend or I was living in a post-apocalyptic fairytale world because no way were we talking about the same man.

"Why is this so hard for you to believe?" I asked.

"Look, Dani. I want nothing more then for you to be right. I really do. But you've met him. You spent five months with him before the earthquake. You know RJ well enough to know that the level-headed dude lying in the hospital bed is not him."

"Um... you forget that I spent five months with the slimy blowfish Chad Woodcock, not RJ."

Bodhi blinked; his face twisted in surprise.

"Dani," Bodhi finally said. "That slimy blowfish *is* RJ. RJ *is* Chad Woodcock. The guy in there?" He shook his head. "*Not* RJ."

The revelation knocked the wind out of me, and I leaned back against the wall. My god. Bodhi was right. What in the living, breathing hell had I been thinking? Of course RJ was Chad. Somehow, in the progression of the unfolding disaster, I'd separated the two in my brain.

RJ, the perfect brave hero.

Chad, the toilet-clogging dipwad.

Two separate entities... but they were one and the same.

Oh, yes, there was most definitely a storm coming... and I was in its direct and destructive path.

26

RJ: MEETING HALFWAY

I ENDED THE PHONE CONVERSATION WITH DANI THE SAME WAY every conversation with her ended. *When are you coming home?* Pathetic, really... begging for her return. She'd been gone for nearly two weeks, and I'd been home from the hospital for one of them.

She kept promising me she was coming back, but there was a hesitancy in her voice, as if she were just saying what she thought I wanted to hear but didn't really believe it herself. What was she doing? Her life was here. She had her job, her siblings, me. I could sense her pulling away. I needed to get to Dani to remind her who I was and what I was willing to do to have her. I'd never fought for a woman before, never felt the need or desire, but this was different. This was my future, and she was threatening to strip it away from me.

"Julio," I called from across the patio. "I need you to drive me to Temecula."

Julio sighed. "We've talked about this, RJ. No traveling long distances in enclosed spaces until the risk of clots has passed."

"It's passed. Just take me. Stop being a douche."

"Not being a douche. I'm doing the job you hired me to do.

Now come sit down and rest."

With the help of my crutches, I crossed the outdoor lounge area in record time and plopped down into an oversized outdoor patio chair.

"Dude," Julio chastised. "Slow down. You have to protect your knee until you strengthen the muscles."

"Dude," I mimicked him. "I sat down. If there's a way to slow gravity, I'm all ears."

"Actually, you set the crutches down and use your hands. You don't need a slide presentation to know that."

Julio was the new Heather, micromanaging my every move... and I paid him for the privilege. Before discharge from the hospital, I'd convinced him to take a temporary leave from his job to become my live-in nurse for a month while I healed from my injuries. I paid him triple his normal income to live at my estate, take care of my health needs, and not to take my shit like Roland Akers before him. I'd told him at the time of hiring that I wanted him to kick my ass so I could be back on my feet in record time. And he had. With the added support of a physical therapist, I was up and moving pretty damn well on the temporary prosthesis while I waited to be fitted into the permanent one currently on order.

As much as I hated the present contraption, which traveled halfway up my thigh, I knew I was luckier than many who undergo emergency amputations. I'd been young and healthy before the accident, which helped with wound healing. So by the time I was finally released from the hospital, I was able to walk my ass out of there.

Once I got home, that was when the real work began, the goal being that I'd be ready to wear my new state-of-the-art foot-and-ankle prosthesis the moment it arrived. I wanted to get back to living an active life as soon as possible. I might have sat around moping back in my Chad Woodcock days, but that was all behind me now. I had plans; ones too big to wait for things to happen. And those plans started and stopped with Dani.

I settled into my chair, sweaty from the walking I'd done while talking to Dani on the phone. As far as resting spots went, this outdoor patio overlooking the expansive pool and water features was a fine one. As an added bonus, my property featured a giant security wall, keeping any unwanted trespassers out.

I watched Julio basking in the sun. It had only taken him a couple of days to acclimate to the good life, spending hours in the pool, in the gym, in the movie theater. With his contract up in three weeks, I wasn't sure if he'd actually leave, not when Rozsika happily waited on him hand and foot.

"What time is it?" I asked.

"You can't check your Apple watch or your phone?"

"I could, but I prefer to hear your sexy voice."

Julio sighed, taking a sip of his Blue Hawaii, complete with an umbrella and fruit kabob, before pulling the phone out of his swim trunks. "Twelve fifteen. Why?"

"Perfect. We can get to Dani's before her surprise comes in."

"No. You didn't hire me to be your chauffeur. I'm not driving you anywhere. Dani can come here."

"That's the problem. She won't."

"I can't believe I'm even saying this, but maybe she's just not that into you."

"She's into me," I assured him. This wasn't an attraction issue; that much I knew. Something else was going on, and I needed to get to the bottom of it, even if that meant going behind Julio's back.

"So, why's she not here? Have you told her you like her?"

"Do I look like an amateur?"

"Then don't ask me for female advice."

"I wasn't. I was asking for a ride."

Julio considered me with an expression that bordered on pity. "Look, dude, I've been dumped a lot in my lifetime. A lot. Are you sure this isn't her telling you to get lost?"

"I'm not being dumped, dick. She's going through something, and I have to figure out what it is and fix it."

"I don't appreciate name-calling, RJ. This is a professional relationship we have here and should be treated as such."

Rozsika appeared with a plate of finger sandwiches, placing them on the table between Julio and me. She laid a hand on Julio's shoulder and smiled as she set a second plate down in front of him, piled high with warm chocolate chip cookies. "And for you."

Professional, my ass. The dude had slipped into my life with ease. If I wasn't mindful, he'd be the lord of the manor in a week.

"Oh, Rozsika," he said. "Where have you been all my life?"

"I make cookie for RJ but he doesn't like," she said in her heavy accent.

"So ungrateful," Julio agreed.

"Or maybe I just don't eat sugar to maintain a healthy body."

Rozsika and Julio exchanged an exasperated look.

"With Julio, I get to show off cooking," Rozsika tsked. "With you, only protein."

Julio patted his impressive belly. "Well, lucky for both of us, I don't worry about my figure quite as much as RJ does."

Rozsika giggled her way back to the kitchen.

"I've got to give you props. For a guy with absolutely no game, you sure know how to charm the Hungarian grandmas."

"It's a gift."

"Right, well, I'm gonna go take a shower," I said, step one of my escape attempt.

"Do you want help?"

"Showering? No, I'd rather lick a gas station toilet seat than have you in there with me, but thank you."

"Jesus Christ, RJ. Your shower's big enough to host the Oscars. Besides, I've already seen your junk more times than I care to remember."

Not emboldening him with a response, I hobbled away.

———

I'd just barely gotten dressed when a call came in from Andrew, my jack-of-all-trades employee... and my driver for the day. I assumed he was calling to let me know the car was waiting for me behind the hedge, where I'd instructed for him to park it. Yes, Julio was my employee and could easily be fired, but technically I *had* hired him to do exactly what he was doing—keep me healthy and on task. And so, I had to sneak out behind his back. If I was lucky, I'd be back before he was done with his outdoor evening nap.

"RJ, someone claiming to be your brother is out front."

"My brother? Which one?"

"Says his name is Manny. This him?"

A still image of Manny at my gate popped up on my screen. What the hell was he doing here? My family never came here. I went there. It was sort of an unwritten rule that, up until today, had never been broken.

"RJ, you still there?"

"I'm here, and yes, that's my brother."

"You want me to let him in?"

I ran my fingers over my now smooth jawline and pondered. The last thing I wanted was to entertain family when I had a mission to complete before rush hour, but I thought back to our last encounter and how he'd stood up for me at the hospital. At the very least, I wanted to know what was up with that.

"Uh... all right. But have the car ready."

"It is. I'll send him in."

I met Manny at the front entrance and figured I'd keep him contained there. No sense in him getting comfortable, as he wouldn't be staying long. I observed him as he stepped into the lobby. Manny was two years older than me, with curly brown locks that were currently being worn longer than I'd ever seen them. He was a near perfect replica of Renato, making it more than clear that he was the man's biological son.

"Hey," he greeted me with a smile. "Wasn't sure if you were going to let me in."

"I wasn't sure myself."

"I don't blame you. Last time was…"

"Every time is," I corrected.

"Sure." He nodded. "Every time is an adventure in our family."

I didn't like the way he said 'our family,' like I was actually a part of it. I had a pretty good idea what he was here for—money—and the sooner I shut him down, the better.

"Not to be rude, Manny but I've actually got somewhere to go, so…"

"Oh, sorry. I'll make it quick. I just came by…" He hesitated, looking nervous as hell. Oh yeah, this was definitely a money grab. "To say thank you."

"Okay," I responded. Definitely not what I was expecting. "You know I cut the family off, right?"

"Yes. I do. And that's actually why I'm thanking you. You finally gave me the push I needed to strike out on my own. I moved out. Got a job. And I'm going to start trade school in a couple of weeks."

In some ways, Manny was so much younger than me. He'd been sheltered all his life, with very few expectations placed on him. While I was off touring the world, he was on the couch, watching TV and living off my dime. But it was never too late for redemption, and I was inclined to give it to him.

"Nice. What trade?"

"I've always been good with cars, repairing them in the garages and stuff. So, I'm going to put that to good use and train to become a diesel mechanic. They're in high demand, and I can make a good living doing it. Not to your standards, but... you know what I mean."

I nodded, surprised to find myself actually happy for him. "Good for you, man."

"I've never actually thanked you for all you've done for us over the years. No one would have blamed you if you'd turned your back, but you never did. Shows your character."

"Or lack thereof."

"True. I suppose it depends on how you look at it. Anyway, I was thinking—and it's just a suggestion, totally up to you—but sometime when you're not busy, maybe we can grab a beer, get to know each other better. Just the two of us. I'd really like the chance to be your big brother. No strings attached."

Stunned was the only word to describe how I felt about the conversation we were having right now. I stood there in silence as I processed the offer. I'd wanted this for so long, but was it a little too late to resurrect a relationship that never was?

Manny must have seen my hesitation and began to backtrack.

"You know, it's okay if you don't. I totally understand. Here's my phone number," he said, stepping forward and handing me a piece of paper. "I'll leave the decision up to you. I live in Los Angeles now, so, you know, not too far away."

I looked down at his name and number in my hand. He was trying to build a bridge. The least I could do was meet him halfway.

"Are you busy right now?"

He jerked his head up. "No. Why?"

"You up for a drive?"

———

Manny and I talked the whole way to Dani's. At first about nothing, but as the miles passed, we dug deeper. He spoke of his regret, of his fear of Luis's reprisal. I knew they weren't empty words, remembering the times he'd reached out to me only to get a beat down from Luis. He'd never been strong like me; never been able to stand up for himself. But as he grew into the man he was meant to be, just as I was doing now, he was finding a strength inside him he never knew he had. And it was in that realm where we slowly began to bond.

"I hate these things," he complained, pulling up to the neighborhood security gate with its touchpad entry. "Who do they think they're keeping out? If I was a thief, I'd just sit out here and wait for a car to open the gate, and then I'd just drive right on through. False sense of security, if you ask me."

"Focus, Manny. The last name is Malone."

"God, you're so type A," he muttered. "And I'm looking. I can't find Malone. Do Dani and her mom have the same last name?"

"Her dad's a test tube, so yeah, I'm thinking they do."

"Oh, there it is."

Manny didn't give me a chance to prepare. He just pushed the button, and we were off to the races.

"Hello?" a female answered. It was not Dani.

"Uh, yes," I said, leaning over Manny. "This is RJ Contreras. I'm here to see Dani."

There was silence on the other line, and then the gate creaked open, and as we drove through, the flatbed delivery truck carrying a brand new four-door Bronco in a steel blue color followed right behind.

27

DANI: POP THE CORK

PULLING THROUGH THE SECURITY GATES TO MY MOTHER'S HOME, my body felt heavy. Another day. Another therapy session. Another promised breakthrough thwarted. I wanted so badly for things to get better, but in fact, they were getting worse. I could almost feel the depression settling into my bones. However, the medication I'd been prescribed had not yet had time to take full effect, and I clung to the hope that when I hit that magical two-week mark, everything would fall back into place, and I could return to RJ the strong, confident woman he admired.

As I turned the corner on my street, I noticed my mother out front speaking with two men. She hadn't mentioned any visitors. And then I saw him. RJ, standing there looking beautiful and healthy and whole. Blood instantly began pumping through my rusty heart as RJ stepped toward the curb and revealed my next surprise... and it was as jaw-dropping as the man himself: the Bronco he'd promised me in the parking garage.

With the help of crutches, RJ walked to my driver's side window and stared down at me through the glass. There was both hope and fear in his eyes. And I felt so bad. So hopeless. Because we wanted the same thing—to resume the fragile life we'd started together before despair brought me down—and I just couldn't give it to him.

RJ helped me from the car, and with my shoulders slumped from the strain, I sagged into his arms. His strength enveloped me, and I cried. RJ didn't let go; held me longer than any man ever had. He let me cry. He let me grieve. And when I'd finally emptied the tank, he pulled away long enough to cup my face in his loving touch and kiss me so gently, so tenderly, I wondered if he thought I might break.

Our lips parted, and I ran my fingertips over his jawline.

"You shaved."

He laughed. "I did. For you. Every day. Just in case."

Just in case I came home, he meant.

Taking my hand, he led me to the Bronco. "My promise to you."

It was beautiful—my dream car, just as he'd promised me. I ran my fingers along the side, marveling at the grand gesture. "RJ, you know you didn't need to do this. That was just a silly conversation."

"Not to me it wasn't. I meant every word. I want you to know, Dani, my gratitude is not contingent on *us*. Don't get me wrong; I want us. And I will fight like hell for us. But this gift is separate from that. This gift is not for the girl I love. It's for the hero who saved me."

Love? His words nearly melted me to the curb. I could not give him up without a fight. "Can we talk?"

"That's why I'm here," he said, then turned to the other man and shook his hand. "Thanks. I owe you one."

"No. You owe me nothing."

"At least a beer."

"Yes. I'll accept a beer. Dani," he said, tipping his head in greeting.

I returned his greeting even without knowing who I was interacting with.

"My brother, Manny," RJ said.

"Oh." I rocked back in surprise. "Your brother."

Manny flashed me a quick wave before heading over to his own car and driving away.

"Come on," I said, leading RJ through the house and up a flight of stairs, his first on his prosthetic leg. By the time we got to my room and I shut the door behind us, he was seriously winded.

"Are you trying to kill me?" he asked.

"If I were, I've had plenty of opportunities."

"This is true."

I crossed to the oversized chaise longue. "Sit."

Once he'd settled into the heavenly cushions, I crawled in after, facing him with legs crossed. We stared at one another for a long moment before he reached out and slid his fingers over my cheeks.

"God, I missed this pretty face. Tell me what I have to do to get you back."

"There isn't anything you can do. It's just something I have to work through on my own."

"Why on your own? I'm fairly certain this all stems back to the earthquake we both survived, so there doesn't seem anyone better suited to help you through this than me."

He was right. I'd tried to get past this on my own. I'd tried to get past it with piping warm soup. I'd tried to get past it with professional help. But I'd never tried to get past it with him, the person who should've been at the top of the list. Edging off the lounger, I retrieved the bag I'd been taking to the therapist even though I'd never revealed the contents. I pulled out a folder with a stack of papers inside. And, as I reclaimed my spot on the chair, RJ's eyes were fixed on what was in my hands.

I looked down at the blue folder, hesitating a moment before handing it over. RJ was slow and methodical as he flipped through the papers. It wasn't until page four or five that he finally realized what he was holding.

"You did this?" he asked. "You gathered all these together?"

I nodded.

RJ slumped back against the cushions; even ran his hands over his face and through his hair. "Why, Dani?"

"I was trying to find closure."

"No," he said, holding up the papers. "You were trying to torture yourself."

I grabbed my precious papers out of his hand. "No, RJ. I was trying to understand."

"Understand what?"

I could barely force the words out through my strangled throat. "Why I lived and they died."

The only sound in the room was the hum of the fan overhead. Every emotion appeared to be cycling over RJ's face. Maybe he didn't understand my methods, but he sure as hell understood my pain.

"Look," I said, holding up the first paper on the stack. "Her name is Doreen Dodd. She was the one in the parking spot you stole from me. She was crushed by concrete near the exit. She lived on our floor, eight doors down. Or Lamond Brown. He was sick, so he stayed behind when his wife and kids went out for ice cream. When they came back, he was dead. They lived in the apartment above us, three to the left. And..."

I paused, trying to catch my breath. "Sarina. She's six. They pulled her from the rubble alive. Her mom and her grandmother and even her dog—all of them died. They lived directly below us, RJ. Directly below."

"Okay, I get it," he said, removing the papers from my hands. "They were living, breathing people, and they died. You don't think I have the same thoughts going through my head? If anyone would understand, I would. Why wouldn't you just share this with me, so we could work through it together?"

"Because I didn't want to drag you down with me, not in your state of mind."

"My state of mind? What are you talking about?"

"Bodhi thinks you're in denial; that you're a hurricane waiting to come ashore. I worried if I burdened you with this, it would put too much stress on you, and it might prevent you from healing."

"Wait, since when are you having discussions with Bodhi... *about me?*"

"We talked in the hospital just before I left. He was concerned by how calm you were. He thinks maybe you haven't fully processed what happened to you, and that at some point, you're going to freak out about your foot."

His fingers were now so tangled in his hair, I thought RJ might pull the strands clean out. "My god, Dani, do you really think I'm that shallow? That I care about my foot more than my life? I'm glad my foot's gone."

"Don't say that. You know it's not true. Bodhi said you'd never be okay with losing it."

"Bodhi wasn't in the parking garage!"

RJ's burst of anger startled us both. He reached for me. "I'm sorry. I didn't mean to..."

"Don't be," I said, folding my fingers into his.

RJ sighed long and hard. "I need to tell you something."

I watched as he flipped through the stack of papers. "There's a man named Albert Arthur Aldrich in that stack, isn't there?"

"I... yes. Did you hear about him on the news?"

"No. I listened to him die."

Chills swept through me as the full scope of his trauma came to light.

"Oh god, RJ, I'm so sorry. I didn't know."

"Because I never told you... just like you never told me about this stack. You and me, we gotta communicate better. We're survivors, Dani, but we're not bullet proof. We need to lean on each other for support. Running away doesn't fix anything. It just pushes it down the road, prolonging the misery."

My misery. His misery. Oh no, what had I done? Cradling his face in my hands, I whispered, "Never again."

"You and me, Dani," he replied, his words heavy with strain. "It has to be. You and me."

"Yes." I kissed him. "You and me to the end."

I drew in a breath and realized it didn't hurt as much as it had when I opened my eyes this morning.

"Tell me about Albert."

He sifted through the pile until he found the man, staring at his picture for a long while before opening up to me. "When you left that first time, to go get help, that's when I realized I wasn't alone. Did you know him? That old guy in apartment 140? Always wore a Dodgers hat and carried a tote bag with him to the mailbox."

"I never spoke with him, but I recognized him from his picture."

"He was in his first-floor apartment when the earthquake struck. Somehow, he ended up above me in the parking garage. By the time I realized he was there, Albert was barely alive... had a rebar skewered through his stomach. He was scared but was talking about how he'd lived his life well and had no regrets. The last thing he said to me," RJ halted, the memory gutting him. "He said, 'I lived a damn good life.'"

I lay my head on RJ's chest, hurting for him. We sat like that a long time before he was ready to talk again.

"When he died... I don't know, something changed in me. I realized that I was doing life all wrong. And if I wanted my last breath to mean something, like Albert's did, then I had to start living. Not like I was doing before—with excess amounts of anger and resentment—but really living. I promised myself if I made it through, I wouldn't waste another day.

"And Bodhi's right about one thing. I'm not the guy he knows. The day I woke up in the hospital was the day I was reborn. So, if you really want to see me freak out, by all means, give me a slow internet connection; but if you're waiting for me to go ballistic over my missing foot, that's never going to happen."

There was power in what he spoke. RJ had changed not because he was forced to but because he had the strength to. And I could rediscover my strength too. I was, after all, the 'pint-size' woman who'd dragged RJ through the debris.

"So, what do we do?" I asked.

"I know what we can't do. We can't bring them back, and we can't trade places. You want to know why you lived and they died but there isn't an answer to that, Dani. It's all random, a game of fate. If Doreen would've backed out of her parking spot even three minutes earlier, she would've lived, and you would've died in your apartment. Or maybe if I hadn't been stuck at the grocery store behind the guy who couldn't remember his PIN number, I would've been there before you, snagged that spot, and died in my apartment. We just got lucky. That's it. You want to play the 'what if' game when what you need to do is accept that we won this round and be grateful for our second chance."

It was all stuff I knew. Of course it wasn't my fault; yet somehow my brain had made it seem that way. This was survivor's guilt at its most destructive, and now that I had RJ to guide me through the fog, I knew everything would eventually be all right. My heart beat faster as a surge of voltage awakened it.

"I am grateful."

"For what, Dani? Say it."

"For you," I replied, my voice strengthening. "And to be alive."

"I'm grateful for the same things."

"Good," I shouted.

He answered back with his own shout. "Why are we yelling?"

"I don't know," I continued at the top of my lungs. "But I like it. The pressure was building. You popped the cork. And now I'm gonna blow!"

"Okay," he mused, a smile jumping to his lips. "Should I get out of the way?"

Lifting to my knees, I leaned over and smacked a kiss to his lips before tossing my arms to the sides and screaming. Seconds later, the door was flung open and my horrified mother rushed toward me, her eyes flooded with panic.

"It's okay." RJ held his hands out to stop her.

"No. No, it's not okay."

"Yes, Gladys. She needs this. Let her empty the bottle."

And they did, both waiting patiently until my throat was raw and I collapsed to the side, laughing.

"I'm just so confused," my mother said.

I reached my hand out to her, and when she grabbed it, I pulled her down and gave her a hug. "I love you. Have I told you that lately?"

Her tense body began to loosen. "No. I don't believe you have."

"Well, I love you," I said, kissing her cheek. "Thank you for everything, Mom. Now I'm ready to go home."

28

DANI: DOCTOR DANI

IT SHOULD HAVE BEEN A GRAND EXPERIENCE—ME GLIDING INTO the stately mansion while attentive staff fussed over my every need.

"Park over there," RJ instructed.

"Behind the shrubs?"

"Yes."

I eyed him but said nothing as I pulled into the dirt, my fancy new Bronco getting her first real taste of adversity. RJ steered me along the outskirts of the property, welcoming me to my new digs through the back door. Again, weird; but I'd never been to his house before and just figured it was sort of a 'garage' entrance. It wasn't until he began tip-toeing through the kitchen —on crutches—that I realized something was up.

"What's going..."

My question was interrupted when RJ abruptly pushed me into the pantry and slapped a hand over my mouth, his lips puckered in a 'shush.'

I squawked indignantly, prying his fingers back. "If you don't explain what's going on right now, I'm going to scream... and then I'm going to knee you in the nuts."

RJ didn't take my threat lightly. "My nurse," he whispered. "Julio. He's pissed. Left me like eighty messages."

"So what? He's your nurse, not Heather! The RJ I know doesn't hide in a pantry the size of my old apartment because he's afraid of the hired help. Who is he, Freddie Krueger?"

The door suddenly blew open, and we both screamed like we were on Elm Street. A short, disgruntled dude in swim trunks stood in the entrance to the pantry.

"Oh, hey, Julio," RJ said, quickly recovering from the shock. "Just getting a snack. Nice to see you threw a shirt on."

RJ hopped past his nurse and into the kitchen. I followed right behind, having no clue what was currently happening but feeling like I was in the middle of a domestic dispute.

"You were getting a snack in the dark?" Julio questioned.

"Yes," RJ confirmed. "It's more fun that way. A surprise every time—like snack roulette."

Julio narrowed in on RJ. "I do not appreciate you leaving..."

"Actually, Julio, sorry to interrupt, but Dani can't keep her hands off me, so we'll have to discuss this in the morning."

I wanted to punch him for putting me in an awkward position, but instead I dutifully followed after RJ because the house was massive enough that I would've gotten lost without him.

"Thanks a lot, Chad!" I smacked him in the pecs. "Now I have to find a new place to live."

"You're not going anywhere," he said, reaching around my back and tugging me to him. "Until I have you quaking on my bed."

"You sound confident in your skills," I teased, biting his luscious bottom lip as my hand dipped to his pants and I took a firm grip of his manhood. He groaned, pulling the shirt over my head before reconnecting our lips. "But I'm a finicky climaxer."

I could feel his lips curving against mine. "You won't be tonight."

"All right, well, I'm rooting for you," I said, between kisses.

"No need. You'll see."

He was so confident in his skillset that I almost believed him. The fact of the matter was, while I was a whiz with a vibrator, I'd always struggled to achieve orgasmic bliss with the Jeremys. But I was more than willing to give the studly pop star a try.

"Bed," I instructed, walking him backward until his legs touched the bed. Dislodging the crutches from under his arms, I pushed him back onto the mattress and wasted no time climbing on top of him and straddling his waist. I leaned over, hands on either side of his head, staring into his lustful eyes. Lifting his head, he took a swipe at my lips with his tongue.

"Do you want me?" I purred, teasing him by rotating my hips over his ever-expanding erection. That I'd worn a skirt with itty bitty silk panties today seemed almost like divine intervention.

He answered by unhooking the clasp of my bra and setting my breasts free. But they weren't really, because RJ's calloused hands were on them in seconds, using his thumb to gently brush against my nipples. I sucked in my lower lip, gripping his chest and grinding deeper onto him. He winced.

I froze. "Did I hurt you?"

"No," he lied. "Don't stop."

"RJ, you're fresh out of the hospital. Still breakable."

He thrust his pulsing dick between my legs; the only thing keeping it from penetrating me was the fact that it was still in his pants. "Does that feel breakable to you?"

"No," I whispered in his ear, squeezing my thighs around him.

He dragged in a sharp breath. "So, stop worrying about me."

"Okay. But I'd feel better if I did a real quick health exam on you," I said, tilting his face toward me, and when he opened his mouth to protest, I stopped him with a finger to his lips. "Yes, just as I suspected. You appear winded. Dr. Dani prescribes mouth to mouth resuscitation."

I lowered my lips to his, inhaling him long and deep. He caught on to the game in record time, slipping his tongue into the resuscitation efforts, a giant no-no in every medical personnel's survival playbook. But this doctor didn't mind, the forbidden excitement of RJ reaching all the way to my core. I was living out a fantasy millions of girls around the world could only dream of. And he'd sought me out, coming to my house to win me back. He was mine for the taking.

RJ pulled back, gazing up at me with heavy-lidded eyes, that look of his all lust. Gripping the back of my neck, he drew me in until our lips were crushed up into each other's. There was nothing gentle this time around. Digging my fingers into his hair, I helped myself, clinging to the promise of a life spent exactly like this.

And when we finally broke apart, I forced myself to breathe as I traced his saliva along my swollen lips with a finger. RJ pulled his shirt up and over his head, giving me my first glimpse of his deeply bruised stomach and torso. It had only been three weeks since the earthquake, and he was still healing. Could he handle the jostling?

RJ saw me staring. "Are we back to this again? Trust me, it'll hurt me more if you stop."

I nodded, lowering my lips to his warm skin, and tenderly kissed each and every bruise. "But just to be sure... I need to check your reflexes."

"My reflexes?"

"Uh-huh. Your medical clearance. Remember?"

Still straddling RJ, I glided my slippery center down past his waist, coming to rest on his jutting erection still frustratingly sheathed. I rubbed my slickness over him. Once, twice... oh my god, yes.

"Reflexes," I grunted. "Working fine."

He thickened between my quivering legs, the expression on his face straight-up lust. I continued to move over him in a slow circular motion. His thumb moved down to my nub, kneading the pulsing spot between my legs and sending a jolt through me. Seeing my electrified reaction, RJ doubled down, his fingers working expertly between my thighs. I writhed against him, my heart racing and my head spinning. Nothing had ever felt quite like this. Under RJ's expert touch, I was leaking like a malfunctioning faucet.

"Do you want more?" he whispered in my ear.

God, yes. More. More. But I couldn't speak. Could barely breathe. My body rumbling with desire. So close. And then nothing. RJ stopped, his fingers abandoning me in my time of need and leaving me throbbing at my core. I think I might have whimpered in response, pressing my thighs together to try and ward off the inevitable. But it was a swift transition. RJ lifted me off him and set me on my back before rising to his knees. He gazed down at me with lascivious eyes, while prying my legs back open.

"I'm not done with you yet," he teased, flashing me a wicked, life-altering grin.

I was supercharged; one touch might shock me dead. My stomach rose and fell with the anticipation of what he was promising me. And when he dipped his head between my legs, touching his tongue to my sex, it forced a squeal from my depths. I closed my thighs around his head and grabbed for whatever might dampen the relentless pressure growing inside. With a wad of sheets in my hands, I dipped my head back waiting, wanting. With his tongue applying the final touches, RJ slid his hand the length of my rigid, arched body, triggering the explosion. For one intense moment I felt weightless, suspended between here and there before crashing back onto the bed in a quivering state of shock.

I watched helplessly as RJ removed his pants, his dick springing from its restraints. He was naked in all his glory, and I'd never seen anything quite like him. Holy shit, he was hung. And that rack of abs. I was not worthy. While RJ sheathed the monster, I curiously traced my fingers along those horizontal muscles in his stomach, reveling in their hard lines. Jeremys did not have these.

RJ returned to his rightful spot between my legs, rigid and ready. I reached for him, wanting to own every bit of him. He pushed in, the wetness easing him through. He filled me up, returning my body to high alert as he slowly eased me into this whole new world of desire until I was once again on the edge of sanity, begging him for more.

His fingers returned to my sex, startling me in the very best away. Currents of pleasure ricocheted through me as I dug my nails into his back. It was wild. Thrilling. I wasn't going to last. He slid through me, the length of him, in and out, sending my mind to places it had never been. And those punishing fingers just seared through me. It was ecstasy and agony all wrapped into one. I couldn't hold on. I couldn't let go. My body shook like the temblor that had started the story of us. He ground into me, bottoming out, and the groan escaping his mouth sounded like a wounded animal.

"RJ, I can't. It's too much. Feels too..."

He thrust harder, and I just held on for dear life until a rolling earthquake of unimaginable magnitude ripped through me. I screamed, not caring who could hear my cries. And when the rumbling finally subsided, I collapsed on top of my superstar lover, panting and calling out his name.

He stroked my hair. Kissed my neck. My face. My eyelids.

And in that moment, I knew my declaration of love in the parking garage had not come from a place of fear or sadness. It had come, very much, from the heart.

29

RJ: FOR A GOOD CAUSE

I SAT ON A STOOL IN THE MIDDLE OF THE STAGE, JUST ME AND MY guitar. Stripped of all conceit, I simply played, lost in that place in my mind where I went when the music was flowing through me like gold. I'd existed here a lot lately, enough that Dani needed to remind me to eat and to sleep and to make her scream.

But the late nights in the studio had paid off with nine solid tracks for my second solo album, each one more deeply felt than the next. I'd been proud of my work before, but never like this. In a few weeks' time, the album would drop, and the world would judge its worth. There was always that chance it would flop, but this time I wouldn't hide, because I no longer measured myself by the opinions of others.

I launched into my final number, Dani's favorite, and one that never failed to bring tears to her eyes. This was the song inspired by that day on the chair in her childhood room. That was the day we'd decided to turn our survivor's guilt into action. And why we were all here tonight—Dani, me, and a few of my famous friends—raising money for earthquake victims throughout the city. The proceeds wouldn't bring back loved ones or replace heirlooms lost, but it would help with funeral costs, put roofs back over people's heads, and provide a future for Sarina, the little girl who'd lost it all.

Steeped in emotion, I sang the last wrenching notes of the song, ending with a crackling of my voice. There was a brief moment of silence as the audience acknowledged my sorrow. Then came the cheers. I stood and waited. Normally I'd take my final bow and exit the stage, but there was nothing normal about this show, nor was this the last song I would sing tonight.

The crowd buzzed with excitement, knowing what was to come. Despite all the notable names on tonight's roster, *AnyDayNow*'s one-night-only reunion had earned top billing and driven the ticket prices through the roof. The audience erupted when the guys joined me at center stage. Although each had been out earlier in the evening to perform solo, this was the first time any of us had been on the stage together since our much-publicized breakup nearly two years ago. There had been renewed interest in us after the quake, our natural disaster dramas drawing the interest of millions and bringing our older music back onto the airwaves. Say what you will about our cheeseball pop songs, but they were generation-defining and as popular today as they'd been at the height of our fame. We'd made our mark on history. *AnyDayNow* was here to stay.

Taking our positions on the stage, I was overly aware that this was the first time I'd be moving around the stage on my prosthetic leg. It was daunting, but I felt confident that my balance was solid enough that I'd be okay. With the extensive physical therapy I'd done, my new energy-storing foot and ankle had become an extension of me, providing a comfortable stride and allowing me to step up on this stage tonight and sing.

The music started, and we launched into the first song. You could barely hear our voices over the screams of the crowd. That only spurred us on, and we gave a vibrant performance reminiscent of the days when we'd been at the top of the charts. It felt good. Natural. I even tried to pants Bodhi on stage, for old times' sake.

Looking to my left, then to my right, I couldn't help but smile. Damn, I'd missed this. If I closed my eyes, I could almost imagine we were back on the tour bus, exhilarated and exhausted after our first stadium concert—fresh-faced teenagers experiencing our first taste of fame. It was from those humble beginnings that we'd forged our tight bonds. Everything had been so new. So exciting. But somewhere along the way, it lost its shine. Tonight was a reminder of who we were and where we were all going—separately, but never far from one another.

———

The after-party was a who's who of Hollywood and the hottest ticket in town. Most who came had no direct connection to the earthquake, nor had they been touched by the destruction it wrought. Yes, they'd felt it and had tweeted about it, but their lives had moved on just like before. Hell, had I ridden out the quake in my mansion, I probably would've come to this party, plunking down an impressive amount of money to show I cared —even if I really couldn't give a shit.

But, hey, I wasn't knocking these people for coming. Their presence generated publicity for the event, which, in turn, brought in private donations from across the world. And then it would be up to Dani and her team of Lucky Swimmers Club volunteers to dole out the money to those most in need.

Me and the guys made our entrance into the after-party an hour late. As part of the documentary for the band, the camera crew filmed our reunion concert then conducted the final interviews before sending us on our way. When we entered the room, there was a different energy. Instead of snickering behind our boy band backs, our peers cheered us. It was almost as if we'd gone from jokes in the industry to legends overnight. And for a second time in just over an hour, we got a standing ovation.

"What the hell is going on here?" Shawn asked, smiling and waving.

"No clue," Bodhi replied.

"Are we..." Dane stopped to mull over the words. "Suddenly cool?"

"Either that or they're mocking us," Hunter said.

"It's the natural evolution of a boy band," I said. "Puberty plus eight, divided by a natural disaster or two, equals legends."

Dani wasn't hard to find in her sparkling silver dress and bouncy hair swept to one side, held in place with Swarovski crystal claw clips. When it had come time to pick her outfit for tonight's gala event, she'd worried it was too much, that glitter and shine was not her, but I'd disagreed. Every ball needed a princess, and there was no one more worthy of the title than her.

She'd saved me a seat at her table, and I squished in next to Parker.

"You made it," I said, shaking his hand.

"Dani did promise me VIP passes for life, so I figured I'd come collect."

"And this is Marissa," Dani said, snuggling closer to me with a teasing smile on her face. "Isn't it cute? Our little Peter Parker has his first real girlfriend."

"Again," Parker laughed, "not a teenager."

"Sure. Sure." She winked, her whole face contracting.

"Hey RJ," Charlie called from across the table. "Shouldn't you be at the cool kids' table?"

I glanced around, and aside from Parker, Marissa, my brother Manny, every other person occupying the seven tables around us was one of Dani's sperm siblings and their significant others. The Lucky Swimmers Club had taken over my life, and they just kept growing in numbers, thanks to Dani's notoriety following the earthquake. It had spurred countless articles about her unusual beginnings and pushed the LSC into the forefront of artificially inseminated insanity.

But while they'd become the butt of a good many jokes, The Lucky Swimmers Club was no laughing matter. Not only had they rallied around Dani in her time of need, but they were also at the forefront of the fundraising efforts for the relief fund. These people were more than just friends to me. They'd become my surrogate family.

"Nah," I replied. "I'm just where I want to be."

30

DANI: ROMANTIC GESTURE

Bing. Bing. Bing.

I grabbed my phone to shut off the alarm, confused by why it was going off in the first place. After last night's event, this was supposed to be a sleep-all-day type morning.

A yellow stinky note was clinging to my phone screen. It read, *You have fifteen minutes to meet me in the kitchen.*

I smiled. Uh-oh. RJ was being romantic again. This ought to be good. I always enjoyed watching him stumble around the art of wooing as if it were such a foreign concept to him. Some of my favorite romantic gestures included 'chick-flick movie night,' where RJ suffered through each and every film, or the 'no strings attached' backrub that always ended in his favor. He'd even once claimed putting the toilet seat down was a romantic gesture that needed rewarding. But I got it. RJ wasn't used to trying. Women had always seduced him, not the other way around.

I hopped out of bed and quickly did my business, contemplating getting more 'picture ready' for my surprise but sort of liking my fresh-out-of-bed look. After last night's benefit concert, I'd only managed to get out of my dress and pull on a pair of cute pajamas before collapsing on top of the mattress, never to be heard from again. The makeup I hadn't removed from my face last night was looking a little rough this morning, but once I wiped the mascara smudges off from under my eyes, I honestly wasn't looking half bad.

I found RJ in the kitchen exactly fifteen minutes later. He was at the stove, in an apron, making eggs. Overwhelmed with affection for this man, I wrapped my arms around his waist and dug my appreciative head into his back.

"You're on time," he said, twisting to kiss me.

"I'm always on time."

"Well, you definitely slept well last night."

"Is that code for 'You were snoring'?"

"If you were, do you think I'd say anything, after the last time?" he asked.

RJ was referring to the time he'd woken me from a dead sleep to inform me that I was snoring. I'd replied in a deep, manly roar, "Whaddaya want me to do about it?"

Since then, he'd let sleeping bears lie.

RJ removed the eggs from the heat and put his spatula down. He then turned around to give me a proper hug. I tipped my head up for my kisses, easily falling under his spell. It was hard to believe we'd once been warring neighbors. I couldn't remember ever not loving him.

"Now, go. Sit down," he said, swatting my butt. "I'll serve you."

"Wow, so domesticated. Who knew all it would take to turn Chad Woodcock into a real live human being was the love of a good woman?"

"Well," he demurred. "That and a 7.1 magnitude earthquake."

"Ehh." I waved off his suggestion. "That too, I suppose."

He pointed to the kitchen island.

"I'm going," I said, slipping onto the stool before getting my first full look at my surroundings. The room was filled with fresh flowers—they were everywhere. "What's all this?"

RJ shrugged. "Rozsika went to the farmer's market, I think."

"Damn. What sort of grocery budget do you give her?"

RJ set two plates down in front of me—scrambled eggs and cut-up fruit. It was the extent of his culinary talents, but somehow it was completely endearing.

"Why do you look better to eat than my breakfast?" he asked, kissing my cheek as he slid into the spot beside me.

I smiled, picking up my fork and taking a bite out of his romantic gesture. "Yum."

RJ didn't respond, but I noticed his leg bouncing up and down on the rung of the stool.

"You okay?"

He met my eye and smiled before dropping his gaze back to the counter. Placing his finger on a stack of Post-it Notes, RJ slid them closer.

"Ah." I laughed. "Like old times."

Without a word, RJ picked up the pencil and wrote one word on the top sticky note in the stack.

I.

He tore it from the pad and set it in front of me.

Love.

He tore that one off too and placed it in front of me.

And then the third. *You.*

I smiled, took the pencil from his hand, and wrote four separate words on four individuals notes and placing them one at a time in front of him.

I. Love. You. Too.

He snagged the pencil back and wrote, *My Hero.*

I replied on three separate notes, *My. Hero. Back.*

We gazed into each other's eyes. Such love. I gripped his jaw and kissed him. We lingered there, our lips attached but not really moving. Lazy love.

He picked up the pencil once more and, hiding the words from me, scribbled onto four separate sticky notes.

Placing them all out in order on the counter in front of me, I read:

Will. You. Marry. Me?

EPILOGUE
RJ

I checked my watch. Shit. Almost eleven. I'd promised the kids to be back by ten-thirty to tuck them in, but the concert had run late, and now I was racing against the clock. Although realistically, they probably wouldn't be asleep anyway, given that bedtime for them was like a twenty-seven-step process that went something like this: Bath. Story. Song. Kisses. Hugs. I love yous. And then the glorious 'See you in the morning.' Dani and I would shut the door behind us, so hopeful, even though we both knew we'd be *seeing* the kids twelve more times before the night was through.

Not that it was really their fault that their sleep patterns were all off. Life on the road wasn't exactly conducive to early bedtimes. But Dani and I had decided early on that staying together was more important than socially acceptable bedtimes, so touring during the summer months had become family vacation time. The kids loved the bus, with all its earthly comforts. We'd go from city to city, picking fun family activities. All the things I'd never done with my own family growing up, I did now with Dani and my own treasured kids... sometimes late into the night. *Making memories*, Dani always said. And damned if I wasn't all in.

For a guy who'd never wanted kids, I'd fallen in line pretty quick. As labor-intensive as our boy and girl were, I wouldn't have traded them for the world. I'd gotten lucky. Mine were better than the rest.

Cutting across the parking lot to the tour bus, I quietly made my way up the steps and unlocked the door. Peggy met me at the entrance, and I bent down to show her some love. The puddle of pee at my feet proved how happy our mini Goldendoodle pup was to see me.

Dani, already on her way over with paper towels and a disinfectant wipe, complained, "My god, RJ. We've talked about this. Can you be less exciting when you come in?"

"Sorry," I said, giving her a kiss before she knelt at my feet to clean up the aftermath of my awesomeness.

"Long show tonight," she said, stating the obvious.

"It was delayed. Electrical issues."

"I heard. Sorry we didn't come to watch, but the kids were wiped out after the movie."

"How was it?"

"The movie? Depends. How do you feel about true love?"

"Not a huge fan."

"Then you probably would've hated it. Oh, and before I forget. Sue messaged. She has a surprise for the kids when we get back. RJ, I don't think I need to remind you that we don't want another surprise that pees on shoes."

"No, we do not. I'll handle Sue. Are the kids asleep?"

"*Are they asleep*, he asks." Dani chuckled, ruffling my hair. "You're so adorable."

"So that would be a no?"

"A giant one."

I groaned. "I can't sing them a song tonight. Too tired."

"They don't need one. All they want is a hug and a kiss. And a hug and a kiss. And a... well, you get the idea."

"I do," I said, heading toward the bunks before stopping and drawing Dani into my arms. "Hey, how tired are you?"

"Not tired enough for what I think you're suggesting."

"Good. I'll be in the room in five. Wear that sexy band shirt."

"The one Parker threw up on?"

"No. The other one."

"The *AnyDayNow* one with your face on it?"

"Fuck no." I cringed. "You know what? On second thought, just be naked."

She saluted me, tiptoeing past the kids' closet, as we called it, on her way to the bedroom.

"I'll be there in five minutes," I promised.

She nodded, waving at me without even turning around.

"I'll see you in twenty."

I opened the door to the bunk room as quietly as possible on the off chance that both might magically be asleep. They weren't. Parker was on his sister's upper bunk, her arm around him as she read him a book.

Right, so, Dani's grand life plan had gone to shit. Not that either of us was complaining. She'd once made me promise to give her a boy and girl—in that order—and a potbellied pig. What we got was a girl, then a boy, and Peggy wasn't a pig.

"Daddy!" they called out as I stepped in and wrapped them both into the same hug.

"What are you doing up here?" I asked three-year-old Parker.

"Reading with sissy. I know five words," he said, holding up four fingers. Yep, chip off the old block, that one.

"No reading after bedtime, you know that."

"We were waiting for you," my daughter said. "I can't go to sleep until I know we are all safe inside."

"I know," I said, kissing her silky brown hair before turning my attention to her little brother. "Come on, bud."

I grabbed Parker off the bunk, his legs wrapping around me as he buried his head in my neck. Was it possible to love this much without bursting the heart? I often thought about the many ways Dani had saved me. It started in the parking garage, but it didn't end there. I credited the person I was today with the man she'd made me. Without her, I wouldn't be here right now cuddling with my baby. This was what Albert had been talking about—living life well enough that there would be no regrets when the end finally came for me.

I tucked Parker into bed, kissing him goodnight before focusing on his sister.

"How's my warrior?" I asked, pulling the blanket up and over her. She held her arms out to me and I dropped in. No one hugged like my little girl did. So solid. So tight.

"Good. I taught Peggy a new trick today."

"How nice. Maybe next you can teach her not to pee on my foot?"

"I'll try," she giggled. "And Mom bought me overalls so I can be like the K-pop boys."

"You know, I used to be a real-life K-pop boy myself, minus the K."

"I know. *AnyDayNow*. But that was in the olden days."

The olden days? I'd just turned thirty. Hardly a relic.

She must have sensed my insecurity and went in for the kill. "I still think you're cool... just, no one else does."

I grabbed my chest, wounded. "Brutal."

I could have told her that I'd just played to a sold-out crowd or that a woman in the audience had found me 'cool' enough to throw her bra up at me on stage tonight, but I didn't bother. She was eleven. Nothing I said would convince her that I was even half as exciting as her K-pop idols.

She giggled. "You're the best dad, though."

I'd take it. "And you're the best daughter."

"I know." She nodded, so confident it made me smile. "Hand-picked."

"Hand-picked," I agreed, so proud of how far this little girl had come.

"I'm glad you're home. Now I can sleep," she whispered, yawning. "I love you."

I kissed the tip of her nose. "I love you more."

Flicking off the light, I backed out of the room and whispered, "Goodnight, Parker. Goodnight, Sarina."

———

I hope you enjoyed reading RJ and Dani's story. Want to know more about the boys of *AnyDayNow*? For Bodhi and Breeze's story and to find out why *AnyDayNow* broke up, check out Like The Wind.

DISCOVER THE BESTSELLING CAKE SERIES

Ten years have passed since Jake survived a stranger abduction.

He now finds himself on top of the world, a singer famous for the music that helped him heal. He thinks he's put his past behind him. He thinks he's okay. It isn't until he meets sweet, quirky Casey at his brother's wedding that he realizes all he's been missing out on.

Casey Caldwell has never had grand plans for her life. She's perfectly happy with the idea of meeting some nice nerdy guy after college and settling down near her family. But once she meets Jake, she can't remember why she ever wanted a simple life.

Whisked away into a world of music, riotous fans, tour buses, and movie-worthy shopping sprees, Casey is introduced to a life she could only have dreamed of.

But every fairytale has a villain ... and theirs lives inside Jake's head.

Together, Jake and Casey fight to keep their love alive, battling both the physical and emotional scars of Jake's abduction.

Each book in the Cake Series delves deeper into how that

one terrible crime continues to impact everyone in Jake's life and how their quest for love will set them free.

Exploring different points in time, we come to know the extraordinary McKallister family as intimately as we might know our own.

Start the beloved Cake Series at book one. Casey and Jake. Cake A Love Story.

Join my newsletter jbengtssonbooks.com/newsletter and Facebook reader group, J. Bengtsson's The Banana Binder, for future release updates.